The World is Neither Stacked for Nor Against You: New and Selected Stories

Corey Mesler

Livingston Press

University of West Alabama

Library of Congress Control Number: 2024938820
Printed on acid-free paper
Printed in the United States of America by
Publishers Graphics

Typesetting and page layout: Joe Taylor
Proofreading: Annsley Johnsey, Angela Brooke Barger, Savannah Beams,
Kaitlyn Clark, Tricia Taylor, Kelly West
Cover drawing by Edward Carey
(with background by Gracen Deerman)
Author photo by Mark Hendren.
Special thanks: Rick Schober, of Tough Poets Press.

For Cheryl and for Bix

6 5 4 3 2 1

The World is Neither Stacked for Nor Against You:

"No matter: we swim in an oceanful of story, but a tumblerful slakes our thirst."

—*John Barth*

"We need something to wake sleepwalkers…To make the world strange and real again."

—*Richard Powers*

Table of Contents

Introduction
Steve Stern

(Steve Stern is the author of The Village Idiot *and a National Jewish Book Award winner for* The Wedding Jester. *He has been a Fulbright lecturer at Bar Elan University in Tel Aviv, and Lecturer in Jewish Studies for the Prague Summer Seminars. He splits his time between Brooklyn and Balston Spa, New York.)*

Full disclosure: Corey Mesler is a decades' long friend of mine, so I reserve the right to feel pride by association. It's been one of the joys of my life to have witnessed the trajectory of Corey's writing, from his early furtive efforts back in the 80s to the kaleidoscopic world he's since created through his prodigious industry. He has become something of a legend in our mutual hometown of Memphis, which he has elevated to myth through a staggering number of poems, novels, and stories; but almost as if Memphians wish to keep his creations to themselves, he remains a rather well-kept secret on the planet at large. This will change as his reputation grows, but for the time being I think of him as a kind of *lamed vovnik*. The lamed vov are the hidden saints of Jewish legend whose presence on earth is God's reason for refraining from its destruction. Their good works, while remaining largely unknown, are the reasons we're allowed, despite all our infamies, to survive.

To my mind, the essential quality of Corey's project is its joyousness. His voice takes its place among the playful company of writers such as Vonnegut, Brautigan, George Saunders, perhaps Laurence Sterne, writers whose antic imaginations refuse to leave base reality alone, and are compelled to distill it through the alchemy of language into something both rollicking and sublime. In Corey's work, humiliations, absurdities, and heartbreak are transfigured—by equal parts humor and pathos, and an unapologetic celebration of sex—into carnivalesque entertainments. His heroes and heroines are drawn from the ranks of the humble, his landscapes populated by losers, misfits, and solitaries—as who could be more deserving candidates for the kind of transformative passions Corey trades in? You might say that, taken all in all, the rhapsodic cycle of his stories constitutes, in its undemonstrative fashion, a somewhat warmer companion to the turbulent metamorphoses of Ovid; for while his characters remain subject to the whims of capricious gods, they never quite succumb to fate so much as adapt to it, in what amounts to a shameless affirmation of lived experience.

Take the eponymous shut-in protagonist of "From the Desk of Jojo Self," who is sprung—through the agency of a species of over-sexed fairy godmother—from the prison of his *self* and catapulted (despite himself) from non-entity to fame. Witness the hapless Effie Sempsh, in the reverse fairy tale of "Monster," who's stuck in the throes of an abusive marriage until her abduction by an actual monster who spirits her away to an arboreal paradise. In a hilarious send-up of (and homage to) classic horror films, a traveler in a gothically fabled Carpathia is attacked by a colossal chicken in the light of a "moon as large as Charon's ferry" and turned into a murderous hen. The titular hero of "Chip" is turned into a sexual athlete after swallowing a dime. True, the metamorphoses may sometimes have catastrophic consequences, but nearly all are in the service of returning a character to their more authentic self. In "Supermarket" a man's otherwise commonplace life is precluded when, owing to a minor faux pas, he is sentenced to spend eternity in a cell beneath the store of the story's title—a situation to which he becomes blithely reconciled. And in "The Day Change Came for James," James's own resolution to improve his woebegone temperament backfires, returning him to the embrace of a doleful familiarity.

From the above you will have gotten an idea of the places a free-range imagination can go. The ports-of-call are seldom on any known map. In one story a husband must concede poetic justice when his wife's former lover, having since become a bear, enters his home to lay claim to his wife and family; in another a pair of teenage twin sisters compete in the new craze of dyeing their shadows in spectral colors for a diabolical purpose. A bookworm/detective in "Blue Positive" seeks a missing person in a pitch-perfect parody of a Raymond Chandler mystery, with all its improbable plot twists and over-the-top conceits: "She had skin the color of the Bosco I drank in short pants." "Anna liked, equally, the shine of bar lighting in a shot glass of whiskey (a glister of fish-hooks, she called it) and depravity."

Language is of course the vehicle by which these narratives reach their unlikely destinations, and Corey's language is instantly identifiable as uniquely his own. Supple, buoyant, sensual, bedizened with indelible imagery—his prose is a medium engineered to render the impossible credible and the reader readily willing to suspend disbelief. It's a language that describes a perfectly recognizable universe while at the same time alluding to dimensions far beyond the literal; and it is peppered with metaphors (for which Corey has an almost visionary gift) that brush the ordinary with a patina of magic. To wit: "the murmur of dreaming books," "the purple flame with a red center like the back of a black widow," "an eeriness in the air like cicadas from another world," "the moon a buttery nightlight," "bright as a holy pyx," "her breasts like sea swells," "her smile like a keyboard," "She smiled like an adder," "She smiled like a ring-dove." I don't know how a ring-dove smiles, but the visceral reverberation of such images gives the narratives their aura of enchantment and lends an element of guilty pleasure to the fundamental enjoyment of an original literary experiment.

Not to mention the words themselves: *pandiculations, cicatricial, hadal, pilliwinks, papyrvore…* Arcane words to be sure, they constantly remind the reader that these fictions are conceived by a writer not only besotted with language but in love with the myriad tales that precede and inform the story at hand. To read Corey Mesler is to be infected by the breadth of *his* reading and to inhale an essence of the authors that have beguiled him. Needless to say, it's a heady atmosphere. Moreover, I'd be remiss if I didn't mention Corey's pitch-perfect ear for dialogue. (I know, I've used the term before, but its abuse is unavoidable here.) An example: in "The Day Change Came for James," James takes to the roof of his house to announce his apotheosis, prompting a neighbor to call the police.

His wife: "James, Mrs. Turra called the cops."

James: "I know, I know. I'll go talk to Mrs. Turra. I'll just tell her it's the new me. I'll tell her I won't need to get on the roof very often."

"James, the police came to our house."

"Just to talk me down, Honey. You know. They were very nice. I told them—"

"James, you didn't—"

And from the rom-com charade of "Barbara and Chuck Said We'd Like Each Other," the moment that breaks the ice:

He: "What is it with green tea?"

She: "Anti-oxidants. I take anti-oxidants. Don't you?"

He: "No. I'm an oxidant waiting to happen."

But make no mistake, there's nothing pure about the whimsy in these stories: the arc of their artful, shape-shifting narratives is always about the messy business of bending toward human intimacy. And sometimes a story will divest itself entirely of its verbal hijinks to deliver a very earthbound truth about mortal need. In "He's Gone," for instance, a pregnant wife, left alone for a day, imagines that she has been abandoned forever by her husband, and his return from an ordinary day's work can do nothing to console her.

It's no secret that Corey is an agoraphobe, bona fide and clinically diagnosed, a condition that evokes a metaphor he's well aware of. Like so many of his characters, he's been forced by a quirk of his sensibility to retreat into a physical seclusion, a withdrawal that naturally has its psychological coefficient. But in Corey's case, the shrinkage of his world to the mere square-footage of a modest house in midtown Memphis has had the paradoxical effect of allowing his imagination to expand to starry magnitudes. I suppose one could say that he's swapped the domain of experience for one defined largely by art, but then, in his stories, the formal stratagems of his art are repeatedly subverted by the chicanery of experience, and life is extolled in the most peculiar ways. The name for such happy proceedings is, I believe, redemption, and if Corey's characters can't always manage to get there on their own steam, then his language—call it, with a nod to his irrepressible penchant for play, "corybantic," or to use one of Corey's favorite terms, "cock-a-hoop"—takes them the rest of the way.

How to be a Man

"And how does it feel to go down into the water with your eyes wide open, and your mouth gaping, so that you can see and taste every inch of the descent?"
—Peter Ackroyd

Waiting in his therapist's office, Rodney Carp was reading a women's magazine, an article about a man who built an entire home underwater. Because Rodney had lived his life with the name Carp and taken a bloody bruising for it, he was fascinated by all things aquatic.

It reminded him of a childhood storybook called *The Fishman Nicolao;* it was about a man who could live both on land and underwater. It was Rodney's favorite book. He was a reader; he lived in books. This was at a time in human history—the mid-1960s—when it was important that a growing boy be only one thing: tough. Rodney was not tough. He could not catch a ball and he could not run fast. He dreamed about living underwater like Nicolao because he imagined there he would be free of bullies.

His mother, mousy and slight, a grin like a cringe, was indulgent. Rodney's father was stoic, like his entire generation, until he grew exasperated with his only child.

"Put the goddamn books down and go outside. The boys are playing corkball. Why don't you join?"

A shudder went through Rodney's slight frame.

One day his father came home wearing a self-satisfied smirk. "You wanna read?" he said. "Read this."

And he threw down in front of Rodney a small pamphlet entitled, "How to be a Man."

Rodney's heart sunk. His father would never love him.

And here Rodney was, 34 years later, in his therapist's office, prepared to talk about the dreams he was having about his now deceased father.

"Whatcha readin?" A voice like a mermaid's.

Rodney looked up from the depths of fancy. It was that receptionist, Clark, with her nails like talons and her hair pulled back so tightly her face seemed inflated.

"*Women's Day*?" Clark tittered.

Rodney flushed royally.

"Article on—" but he stopped. Why explain?

"How were your dreams this week?" Dr. Moscoe asked, once Rodney had settled onto the settee and made himself receptive to transformation.

"Same," Rodney said.

"Underwater?" Dr. M asked.

Rodney nodded. "Dad dead."

"Been out any? Did you tell me you were going to start going out evenings?"

"No."

"I believe you did promise that, Rodney."

"I meant yes, I promised. And no, I didn't. Go out."

"What about—the woman, the girl, you went to school with, the one you ran into at the supermarket?"

"Candy."

"Yes. You told me you had a nice chat. Perhaps you could look her up."

"I told her I liked her dress. It wasn't much of a chat."

"Still, before next time…"

After his session Rodney went home. Rodney worked from

home as a remote designer for one of the major electronics companies. He spent his time in front of a computer. Tonight, as the screen whirled into view, he walked away. He opened the pull-down staircase to the attic and climbed the rickety ladder into the depressing fusc of his collected past. He thought he might find his old high school annual and look up Candy's picture. Maybe he would call her.

He brought down a box marked "Childhood—Teen Years." He emptied it onto his dining room table. It was a horrible agglomeration. The detritus of a life lived indoors, a life apart. Old report cards, snapshots, pieces of toys, which, it can only be assumed, once gave joy.

And there, lying atop the ruins, like a fish floating in an aquarium, the damned pamphlet, "How to Be a Man." It was yellowed and foxed and gave off an odor like a sour tarn.

Rodney opened it as if it were bad news from afar. The words swam upward. They were unfamiliar. Had he ever read it? Had he ever pleased his father? He could not remember. The page he turned to was headed: *Are you a man or a fish?* Surely, he was hallucinating. His history was contaminating the pool of his rational mind.

The more he stared the more it hypnotized him. The print began to spin like a maelstrom, dizzying Rodney. A vision erupted in his corrupted noodle: a man swirling down a drain, a deadly eddy. The booklet slipped from his hands. He *was* spinning, traveling. He was leaving the earthbound world. "This is it," Rodney thought. "Now I leave my life behind."

"This is how the great Nicolao was transformed." The very earth under Rodney's feet gave way. It was a sinkhole, a gateway to the pelagic depths. *Goodbye*, Rodney said. *Goodbye, world*, as he moved downward until there was no up and down, no direction. There was only this watery place, this atmosphere of airless serenity, his abundance, his hadal hideaway, his new home.

Supermarket

"The A&P is a supermarket, a higher exchange, an inexhaustible reservoir, a place so complete it can embrace its own contradictions: it is both abattoir and garden, sacrifice and harvest, death and life."

James P. Carse, from *Breakfast at the Victory*

Robert Caldwell was a man like a lot of us, who did not enjoy random human encounters, who, indeed, avoided them at all costs. He did not mesh well with the workaday world, or, at least, he believed he did not. And this is the same thing.

On bad days the smallest task was beyond him. He dodged the duties which require confrontations with official servants of the public good: arguing traffic tickets, getting the car inspected, taking out a loan. Normally, his wife, Gayla, accomplished these assignments for him. When they bought their house, it was painful for Robert to meet with the real estate agent (even though she was a friend) and even more painful when they had to close and meet with a lawyer.

In the circle of his friends Robert was known as an affable, pleasant man, one given to jokes and reassuring pats on the back. So, he was high-functioning, to use a fancy word, in his day-to-day life, a manager of a small, independent movie theater, who was known in the narrow circle of midtown Memphis for his good taste and knowledge of films. Not a public figure, certainly, but, in his particular artistic domain, he had a reputation.

Such are the mysteries of the human heart that such a dichotomy exists. The chasm between public persona and private sensitivity is wide, is extraordinary. But, there's nothing overridingly unconventional about

Robert Caldwell; he's no better or worse off than the majority of men, who, as Thoreau said, lead lives of quiet desperation.

Enough said, then. One Sunday morning Robert Caldwell went to the grocery store, the same grocery store where he had been going for the last ten years, with no foreboding, a man on a simple errand, out for his weekly food run.

There was no trepidation attached to this particular visit. It was routine, practiced. Robert did it every week with no more thought than he used to sign the monthly mortgage bill. He had a list. He methodically checked items off his list as he located them in the store. He located items in the store with little or no searching, due to his familiarity with this specific grocery store.

And, if the store personnel did not know Robert Caldwell, it was due to the volume of traffic they encountered in their necessarily very public jobs, or due to Robert's regular good looks, neither overly handsome, nor remarkably bad looking.

Robert wheeled his crippled cart deliberately down one aisle and up another, never skipping one, not even the diaper/pet food/hardware aisle, though the Caldwells had neither child nor animal nor were particularly inclined to do their own repairs, however minor. Still, aisle 11 was part of the route, the prescribed circuit.

Today the stock boys seemed lethargic, surly, as if some exotic flu had overtaken them all. Robert reached in front of one young man clad in excessively baggy jeans and required white apron, in the produce aisle, to squeeze a cantaloupe, and the boy's expression reminded Robert of one of the undead. Robert moved on.

While scrutinizing the fish selection Robert paused to catch the tune the muzak was cloning. It was Dylan's "Ballad of a Thin Man," an odd choice for a syrupy string arrangement. Robert smiled a bemused smile at the absurdity of modern existence.

As Robert neared the checkout his heart did a brief tattoo, nothing major, a slight dipping in its accentuation. The open cashier suddenly before him, her aisle as free of business as a cloudless sky, he found a tad severe, a large, black woman who perpetually scowled. Robert, as we know, was not the type to engage her in small talk anyway, but this woman was menacing in her every movement; she had a body language which whispered intimidation. "Clairice" her name tag read, a most unlikely moniker. Robert regularly avoided her aisle.

Her blackness had nothing to do with Robert's fear. He was satisfied in his own heart that this was so. He did not fear other cultures— at least, no more than he feared his own. It had more to do with her size, her furrowed brow, her habit of sliding products across her scanner with a rapid right to left movement, as if she were slinging mucus from her spread fingers. A motion of disgust, of an unwillingness to work with the objects of the world, an antipathy for things.

Clairice looked up and took in Robert's hesitation at the mouth of her pathway, the territory she policed. Her ebony face was a mask of unfeeling; her stillness spoke volumes. It said *Come on, ofay, move your ass.*

Robert smiled a tight little smile and pushed his cart forward a tad too quickly. It did not clear the ridge over which it was supposed to rest but shocked him with a dull encounter which shook his teeth. Clairice registered no emotion but, instead, began to drag items across the computerized eye under her glass counter top. Her substantial hands worked with world-weary accuracy. Robert noticed that each nail on each finger had been painted a sky-blue and garnished with a black ace of spades.

Robert prepared his checkbook and pen, already writing in the name of the store and signing his name. No good to keep the customers behind him waiting—he was considerate. He waited patiently for the foodstuffs to file one by one over the scanner.

Then it happened. The Red Baron frozen pizzas, clearly marked with a sale tag on their shelf, at 2 for $6.00, rang in at $3.99 each. Robert paused and then cleared his throat. Clairice rested not, the items flying now, a blur of colored cardboard packaging. Robert tried another preparatory cough, one which would arrest any ordinary retail clerk, one which, in all societies signaled the beginning of an interruption, the cessation of all previous activity for the coming on of speech.

"I'm sorry," Robert now had to toss out.

Clairice lifted her large, round, expressionless face.

"Those pizzas," Robert nodded toward his groceries, already bagged by the efficient young man at the end of the counter.

"Yeah," Clairice intoned.

"I think they rang up wrong."

Clairice breathed out a sigh which carried historical significance.

The young bagger stuck his face over the bags, his sleepy eyes searching out miscreants. He reached down, like a young Arthur, and pulled the two pizza boxes back out into the swirling air.

"They're on sale," Robert said, pleasantly.

"Uh huh," Clairice said, giving the receipt a perfunctory perusal.

"I think they're 2 for 6," Robert said, trying to sound breezy, trying to sound as if he were tapped into stock boy lingo. "They're on sale," he repeated, unnecessarily.

"You wanna go back and look again?" Clairice deadpanned.

"Uh," Robert hesitated and in that moment of hesitation lost whatever power he had had up to that point.

Clairice bent her head back to her task and the food began again gliding over the scanner. She was impervious, regal.

Robert felt the gall rise in his throat. He felt the beat of his heart quicken. Injustice was a heady tonic and it bubbled now in Robert's white, middle-class veins.

"You check it," Robert said, with perhaps a little more heat than intended, his voice breaking on the penultimate syllable. "Or him," Robert threw in, tossing his head in the silent stock boy's direction.

Clairice did a slow burn. Her voice, when it finally emerged from her ancient mask, was measured and sure.

"That sale over," was what she said.

But Robert had come too far now. He stood on the podium of truth and his gaze was austere, his jaw firm.

"You must honor the sign," he said, his voice gaining in timbre and vitality.

Clairice stood stock still for one moment only. And then she managed something truly impressive. She smiled, an overly large, lopsided smile.

"Fuck you, Charlie," she said under her breath and bent inexorably to the task at hand. She slid the last remaining items over the center of her private principality and spoke with tried and tired regularity.

"$98.69," Clairice said.

Robert stared at his nemesis with a stony resolve. There was a clarity to him now. He stood defined against the background of mass commercialism, a warrior. Around his tunnel vision was a mist of delineation, simplifying his certitude. His heart beat a steady and inspiring cadence, the drumming of what is right. He would not falter now.

"I need to see your supervisor," he said, and then added with a dash of impropriety, "Clairice."

The on-duty supervisor that day was Delray Pervus, a gangly youth of 19, who looked 15, even though what was once a bad case of acne had now been diminished to a bad case of pitted scars. Delray was summoned to register 6 over the store loudspeaker and he approached the register area with a smirky, pursed grin affixed in the center of his cicatricial cheeks.

"Whatsa problem here," he leaked from his rident visage.

Clairice jerked a thumb toward Robert, who was reduced to a momentary sticky wicket, a speed bump in the inconversable clerk's busy day.

Robert cleared his already clear throat and said, reasonably, "We had a disagreement over an item's price and she became very rude."

"A disagreement?" the supervisor simpered.

"You rude," Clairice proclaimed, succinctly.

"Well, that's not important. She swore at me," Robert said.

"The disagreement may be important, sir. Our prices are fair and firm," Delray spoke, the company line ready on his tongue.

"Yes, yes," Robert said, impatiently. "The point is she was rude to me. She swore at me."

"What did she say?"

Robert hesitated a crucial second.

"She said, 'Fuck you.'"

"I dint," Clairice said.

"Hmm," Delray said, ruminative hand on chin.

"Look," Robert began.

"I think we'll have to refer this to downstairs," Delray pronounced.

Robert saw Clairice register a moment of surprise, a slight widening of the eyes, which betrayed—what? Robert looked from Delray to Clairice awkwardly. Maybe this was getting a little out of hand.

"Follow me," Delray Pervus said and set off down the Pasta/Sauces/Spices aisle with military determination.

Robert bumbled along after him, feeling foolish, as if he were following a teacher to the principal's office.

"Wait," he said, weakly, toward the rapidly moving back of the floor supervisor.

Delray disappeared through one-half of a pair of swinging doors beside the meat counter and Robert just caught the door on the backswing and toddled after. The cinder-block corridor was dark and damp and smelled of blood and sweat. To his right he flashed by a heavy-set butcher, whose apron wore the imprint of a life of slaughter. Robert may have seen a large, ensanguined cleaver in the meaty hand at the butcher's side or he may have imagined it.

The slender supervisor stepped off to his left at the end of the corridor and when Robert caught up he almost fell headfirst down a steep embankment of concrete stairs. He righted himself on the narrow walls of the passageway and saw Delray vanish behind a door at the foot of the stairway.

Through that door and down another long concrete-block passageway to another flight of cold, hard stairs, Robert felt as if he were descending into the Earth. It was cold and unforgiving, hard like he imagined a prison was. He hurdled on, trying to catch the descending supervisor's attention. He wanted to call the whole thing off; he wanted to go home.

Eventually Robert emerged through another white, metallic door into a room lit with a thousand lamps. After the murk of the halls the room was an assault on the eyes, the bright white like the blankness after death. Robert gasped and squeezed a hand over his pained peepers.

When he could see again he found himself in an anteroom, such as one finds in a hospital ER, a sterile place of waiting. Delray Pervus was right at his side.

"If you'll just wait here," he intoned.

Robert raised a jaded hand.

"I think this is a bit much," he began.

Delray Pervus seemed offended.

"How so?" he inquired.

"Well, I mean," Robert grabbled. "I guess, it's only a few cents..."

Delray Pervus seemed to gather himself like a diva about to solo.

His moony face squinched into a twisted mask.

"How dare you!"

"What?" Robert returned.

"You impugn our integrity, you insult our clerk, and now you wanna just go home and put your feet up."

Robert's sense of injustice was newly inflamed. His ire went beyond the spiny toad immediately before him: it took in the room, the store, the cold-blooded, uncaring planet.

"OK, dammit, let's do it all, let's see it through to the end, let's just see the head honcho, let's get his straightened out. Maybe someone around here has some sense about how to treat a customer. Let's go—let's see your superior!" Robert fairly spat out.

Delray Pervus grew calmer in the face of Robert's outburst. He seemed to say, *Now I know what I'm dealing with.*

"Sit there," he said, like a prim schoolmaster, pointing his bony hand at a row of industrial chairs. He turned on his heel and once again was gone behind a forbidding door.

Robert dropped onto one of the hard cushions of the chairs and expelled a pent-up breath. Rage rattled in his chest; he found himself wringing his hands like some bad actor's imitation of Uriah Heep. He ran a sweaty palm over his hair.

A long time passed. His palms had dried. Robert began to suspect he had been abandoned. He stood up and stepped toward the door and tentatively reached a hand toward the knob. As if he were being watched the door sprung open right underneath his outstretched reach, freezing Robert in an embarrassing posture.

Delray Pervus stood on the other side, the picture of grim foreboding. There was something funereal about his pose, upright and somber, as if he were welcoming another sinner into hell.

"Down the hall, to the left," he said.

Robert started to say something, something slightly apologetic, peace-offering.

Delray raised an attenuated hand.

"Down the hall, to the left," he repeated.

Robert gathered his uneasy dignity and sidestepped past the ghastly supervisor and walked slowly down the hall.

At the end, on the left, was another door. This one, however, was wooden, warm, painted a forest green. It was like a door in a home, welcoming and friendly. Robert felt better suddenly. He didn't know whether to knock or just walk in. He settled for a light rap as he opened the door.

"Hi," he said, with as benevolent a grin as he could muster. He faced a desk the size of a battleship, as devoid of clutter as an airport tarmac; not even a phone marred its perfect, black surface. The only thing resting on the desktop were the muscular hands of the store's manager. These hands drew Robert's attention: they were lightly coated with thin black hair and the interlaced fingers exuded a strength Robert could only admire, a strength which *ruled*.

Gradually Robert took in the rest of the individual before him, who seemed content to sit quietly while Robert made his assessments. The face above the exquisitely cut suit was the face of a devil, if one can conceive of the devil as movie-star handsome. There was something of the young Robert DeNiro about him, something equally princely and evil. Then, as if a conjuring act had been achieved before his wondering eyes, Robert saw his ghastly mistake. This was not a handsome man sitting before him in stately silence, but a woman, a woman in a business suit, with hair slicked back from her well-defined face with cunning severity. It was a face to be reckoned with, a beatific appearance; it was Oz. As Robert made the adjustment the face cracked ever so slightly with what Robert eventually realized was a smile. She smiled at the dawning of intelligence in Robert's countenance, and at Robert's smallness.

Robert crept forward in slow motion and took the chair in front of the desk as if it had been offered him. He could not speak and waited only to be told what to do, crawl away, kiss her shoes, prostrate himself before the store's *Maya*. This was not a mere grocery store he was dealing with, he realized, but a power, a presence, a principality ruled by empirism, judiciousness, love. He was nothing before it. He was less than nothing.

Finally the beautiful face opened and spoke.

"What is your name?" she asked, as if she were picking him up in a bar.

"Robert," Robert said. "Robert Caldwell."

She seemed to think about this.

Maybe he was wrong. Maybe Robert Caldwell was known to her and he was not him.

"You have insulted our clerk, I understand, Mr. Caldwell?"

"Well, no," Robert began. "That is, it was I, me, I who was insulted. Your clerk swore at me."

"That is not what she says," came the answer.

Was it possible this preeminence had already spoken to all available parties, had already called all the witnesses, had adjudicated and found him blameworthy?

"Well," Robert said again. "I merely questioned a price on some frozen pizzas and she..." Robert trailed off. "It sounds kind of silly now," he added.

"Is it silly?"

"I mean, it's just some crummy pizzas—"

"You're dissatisfied with our pizzas?"

"No," Robert said quickly. "No. I mean, it's not as important as all this."

"All what, Mr. Caldwell?"

"This folderol," Robert said, grandly.

She thought for a moment more.

"I'm quite at a loss what to do with you, Mr. Caldwell," she said with some stress.

Robert felt a tingling along the base of his neck.

The manager slowly rose from behind the desk, uncoiling her body like a constrictor. She moved from behind her judge's bench and Robert turned in his chair toward her. She moved as if she were an automaton, her feet seemingly rolling across the carpeted floor. As she emerged from behind her monstrous desk Robert comprehended her full majesty. She wore a short skirt with her suit and her legs were strong and lithe; unstockinged, they shone with a rosy glare. She stood next to his chair and her large, fulsome body exuded an animal musk. Despite his fear Robert felt a stiffening in his trousers, inappropriate as an erection on the gallows.

She turned Robert toward her and he realized for the first time that his chair was on wheels. She stood almost astride him, her legs slightly parted and her powerful thighs on each side of his. She took his face in her warm, moist hands and lifted his gaze upwards. She bent to look closely into his eyes and Robert saw revealed underneath the suit coat and lacy shirt the swell of life, two onerous mammaries.

"So, Robert Caldwell," she said, peering into his very soul, her hands moving gently on his cheeks.

The air was full of static. Robert was warmed by her proximity.

"I'm sorry," she said after a moment. "I'm not going to be able to let you go."

Robert wasn't sure he had heard her. He was muddled, sweating. His ears seemed to be filled with a low-range rumble as of some incessant machine deep in the bowels of the store. He was afraid, aroused—save for the blood flow to his genitals he could not feel his body. He was sure at any moment she would laugh and they would exchange companionable touches and it would all be over. A deeper, insane urge flashed through him. Momentarily he became afraid he would never see her again. He wanted to extend the agony just a little longer before being released with a chuckle and a pat on the back. He wanted to be her prisoner, just a little longer.

"We can't have you running around badmouthing our employees, can we?" She sounded almost reasonable. Her right hand left his cheek, nestled in the hair at the back of his head, caressing him for an instant. Robert closed his eyes.

Her fingers entwined in his hair tightened suddenly and she snapped Robert's head back and his eyes shot open. She lowered her face over his and Robert thought—oh briefly—she was going to kiss him. Her mouth would be hot and wet, like a jungle. He anticipated the contact.

"Worm," she said and her inviolate mouth pursed to a sneer.

"Look," Robert said, half strangled.

"Your time to talk is over," she said, pulling harder on his hair. "Your time to talk is history. It's Babylon. It's Persia."

She had Robert's head in a death grip. He believed his hair was beginning to tear. He raised an arm in a half-hearted attempt at freeing himself only to find her knee quickly in his crotch. She wiggled it in tight and pressed firmly on his most tender center.

She looked intently into his eyes one last time and released his hair with a dismissive gesture. She stood up and straightened her suit.

Again the face showed its feral smile and then she was at the door and there were hands on Robert and he was being dragged down the corridor and, before he could protest he was thrown into a room and the door was closed.

Robert looked at his cell, with a searching eye, still dazzled from the rough handling, tempering his outrage. He was looking for signs of comfort, for a human touch, for a feeling that here he could sort things out. There was a certain relief to being left alone.

It was a small room, but it was well appointed. There was a couch (which Robert found out later was a hide-a-bed), a wash basin, a commode, a chair such as one might find in chain motel rooms, a plastic plant in a bucket. No window. No television. No books.

Other than the aforementioned plant—what was it supposed to resemble, a palm? eucalyptus?—the only nod to aesthetics was a cheap art reproduction scotch-taped to the back of the door: Breughel's *The Fall of Icarus*.

Robert stretched out on the couch and tried to order his thoughts. He had been insulted, mocked, embarrassed, roughly treated, and, finally, thrown into a small room, apparently to frighten him. He took several deep breaths. Ok, he told himself, overall it wasn't that bad. He had not been physically hurt. What they intended to do with him was a mystery but they would surely come back and talk to him further. Perhaps she would come again. Perhaps they could start over again. This was all a misunderstanding. It could be rectified.

When they slid his evening meal under the door was the first time Robert noticed the slit in the door built just for that purpose. And, for the first time, Robert felt nauseatingly afraid. He was actively sick into his commode and the food was left there to spoil. The next morning—had he slept? had he really slept here all night?—another tray of food was passed under the door and Robert understood he was to slide the old plate out. This he did.

That morning the eggs and sausage looked highly edible and Robert cleaned the plate, again sliding his dishes back out when he was finished. At lunch the process was repeated.

As the days went by Robert realized the real test facing him would be the lack of human contact, and this interested him and amused him. He spoke to no one and no one spoke to him. He tried once to shout through the door when his dinner plate arrived, but there was no reply.

After many months Robert's routine became sacred to him. He slept eight hours every night and in the morning made the bed back into a couch. He was disciplined. Once, when the lunch plate was not delivered until mid-afternoon, Robert grew restless and morose. But he was immediately cheered when the food arrived, especially since his desert was tapioca pudding.

One day was like the next, soldiering on into the unforeseeable future, and Robert found himself living an inner life which surprised him with its richness. His imagination became a flexible, athletic, living thing. He kept his senses alive, his brain sharp. Sometimes he thought of Gayla, but he knew she was young and strong and would make it without him. He smiled a rueful smile and wished her well.

His diet was good thanks to his keepers and he even exercised. His body became an important part of him, no longer just a tool for mobility, but a soul-cage, and he began to marvel daily at the imposing size of his chest and the slate-hard curve of his thighs.

He stayed alive and alert and at the ready. Someday, again, soon perhaps, something would happen to Robert, again a twist, a curve in life's numinous and pedagogic road, and this thing which happened would gladden and astound him. Maybe *she* would return, or maybe it would be something else. But Robert stayed ready, alone in his room beneath the supermarket, a coiled spring of possibility.

God and the Devil: The Exit Interview

—Satan, Satan, come in. Sit down.

—Thank you.

—Comfortable?

—Yes, of course. Your amenities have always been first class.

—Drink?

—Nothing, thank you.

—Smoke.

—Hm.

—Sorry.

—It's alright. I see you've got a Bosch.

—An original. Bet they'd like to see this one down on Number One, eh?

—Mine also.

—Yes. A Bosch? Yes, I can imagine.

—Of course you can. You are the First Imagination.

—Flatterer.

—Not at all.

—So—sure you won't have a drink?

—No, thank you. I only have a little time left. As you know.

—Right. Sorry.

—Stop apologizing.

—Ahem. This might not seem fair after, you know, kicking you out of Paradise.

—What do I know from fair?

—Right, ha. So, listen, have you had a chance to look over what I've written. I trust your opinion because, you know, the devil is in the details.

—The devil is in the fine print.

—Right. That's the kind of thing I'm looking for.

—Well, I have read it through. It's good.

—But…

—No, really, it's good. There are a few things I would have done differently.

—Tell me.

—You're presumably writing this with one of them.

—Yes, I am the—ghost writer.

—This opening chapter, *I Made a Little Mistake: I Call it Man.*

—Yes?

—A little harsh, isn't it? I mean, consider your audience.

—I see your point. Better idea?

—How about keeping it simple? *Commencement.*

—Hm.

—Or, *So It Begins.*

—Yes, I like that one.

—*Genesis.*

—Now, that's a beautiful name. Hasn't been used before?

—Not to my knowledge.

—Good, good. Done. Anything else?

—Put some more jokes in. You're so damned solemn. Use your humor.

—I'm not funny like you.

—You have your own special brand of humor. The platypus for example. Gnats. Twisters. Those little fluke things that penetrate their soles and worm upward. Kneecaps that last only 30 years.

—(stifles chortle)

—Sexual *desire.*

—(Snorts) Partly yours.

—Still. You had final approval.

—(chuckling) Giving them a right royal amount of turmoil, isn't it?

—Yes. I am particularly pleased with how out of control the males are.

—Ha. I know. Anyway. More humor. Okay. I'll work on that but I can't promise.

—You can.

—But I have to follow through.

—Unlike yours truly.

—Exactly. Did you like the action scenes?

—The wars. The murders, rapes, haircuts. Of course.

—Good, good. Job is all over me about promoting violence. It's not like it's a video game, right?

—Video game?

—It comes later. They make them.

—Ah. Leave it to the monkeys to even raise you on the violence scale.

—What about the ending?

—*Polecats and Carrion in the Kiln House*?

—Yes. Good, right?

—My favorite chapter. Should scare the holy shit out of them.

—I know. A little fear never hurt, right? A little warning shot across the bow.

—Yes. Keep the monkeys harried and unsure. The title though?

—Again? Not good?

—Too...*literary*. You're showing your hand. Let them come to it suddenly, like a spectre around a dark corner. Let them draw their own conclusions.

—I see.

—How about *Pilliwinks*?

—I don't know what that means.

—Neither will they.

—I see.

—Ok, too obscure. You're right. How about *Revolutions*? No—wait— *Revelation*.

—*Revelation*. Hm. You think that's a kind of, what? Teaser?

—Exactly.

—Could work.

—It will.

—Great then. *Revelation*. To close. Just so.

—Is that all? Free to fall now?

—Don't do me that way. I'm sorry.

—Stop.

—Ok. Anything before you go? Really. I appreciate the help. What would you like?

—10,000 virgins?

—You'll have your little joke. I told you your sense of humor is better than mine.

—How about some of the lesser angels? Someone to add to my army.

—Army?

—Just kidding.

—Right. Ok. Sure. Got anyone in mind?

—Mammon?

—Greedy little bastard.

—Exactly.

—He's yours.

—Thanks.

—Ok, listen. Thanks. Sorry about the expulsion. Keep in touch.

—Count on it.

Monster

Prior to the monster taking Effie Sempsh into the woods on August 21st, some things had happened in Effie's life that require delineating. Effie was a complex woman and, though the temptation to simplify her story is strong, in the end truth must be served and details must be brought to light.

Effie and her husband, Robert Sempsh, lived in a neighborhood not far from the airport, not far from the chemical plants, the kind of neighborhood one passes in one's car and either turns away from or notices with only half one's attention. Nondescript is perhaps descriptive. Run-down certainly.

Robert worked at a bottling plant in nearby Millington. They bottled a lesser known soft drink, something called Flip, a mixture of citrusy extracts and corn syrup. Robert was not a boss. He was a drone on the line and he hated every single day he worked there. We could say more about Robert but you probably know his type. Perhaps you went to high school with someone like him. Robert drank. Robert was lazy. Robert abused his wife with an acid tongue and an unassailable sense of his own superiority.

Effie was not happy that she had married Robert. When they were younger he seemed exciting, a sort of poor man's James Dean. Soon, it became clear that his anarchic charm was thin like a coating of sweat, and that he was self-centered and mean. Effie contemplated leaving him, of course. But she was afraid. Robert could get violent, though, so far, he had never hit Effie. He'd broken things, thrown bottles, put his fist through a bedroom door, kicked the neighbor's dog, but he had never hit Effie. Instead he spoke to her as if he hated her. Some part of Robert, some underdeveloped part of Robert, thought that this was how husbands treated wives. Effie never thought so. She thought Robert was unhappy with his life and his unhappiness took the form of mental abuse and coarseness and alcoholism and drug taking.

Effie's father used to hit her. He called her whore and tramp because she had sex with boys in cars. Effie's father was a Baptist preacher.

Effie's best friend, Tammy Northern, lived across the street in a house only a modest modicum nicer than Effie's. Tammy's husband had taken off a few years ago, leaving her with an infant daughter, Rebecca, and a house note. He had taken their only car, a Yugo. Yet, Tammy did not lie down and die. Instead she took a class at a vo-tech school and learned how to be a veterinary assistant. She now made pretty good money, had a new Volkswagen, and kept herself and Becca in most of what is called the necessities. Tammy's home was a pretty happy place to visit, it seemed to Effie, and Effie took advantage of that, escaping her own plight with long lunches at the Northern's. Also, Effie loved Becca, little butterball with jet black hair and eyes like a bush baby's, and often, happily, babysat for her. She would not take Tammy's money for this.

Naturally, Effie envied Tammy her life as a single mom and independent operator. Often before falling asleep at night she imagined such a life for herself. What kind of profession would she like to try? Would she like to date numerous eligible bachelors? Would she, eventually, like to be a mother also? This self-interview was like counting sheep for Effie. After a few minutes of interrogation she would slip gently into Morpheus' tender clench, the god of dreams deferred.

About the same time the monster was first sighted Robert increased the intensity and frequency of his abuse. A couple times, after cursing and throwing things failed to sate his ire, he raised his fist and wondered in that frozen second what it would feel like to strike Effie's once pretty face. Effie stared at that fist and grew more tired and grew more afraid and felt more trapped than ever.

The monster was first reported in Shelbyville, a town about 13 miles up Highway 69. Three kids, age 10, 12 and 12, were camping in the woods near their home and were awakened by a loud rustling and grunting that sounded like a wild boar. They quietly unzipped their tent expecting to be face to face with a bear, or boar, or panther. Instead they saw an upright creature with the feathery head of a cockatoo, the orange body hair of an ape, the shoulders of a linebacker and a face as hideous as a nightmare. There were tusks protruding from its slobbery mouth, a nose like an anteater's and eyes as red as a devil's. This was how the boys described the monster to the police. And they further reported how the thing stood stock still when the boys emerged from their tent, caught reaching into the remnants of their campfire for burnt pieces of hot dog or marshmallow. And, the boys said, the thing seemed frightened of them and scurried off into the woods, running upright like a gorilla, but with the speed of an ocelot.

"Did you see this story about the creature in Shelbyville?" Tammy asked Effie over morning coffee. "Kids."

"Yeah. Probably about as real as Bigfoot and Nessie. Years from now the boys will admit to manufacturing their ogre, just like the Nessie photograph is now known to be a trick."

"Probly," Tammy agreed.

"Of course our woods are dark and deep. No telling what all could be living up in there," Effie added, being of two minds as usual.

"Yeah. Maybe a beast like in that Disney cartoon. A scary beast but ultimately sweet," Tammy said. And then, giggling, added, "And really well hung you'd have to think."

"It would be an upgrade for me," Effie said, and the two women laughed together, sipping coffee, nibbling scones, and then moving on to other topics of interest.

A week later another sighting, this time right in Millington, raised the level of consternation, as well as the level of fear. A busboy for Peter and Samuel's Restaurant, who was working the early morning shift, opened the back door of the restaurant to empty the trash and startled a creature going through their dumpster. The busboy said it was a good eight feet tall, hairy as an ape and ugly as a scarecrow. He (it) glared momentarily at the frozen busboy, then turned and ran in the direction of the nearby coppice. He also said the creature was fast. "Like Rajon Rondo," the busboy said.

Now everyone was talking about the monster. Tammy shrugged when Effie asked her what she thought. "Can it be real?" Effie asked.

"Sure. What the hell," Tammy said, turning a couple pancakes in a small frying pan. "You ever seen a crocodile up close? We'd call that a monster if we had never seen it before."

"I guess," Effie said.

"You know Bert, Bert Pipkin, lives in the cove?"

"Um," Effie said, but Tammy was moving on.

"Bert teaches at the university. Maybe he doesn't anymore. He's a real smart man. He teaches anthropology. I think. Maybe it's archeology. Or zoology. Anyway. Bert says, folktales often have real life something or others. Correlations?"

"Huh," Effie said.

"Yeah, Bert says there's always a little grain of truth in any myth. Like sailors thinking narwhals were mermaids. Or was it unicorns?"

"I think I've seen Bert," Effie said, now. "He wear suspenders?"

"Yeah," Tammy laughed. "That's Bert."

"I think I talked to him once," Effie said.

Effie had indeed once talked to the neighborhood rascal, Bert. The way the old guy looked at her made Effie's heart go ker-plunk. He was the sort of man who didn't disguise his baser instincts, yet manages to, somehow, not seem a masher. Effie was embarrassed the morning she went to the mailbox and Bert was in the street, cursing and pulling at the tangled whipcord of his weed whacker. She was embarrassed because she was wearing a rock band (Whitesnake) t-shirt and plum sweatpants. Yet, she thought, why should it matter if this stranger, this eccentric old man with his *Godspell* suspenders, see her in sweatpants?

Bert came over to her.

"Sorry about my language, Mrs. Sempsh," Bert said. "Goddamn weed whacker." And he laughed.

Effie laughed, too.

They stood and grinned at each other. It was obvious Bert didn't care that she was in sweatpants. It was obvious because he couldn't take his eyes off her bra-less breasts and their neat little nipples showing through the t-shirt. Effie was stirred. It had been a long time since Effie had been stirred. And by this inappropriate neighbor, for goodness' sake. How old must he be, 70?

"I'm Bert Pipkin," Bert said and put out a thin, strong hand, with gnarly veins. Effie took the hand and the man's skin was surprisingly soft.

"Effie Sempsh," Effie said and then laughed again. He obviously knew her name.

"Effie," Bert said. His eyes were tickling her nipples.

"Ok," Effie said. "See ya." And she went back inside her house.

Later it occurred to her that she had forgotten her mail. She would have to return to the box after Bert went inside. She sat in her living room staring at the TV which was off. She was stirred. "I'm not dead yet," she thought.

The third time the monster made the news was a week after the restaurant sighting. This time he boldly came into someone's back yard.

And this was only a half mile or so from Effie's house. The monster had made off with a family's dog.

"He's getting closer," Tammy said, smiling and stirring her coffee.

"I know," Effie said. She was a bit distracted. She had found a rubber in Robert's pants pocket that morning while doing laundry. Why was Robert carrying rubbers around with him? The answer was obvious.

"Bert says he's genuine but he doesn't like the term monster. Bert said, 'Be careful who you're calling a monster. The real monsters might object.'"

"Robert is a real monster," Effie said, matter-of-factly.

"Another fight?" Tammy asked, her face all concern now.

"Not yet," Effie said and she managed a sardonic grin.

That evening during dinner Effie pulled the rubber out of her pocket and placed it next to Robert's plate, alongside his knife and fork.

"What's that?" Robert said.

"I think you know what it is, Robert."

"You wanna fuck?" he asked. It was the sort of trashy swagger that turned Effie's stomach. She wanted to spit.

"Why are you carrying rubbers in your pockets?" she asked, trying to keep the rise of her voice composed. Tears were marshaling behind her eyes.

Robert looked at her. He picked up the rubber and held the package in the palm of his hand. He looked at it as if it were a small toy. He smiled at Effie and stuck the rubber in his pants pocket. "Bring me dinner," he said.

"Robert," Effie said. "Why are you carrying a goddamn rubber?"

It was then that Robert hit Effie for the first time. He backhanded her as neatly as a gunslinger pulling a gun. Effie's nose shot out a bright upsurge of blood. She ran to the bathroom and locked the door. Robert sat still for a moment. Then he got up and got his own food.

So now it is complete, Effie thought. I have gone from my father's fist to my husband's. Some kind of evil circle has completed itself.

The next morning, after Robert had gone to work, Effie made her solitary way to her friend's house. She wanted comfort but she didn't want to talk about her nose, now red with what looked like a black streak through it, as if someone had drawn there with lipstick and an eyebrow pencil.

"Oh, Jesus!" Tammy screeched. "That bastard!"

She lead Effie into the house by the elbow as if she suspected that Effie might be wobbly on her pins from being popped on the whiffer. In the kitchen Bert Pipkin sat at Tammy's table, a cup of coffee in front of him. On one of his suspenders was a button, like a Your Name Here badge at a school reunion. The button said, *Think Green*.

"What happened, Mrs. Sempsh?" Bert said, his voice warm and caressing.

"Please call me Effie," Effie said, sitting down across from him. Bert reached across and touched the back of her hand. The gesture was affectionate, friendly. Bert's eyes, Effie noticed now, were blue with a light rim of water as if he could cry at any moment. He was still a very attractive man, leonine and assured. Tammy had told Effie that Bert had lived on their street since he was a young newlywed. He had owned that house for most of his life and had watched the neighborhood slowly deteriorate. He retired from the local university five years ago.

"I tripped over our throw rug," Effie said to the room.

Tammy said, "I'll kill that bastard. I swear I will."

"Tammy," Effie said.

"Bert, will you kill her slimeball husband for me? I mean it, will you?"

"Does he hit you often?" Bert said, again in soothing, warm tones.

"No, no," Effie said a bit too quickly. "He's never hit me before. I mean, he has a temper but—" And here Effie began to sob quietly. Bert and Tammy watched her for a moment to see if she could collect herself quickly.

Tammy sat next to her and put a hand on her shoulder.

"He's trash, Bert," Tammy now said. "He's just trash."

The monster was next seen that afternoon, moving along the edge of the wooded area two streets over from Effie's street. He looked like a man in a hurry, a large hairy man. He glanced toward the small group of people who stood stock still watching him. No one spoke.

Then suddenly the monster was gone. He had disappeared into a gap in the woods the way a mouse can become almost two-dimensional to squeeze into your house. The darkness of the woods swallowed him, *blip*.

Finally someone spoke.

"Should we go get some hunters or somebody, some guns, and go after that thing?" someone said. It was the beginning of something impure, something precarious. It was the beginning of the contagious idea that their neighborhood, as rundown as it was, was in danger and no amount of vigilance or level of retaliation would be an overreaction.

The morning of August 21st was like most mornings at the Sempsh home. A few days ago Robert had apologized for his smack to Effie's face. He had apologized, as they say, in his way.

In his way.

That's what I am, thought Effie. Just something else he has to move around to gain the things he wants from the world: another drink, food prepared for him, a fresh-faced fuck every once in a while.

Effie set Robert's pancakes and sausage in front of him on the morning of August 21st. She put the preserves and syrup within his reach. He barely looked at her. Food arrived for Robert as if pixie-borne.

Effie's nose now was the yellow of a dull bug light. "Yellow as a hopeless lover," Effie's Aunt Pat used to say.

"The coffee's not very hot," Robert said, after a while. He was reading the paper, the news on August 21st. Effie was leaning against the sink, chewing on a cuticle, staring out across their small yard at the rubbish in the small yard backed up to theirs.

Effie looked at her husband. There was hot coffee on the stove. Admittedly, she was closer to it. Effie gave a moment's thought to throwing the coffee in her husband's face. Wearily, instead, she hoisted the pot and topped off Robert's cup. He didn't move or say a word. He was reading another article about the monster. This morning's editorial speculated that he was more akin to the Yeti than to Bigfoot. The distinction was a fine one, it seemed.

That afternoon, at home alone, Effie found herself staring out her front window. She had been listless all day. She had wandered from room to room like a stink. She was moony and sad.

Outside she saw Bert Pipkin digging around the base of his mailbox. His thin old back showed a semi-circle of perspiration on his carmine shirt. There was something about that arc of sweat that attracted Effie. She woke up.

Effie found herself in the bedroom looking frantically through drawers. She had to hurry. Bert could go inside any moment. What Effie chose to put on was a pair of thin running shorts, her briefest panties and a t-shirt with the arms cut off. Before putting the shirt on Effie removed her bra. She willed her nipples to stand at attention. She wanted Bert to see those nipples. Effie had a fine new idea, one that had been brewing inside her for a while. She was going to fuck Bert Pipkin.

In the bathroom Effie put in her diaphragm. She was wet. She was surprised at how wet she was already. She actually smiled at herself in the mirror. This was something she could do. She was not dead. She could still have sex.

Leaving the bathroom in a rush she ran into her husband, home unexpectedly. She hit his chest and fell backwards as if she had tripped or been thrown aside. Robert looked at his wife in her short shorts and skimpy t-shirt. He studied her for a second. Then he saw the diaphragm case open on the back of the toilet. In her haste Effie had left it there.

Robert grabbed Effie by the hair. Effie did not scream. Robert slapped her once. Effie took it. She was guilty. She was about to be punished.

Robert practically dragged his wife into the kitchen. He threw her down into a kitchen chair. Then he went to the silverware drawer and began to rummage through it. He was looking for something but he did not know what. Something heavy, something that would hurt his wife but not kill her. He found a mace-like object made of wood. It had a flanged head. He didn't know what it was used for but it fit his hand like a weapon.

He turned toward Effie who sat in the chair, slump-shouldered and afraid. Tears ran down her cheeks. Effie saw the mallet, the meat tenderizer.

"No, Robert," she said, quietly. But she knew it was too late to protest. It was years too late.

Robert walked toward his wife. He hit her once with the back of his hand. Effie put a hand to the cheek but otherwise did not move. She did not raise her hands to protect herself.

"Who?" Robert said, raising the weapon. "Who?"

Effie looked up at him. What did it matter? she said in her head.

"Who?" Robert said, and swung the mace, one time, half-heartedly. It met the side of Effie's head with a dull sound and she was deafened. There was a roar inside her. It was her blood answering her attacker.

Effie was not sure quite what happened next. Suddenly a darkness crossed their kitchen window, a strong, angry cloud. She did not hear the back door wrenched open. Suddenly Robert was not standing in front of her any longer. Blood ran into Effie's eyes.

Robert was not standing in front of her any longer. The monster had picked him up and thrown him out the back door. The monster had then gone out into the yard for a few minutes, maybe two or three. Effie sat in her chair. Her hand was caressing her sore cheek, her fingers now coated in blood. She did not know what was happening. She was dizzy. She was perhaps hallucinating.

The monster returned and picked Effie up. He gently swung her over his shoulder. As they exited the house the monster stepped over Robert, where he was lying at the bottom of the steps, mired in mud and blood. Robert had landed on the cheap lawn sprinkler and now it bent around his head like a cracked headset. It looked comic and cheerless. Robert watched the monster take his wife away but Robert could not move. There were broken bones involved. Robert watched the monster take his wife into the woods. They disappeared into the darkness of the woods as if they had walked through a door into another dimension.

"Fuck," Robert said, right before he passed out.

Slung over the monster's shoulder Effie was surprisingly calm. She thought about an expression she had heard, something about the devil you know versus the devil you do not. She didn't want to know the devil she knew anymore.

Effie had no idea how long she rode that great bony shoulder. She may have swooned, or dozed. It seemed as if they had traveled miles. She did not know the wooded area near her home was so deep, so dark, so tangled and spackled with only tiny spears of sunlight. The monster moved swiftly but smoothly. Effie felt as if she were gliding, flying.

On they went. For miles they went.

Effie let her hands, which dangled over the creature's back, feel the muscular landscape beneath its matted fur. He was a powerful animal.

Some time later, an hour, a day, the monster stopped. The ground cover was thick and extraordinary. Effie thought she couldn't possibly be in the woods near her home, the plain, kudzuey, Southern woods she had grown up with. All around her was a lush explosion of greenery, thick and twisted and strange. It was a nightmare's forest, a place of florid black-magic, except that Effie was calm, was unafraid.

The monster had stopped near the base of an enormous tree, an oak perhaps. Effie wished she knew plant life. The tree was thick and covered with gnarly, shaggy vines, thick vines that wound around the tree like constrictors. The beast readjusted Effie on his shoulder. His strong hand on her back felt reassuring, even affectionate. Effie thought she might swoon again.

Then as sudden as the crack of a rifle the monster grasped one vine and began to move upward at an expeditious clip. He was carrying Effie into the trees. They rose like a column of smoke, swiftly and smoothly into the darkness near the top. The leaves, damp with nature, slid across Effie's cheeks and arms. She felt bedewed, refreshed. And still up they went. It got darker.

Until they came to a stopping point. The monster set her down. She was standing on a plank floor. She was standing on a solid oak plank floor. Her eyes widened in amazement. Above her she could see tree-top, the sun a dappling brightness through the arabesque of foliage. She was on the porch of a house, a house built in the trees. It was small but beautifully made. Everything, door to hinge, boards to logs, window to wall, was finely connected. It was gorgeous. Effie tentatively stepped inside. There was an actual door! The monster moved backwards, slowly, cautiously. He was afraid to let her see.

She stood in the middle of the room, amid rugs and handmade furniture and oil lamps and cooking stove and bookshelves (bookshelves!) and she was positively dizzy with what she was witnessing. She turned her wide-eyed wonder toward the monster. She smiled encouragement. Finally, she found her voice.

"Did you, did you build this?" Effie asked, tentatively, as if speaking to a child. "I'm sorry, can you understand me?"

"Yes," the monster said. He cleared his jumbo throat. "I understand you. Though I am out of practice conversing."

"You—you," Effie didn't know what she wanted to say. "You-—saved me."

"Mm," the monster said. "He seemed a very bad man."

"He's an awful man, yes," Effie said, and suddenly felt shy before this creature, so colossal and strong and exotic.

"I hurt him," the monster said.

"Yes," Effie said, and she smiled sweetly at him.

"I don't understand," Effie said, after a while. "You talk, you build, you—you read! Where did you come from?"

The monster looked sad. He put a large hand on a globe and spun it absentmindedly.

"I'm sorry," Effie said. "It doesn't matter."

"Sit," the monster said.

Effie sat on the couch, her legs drawn up under her.

The monster sat on the couch also. His hair was thick like a cross between a boar's and an orangutan's. And it smelled slightly like wet leather, or creosote, a musky but not unpleasant funk.

"I'm sorry, I don't know your name," Effie said. "Mine is Effie."

"Effie," he said. And for a second she thought he meant that was his name, too.

"I am called, was called Genet."

Now it was Effie's turn to repeat. "Genet." She said it softly the way one might say the name of a magical place, a new Eden.

In the days that followed Genet and Effie became closer. She could cook some things he could not. He brought her squirrels and possums and snakes. She improvised meals that pleased them both. Gradually a warmth grew between them. Effie almost forgot about her life down below. She was enchanted, captivated if not captured.

Some nights they sat on the couch holding hands and talking about their past lives. Effie still never understood where Genet had come from. He would only speak about it in vague terms as if it had passed away into myth, like Atlantis. He seemed lost, out of his element. He had taken to eating trash. Was he a victim like her?

And as they grew closer it was inevitable that they should finally share one bed. Effie had often been nude in front of her host (there was little privacy in their small quarters) but nothing sexual had arisen from that. But on this night, as if by mutual agreement, they ended up at the same bed. Genet was modest, reticent. He told her he had not been with a woman in over ten years. Where had he lived then? Effie wondered. Effie wondered if he meant a human woman like her. Effie allowed as to how she was pretty sexually pent up herself.

They lay under the thin cotton sheet for a while. Effie's nakedness was stimulating her giant friend. He seemed impatient now, and a low growl rumbled through him.

"Genet," she whispered in his ear.

"I'm not a monster," Genet said. "I am just a very ugly man."

And, at that moment, I wish I could tell you that Effie found him beautiful, but it was not so. He was hideous, as ugly as a devil born of mud.

But it didn't matter. She reached down and felt for his pizzle. It was already erect and as big and thick as a horse's. My stars, she thought, if Tammy could see me now. And right before she mounted the monster Effie wondered for a moment if she had put in her diaphragm. But then, in an incandescent flash of epiphany and joy and optimism and prescience, she thought to herself, it does not matter. He is my one lover now.

Everything $20

Jim, the writer, was jogging in an unfamiliar part of town when he had an inspiration. He'd brought no paper with him but his fanny pack held a pen. He eyed the businesses nearby and saw a sign over what looked like a sundry store, *Everything $20.*

He jogged in.

"Paper?" he asked the slim, disinterested young fellow behind the narrow counter.

The fellow gestured toward some pads and post-it notes. Jim grabbed a small package of the latter, stripped it of its cellophane and made a frantic scribble on the top note.

"Ok," Jim said, as if the clerk would share his enthusiasm. "How much?"

"$20," the clerk said.

"Ha," Jim answered. "Seriously, how much?"

"Everything $20."

"No, look, I've got, what here…$3. Surely it's not more than $3."

"$20," the clerk reiterated.

"I'm not paying $20 for a pack of post-it notes."

"You will or I'll call the cops," came the surly answer.

"Right, you'll call the cops over post-it notes. That I'd like to see."

Sam and Janet had just gotten married. It was early in the morning after the first night in their honeymoon city and its tony hotel. They were strolling, hand-in-hand.

"I need a newspaper," Sam said.

"Here." Janet pointed toward a store.

There was a stack of newspapers on the counter. Sam picked one up.

"Look at the headline," Janet said. "It's about that missing writer."

"I see," Sam said. "How much?" he asked the clerk.

"$20," came back the reply.

"Oh, come on," Sam said with some heat.

The Slim Harpo Blues

I woke up needing music. I have an extensive CD collection, with a smattering of vinyl. This morning I needed music before anything else. I flipped through the CDs. Nothing was opening up for me; nothing seemed right. Who was it Nimuë mentioned last night? Slim Somebody. I looked through the CDs again. My mind was blurry, a fuzzy base. Slim Whitman? I checked my Ws. No Slim Whitman but Slim Whitman didn't sound right. Slim…Pickens, no….Slim….Harpo! She was talking about Slim Harpo. I checked: no Slim Harpo.

This occasioned an early morning dilemma. I didn't want the day to go all pear-shaped because I didn't have Slim Harpo. Who was Slim Harpo? Someone cool, someone with élan. Someone missing. He could be just what I need. Then, just that suddenly, I realized that my life would be bereft without hearing Slim Harpo. It felt as if only Slim Harpo could make my life complete. Perhaps I could relax a bit. Perhaps this was a step that was important and afterward I could feel that my extensive CD collection was complete, and thus my life. Perhaps this sounds absurd to you. There is something in me, in the universe, if that's not overstating it, which needs completion. Close the circle. That felt like a mantra for what was happening inside me: Close the circle.

And you know Nimuë and I are having troubles. That's what they euphemistically call it: having troubles. In short, the love is gone. From her side. My love is on the other end of the teeter-totter. As her love sinks mine rises. I love Nimuë. She makes me a me I like better than the me without her. She told me about Slim Harpo. She recognizes gaps. She knows how to work on me, how to build me up, how to take the clay and form a pitcher.

It was cold out. You know. The weather we've been having is uncharacteristically cold for this particular piece of geography. And, since it was cold outside, I didn't really want to get all bundled up to go to the music store and get some Slim Harpo. But I thought I should.

Also, I am broke. Not homeless broke but a CD is an extravagance at this point. Where did my money go? To Nimuë, of course. I spend money on her because I don't know what else to do. I buy her things, love tokens. I give her gifts the way water gives us wet.

I looked at my clothes. They seemed to be especially sucky. I was trying to remember the last thing I wore that Nimuë liked. The jacket with the elbow patches. I hate that jacket but once when I wore it she said, You look all right. Just like that, without prompting. I love that.

I dressed warmly enough. I had a scarf. I don't remember where I got it. Perhaps my mother knitted it for me but I couldn't remember whether my mother knitted or not. And besides it didn't look knitted. I wore it wrapped around my neck like a tourniquet.

The car started. That was a plus. This was going to be a good day, an outing. Sometimes an outing is all we need. Get out of the cage. I had one moment of panic as I drove down my street. I suddenly thought it was a week day and I had forgotten that it was a week day and hence I was missing work. I could not afford to miss work. Mr. Gribble wouldn't stand for it.

Sunday. I told myself, it's Sunday. I knew this because yesterday was Saturday and on Saturday nights Nimuë and I have a standing date. We didn't last night which brought on an ugly telephone conversation after which I wept quietly by myself on the sofa while watching *Jeopardy* and not just *Jeopardy* but a rerun of *Jeopardy* where I already knew the answers. I just sat there and wept and wondered why Nimuë didn't want to have our usual date. She said, For God's sake, can't we miss one week? I snuffled. She hung up. But before all that, during the part of the telephone conversation when I thought we were still about to have our Saturday night date, she told me about Slim Harpo.

"Have you heard Slim Harpo?" she asked. I didn't want to appear ignorant. so I gave with one of those noncommittal, hmms. "You should. You should hear Slim Harpo. He's right up your alley," Nimuë said.

Now, bundled in clothing that was none too flattering, I drove the mile or so to the music store. This was an old converted Quaker meeting house, taken over by some slackers with a desire to start their own record label. Their stock, mostly, reflected their musical bent, which was toward a post-punk, thrash rock. If that's what it's called. Frankly, after New Wave, all the categories began to run like bleeding madras to me. Sometimes the music in the shop made my head hurt. Nimuë loved the store so I assumed they would have Slim Harpo. Inside it was dark as Egypt's night.

Re-Records was run by two musicians, Oswald and Pelleas. They are virtually indistinguishable from each other. I never know which one I am talking to. One of them greeted me as I entered. "Hail," he said. "Hey, man," I answered because you know why. "Where's Nim?" he further inquired. The conversation was already running long for me.

"Slim Harpo," I said.

Oswald or Pelleas looked at me and a snicker escaped his rock-and-roll mouth. He got himself under control.

"Uh huh," he said.

I waited patiently. I thought I had made my mission clear.

Quietly, Oswald or Pelleas came from behind the counter and walked slowly toward a section of used LPs. He riffled through them with a professional panache. He put his hand in. When he pulled his hand out it held an LP. He smiled as he carried it to me. The cover of the album sported a handsome picture of a handsome singer. His face looked like a marriage of Robert Johnson's and the basketball player, Hersey Hawkins'. "I'm a King Bee," the cover said.

"Slim Harpo," Oswald or Pelleas said.

It seemed costly to me. I expect to pay little for old used LPs. I ran my thumb over the price sticker. It seemed to be on there pretty much to stay.

"I'll throw this in," Oswald or Pelleas said. It was a plain white sleeve 45. "Lick it or Kick It" b/w "Mitmensch in Love." It was by Oswald and Pelleas' band The Agoraphobic Postmen. I smiled and ponied up the money.

Once home I was alone with Slim Harpo (and The Agoraphobic Postmen). I looked at Slim's face and I ached. I ached for Slim's face. I traced his severe cheek with a fingertip and whispered, "Nimuë."

I had to lie down for a while.

When I awoke I felt as if I had been dreaming of Paradise. I couldn't put my finger on any particulars, no streets of gold, no women made of honey. I chased that dream around in my head as if it were a blob of mercury under my thumb. "What is Paradise?" I asked myself. And myself would not answer. Close the circle.

Once I got the locusts out of my head I rose from the couch. My apartment looked strange to me, as if while I was sleeping someone had been leaching the color out of the room. I swung my body around and stood. There was a cracking sound under my foot. My heart sank. I was standing on Slim Harpo. His eyes looked from beneath my foot the way a chicken's eyes look right before you lower the ax.

I was slightly sick. I picked up Slim Harpo and slid the record from the sleeve. I had broken off a good sized chip from the edge. By my estimation I had about a song and a half left that was playable. I was sure that the song and a half I had left would be the worst song and a half on the entire LP. I wanted to cry. I picked up The Agoraphobic Postmen and flung them against the wall. They hit the wall with a satisfying smack and fell onto a chair, still whole.

I made my way into the kitchen. I made some coffee. I was on automatic pilot.

Then I noticed the blinking light on my answering machine. I had two messages. Nimuë hated that I wouldn't get a cell phone. She hated my answering machine. I took my coffee with me and sat down to play the messages.

The first message was from Nimuë. She said: "I am sorry. I am really really sorry. I wish it were different but it is not. I hope you will be happy later once you get over me. You will be a long time getting over me. Listen to Slim Harpo."

I began to cry. The other message blinked like the Cyclops looking out from Tartarus.

I put the Slim Harpo record on my turntable and tears dropped onto its spinning midnight. I heard the last notes of a song. Then the final song on that side began. I hated it. I hated Slim Harpo as I do hell pains. His voice was a screech, a banshee's cry.

The other message was from you. When did you leave it? What do you want? Can you just tell me? What the hell do you want from me?

He's Gone

The waiting. The goddamn hours stretching out like a winding sheet. She hated the waiting above all else. The apartment as still as a tomb. It was a tomb. Her thoughts were full of death, of endings. The apartment she loved for so long, her home, their home. They found it together. She found it. She called him and he came and he loved it straight away as she did.

"I knew you would love it," she told him.

"Yes," he said, "Yes, it's quite perfect for us, isn't it? There's a room there for my—for, you know—my—and another for you, next to the bedroom. It's a nice bedroom, isn't it?"

He loved it. He loved their apartment. So why did he stay away so much? Why had he been untrue to her? And, worse, why now, why is he gone forever? How could he do this to her? How could he leave her? Every day she had waited for him to come home. This is what the pregnancy brought them. Initially, she didn't want the baby, she made that clear. But he loved the idea of her pregnant.

"You'll have to quit your job, of course," he told her. "Won't that be delicious, just staying home, getting the room ready for the baby? Won't you love that?"

But she didn't love it. She waited every afternoon, every dead, long afternoon, for him to come home so she could tell him how awful it was, how the hours without him were torture for her. She told him she loved the baby, of course she did. What mother wouldn't? But she hated being alone. *Alone*, the word hurt.

But because of the baby she had all this time to herself. All those long days. The afternoons were the worst. As the light slipped from the sky and she sat in her chair, a book propped open on her lap, a book she would never read, a dead book. The afternoons were deadly.

The apartment they had loved was a cage now. He must have thought so, he must have hated the apartment really to turn his back on it, on her. He had loved the apartment. It was their home. So, now she hated the apartment. She hated its tasteful ecru walls, its wood floors, its breakfast nook. She hated the bistro table, the bookcases, the brass sconces, the linen dromedary love seat. She wanted out, out.

And now, just as she knew would happen, he had left her for good. He hated her whining. He hated her. He had never really loved her. Was it all pretend? Because she was pretty when she was young, pretty and easy going? She didn't know. She didn't know why he loved her. When he did.

Now that's all over.

She was abandoned. That's what they called it.

She sat in the chair and day would turn to dusk and dusk to midnight and she would be alone forever. When the baby came—when it did—and she had to decide—no. She would not think of that now. But, oh, how sorry he would be for leaving her—for leaving them. He would be so sorry.

She sat and waited. She sat in the chair that faced the door. The apartment ticked like a ship in harbor, beams settling, as if everything were in flux. But everything is not in flux. It's all settled. It's settled for all time. She knew what she would do—when it came—what she had to do. She was all alone. She had no one but him and he knew that and now he was gone. This time, this time he was gone for good.

She knew this day would come. She had told him so. You will leave me, she told him. I know it. Just when things get a little sticky, you will leave me. He had held her then but there was reserve in his gestures. He was holding himself back. He was holding his loathing in check so that she would not know he was planning on leaving her.

And now it had come. That day had come. She was alone at last.

Now she looked at her book. Its pages made no sense to her. She didn't think she had really read that far in it. There was a bookmark. Had she put it there? The words in the book were inane. They mocked her.

She felt the baby move. It wasn't a kick, just movement, like something underwater that wants to see the light of day, something malevolent. She hated how it made her feel. She hated it when it moved.

Now she stared straight ahead. There were sounds in the hallway.

Probably that damned neighbor with her boyfriend, the fat musician who thought he could sing the old songs, the standards.

Now the movement stopped before her door. She straightened her spine.

A key turned in the lock. And the door opened and he came in.

He stopped before her. In his arms were flowers. He looked at her for a long time. His shoulders sagged. Wearily, he lay the flowers down on a table and knelt before her.

"What is it this time, Dear?" he asked her. "Why are you crying today?"

"I thought you were gone for good," she said.

He sighed. It was an awful sound.

He put his head on her legs as if he had come from far away just to do that. They both were still for a while. She would not put her hands on his head. She would not.

"I thought you were really gone for good this time," she said.

Her words hung there in the air above them. He had no idea what to say next.

Any Day is a Good Day that Doesn't Start with Killing a Rat with a Hammer

Ibby was the kind of teenager that most other school kids avoided. In the boys he engendered fear or disgust, and in the girls fear or pity. He didn't talk much and he dressed like he didn't care what he wore, often the same wrinkled, stained, mismatched outfit two or three days in a row. Salvation Army off the rack. Also, Ibby was hulking and had an almost Neanderthal brow, capped with a great mop of tangled black hair.

Ibby lived with his put-upon mother and his scrawny sister, Pif, in a double-wide in the trailer park south of the highway. No one knew where the father was if there ever was one. Some said Ibby was born in a pond, the child of algae and tadpoles.

His mother made ends meet by collecting scrap in a grocery cart and selling it to Peat the Junkman, who also lived in the trailer park. Peat didn't really need Mrs. Sankta's contributions but accepted them in the hope that one day she would let him cross the threshold of her trailer and show him what she looked like in her underwear.

"How was your day?" Min Sankta asked Ibby when he came from home from school.

"Any day is a good day that doesn't start with killing a rat with a hammer," Ibby said.

"Don't you have homework? Where are your books?" his mother pressed on, attempting in her despoiled way to be pleasant.

"I can't remember. Is there bologna?"

At school the only kid who talked to Ibby was Haro Bilsun. Haro was a genius—some said—but he was as ugly as a Mudboy. He had no eyebrows, wore glasses as thick as a double-stack Oreo, and his mouth stayed open due to some dental irregularity.

"Hey," Haro said, one day in the lunchroom, taking a seat next to Ibby. "You want my bologna cup?"

"Fft," Ibby said, scooping said cup onto his plate.

"I'm not hungry anyway," Haro said.

"What's that book?" Ibby asked, pointing with a forkful of bologna-dyed mashed potatoes.

"*Beowulf*," Haro said, picking up the book and holding it out like an offering.

"Whassit about?"

"Kick-ass monster."

"Hmf."

"You wanna read it?"

Ibby looked at Haro as if he had just fallen into the seat next to him, something old that had previously been stuck to the ceiling.

Haro sucked at his orange juice, averting his face.

"Donaport Evans at high noon," Haro said, after a while, because silence made him anxious.

"What?"

"Donaport. Evans." Haro pointed with his pencil.

"Her?"

"Yeah, cheerleader. Big bosom."

"So."

"Nothing. She's interesting, I think." Here Haro's imagination failed him.

"Hmf."

That afternoon Ibby went to Haro's house. It was a far nicer place than his own. They kept all the furniture covered in Saran Wrap. They had a stereo console.

"Wanna see my Matchbox cars?" Haro asked.

Ibby gave him another of his looks.

"You want something to drink?"

"You got beer?" Ibby said, nonchalantly. It made Haro's heart beat fast.

"My dad has some Schlitz."

"Pop a couple," Ibby said.

They took the beers into Haro's room. There were shelves of books, collections of cars and little soldiers on every surface, plastic planes hanging from the ceiling, posters of Einstein and Edgar Allan Poe on the wall.

"You read all those books?" Ibby sloshed some Schlitz in that direction.

"Oh. No. That is, some of them. For school you know. Drag, right?"

Haro sat on his bed and Ibby took the only chair.

"I've got records."

"I got a record, too," Ibby said. He didn't smile. Now that Haro thought about it he had never seen Ibby Sankta smile.

Haro put on a record anyway. It was Rockabye Caruso doing "Mess Me Up."

"I like the drums on this one," Haro said. He was feeling light-headed.

"I guess I'll go home," Ibby said.

"What's at home?"

"I got a sister. You want her?"

"Would she?"

"She's yours for a dollar."

"Heh heh, no. Thanks, though. This brew has gone head to my straight."

"Guess I'll go then," Ibby said, draining his can.

Haro attempted to emulate and poured as much onto his chest as into his mouth.

"Thish waz great," Haro said at the door.

"Any day is a good day that doesn't start with killing a rat with a hammer," Ibby said, walking away.

In the trailer Pif was trying to twirl a baton she found in Peat's junkyard.

"Watch this," she said, and holding it at arm's length she sent it spinning into her own nose. "Ouch, dammit."

"Wheredya get that?"

"Peat's," Pif said, rubbing her red nose.

"Mom over there again?"

"Yeah."

Ibby went to his room and pulled the accordion door shut.

"Oh, some girl called for you," Pif shouted through the door. "Ouch!"

Pif had put a note on his dresser. It read, "You want to get together after school some time?" And it was signed, Donaport. The i was dotted with a heart.

Ibby went to sleep that night with a lightness in his chest he had never felt before. He thought about the cheerleader and he thought about her big tits and he fell asleep with a new sensation aborning—was it hope?

Next morning he saw Haro first thing and hailed him.

"C'mere," he said.

Haro's eyes opened wide. Ibby was hailing him!

"I got a note from Donaport. She wants to get together with me."

"Ibby! That's great! She's the prettiest girl in the world!"

"I want you to give her a message."

"Oh. Oh, no. I'm not sure," Haro said.

"What's the problem?"

"She wouldn't talk to me."

"Tell her you're coming from me."

"Yeah. Alright."

At lunch Haro didn't even stop in the food line. He raced to the table and dropped breathlessly down next to Ibby.

"She spoke to me," Haro said, panting.

Ibby gave him another of his looks.

"Oh, right. It's not about me. She said, 3 o'clock at the bleachers. Not the new bleachers but the old bleachers at the abandoned park. The old bleachers."

It was a make-out spot.

After his last class Ibby moved in a steady pace toward his destination. Was he anxious? Pleased? He was holding himself in check.

As he approached the bleachers he saw her. She was wearing her cheerleader uniform and her legs shone like the polished floors in the new Eastern Annex.

She raised a hand as she recognized him.

He slowed his step. He stopped once and lit a cigarette, blew smoke to the east, and then moved on.

"Hi," Donaport Evans said. "You don't know me, I know."

"I know you."

Ibby didn't know whether to sit next to her or not. He had never felt indecisive before. Was he feeling good or bad? He had never asked that of himself either.

"I've been watching you," Donaport Evans said, and she ran a hand absentmindedly up her gleaming thigh.

"Oh yeah?"

"I understand you have a big one."

Ibby was not sure he'd heard right.

"What?" he rightly asked.

"You know. The word is that yours is *big*."

"My cock," Ibby said with a hint of exasperation.

"Oh I love it when a man talks dirty," Donaport Evans said. Now she licked her lips which were a glossy pink.

"You want it then?" Ibby said.

"Oh. Please show it to me," she said.

Ibby hesitated. He looked behind him. Then he slowly unzipped his dirty plaid, double-knit pants. He hesitated.

"Ooh," Donaport Evans said. "I'm getting excited."

Ibby's cock was swollen. He pulled it out.

There was a small explosion from somewhere behind the bleachers. A bright light shot through Ibby's brain.

Donaport Evans was on her feet, laughing and fleeing. From behind the old dugout came a roll of laughter. Ibby zipped up and stepped in that direction.

Behind the dugout he found a small cluster of his classmates: a couple football players, the cute blond secretary of the senior class, a guy Ibby knew from school assemblies, another cheerleader. A black guy with a camera.

"Ibby! I'm sorry," Donaport Evans snorted between guffaws. "It's just a stupid game. A sort of bad-idea scavenger hunt. I got 'See Ibby Bilsun's penis.' See—"

She was holding out a wrinkled piece of paper.

"You were worth 50 points!"

They all laughed some more, some a little uneasily now.

Ibby stood stock still. He let the laughter roll around him in waves but he did not move. He was a black pillar of hate. Suddenly, like a door closing, the happy sounds disappeared.

"Take it easy, old man," one of the football players said.

When Ibby got home he looked a mess. He had a swollen cut above one eye, blood in one ear, dirt in his hair, blood on his corduroy shirt, and his pants were gone.

"Ibby!" his mom squealed.

"Eek!" Pif said.

"Salright," Ibby said and muscled past them into his room, closing his plastic door.

Mother and daughter exchanged a look. The trailer grew silent. It was the kind of silence found in ancient tombs, an old silence, one the world has carried from the first days, the silence between death and birth.

"Did you have a nice day?" his mom called, after a while.

The air inside the trailer was dense. They could not hear Ibby's reply.

The Hen Man

> *"Even a man who is pure of heart*
> *And says his prayers at night*
> *May become a hen when the henbane blooms*
> *And the autumn moon is bright."*
> —*Ancient legend*

—Ms. Ouspenskaya, you're Mr. Toblat's agent, is that correct?

—Please call me Mary.

—Mary then.

—Yes, his agent, his friend, his lady confessor.

—So, you know the story as well as anybody.

—Yes, the only person more closely associated with this extraordinary tale is Larry himself.

—Can you tell us how it started?

—How it started. My. It's been so long. I suppose it began when Larry knocked on the wrong door.

—Go on.

—He was looking for a therapist. My door is one floor up, 999 instead of 899.

—And you were, are a literary agent?

—Yes, multimedia really. Anyway. Larry knocked timidly, stuck his head inside. I said, Can I help you? He looked a sight. Hair mussed, unshaven, the two-day or more whisker growth looked like…well, perhaps I'm projecting. Anyway, he looked a sight. And his voice was a whisper. Dr. Kluckatt? he said. He hit those consonants hard. No, I said, Dr. Kluckatt is right below me, I believe. Larry ran a hand over his face—his distress was evident. He put a hand on the jamb to steady himself and I thought he was going to keel over. I stood and guided him to a chair, got him a glass of water. It was many minutes before he could speak again.

—And it was then—during this very first visit that he told you a tale?

—Some of the tale, yes.

—Go on, please.

—Well, after he recovered more or less, he looked about as if eying the bars of a cage. Then his eyes locked onto mine. He has very small eyes, and in the center, black, jet black. His gaze bore into me—like the Ancient Mariner's. And, I suppose, he had an analogous narrative, one that would not let him go. To this day I do not know why he opened up so readily—he was about to burst I think and could not have made it back down a flight to good Dr. Kluckatt, to unburden himself. I told him who I was, where he was, and bang! he just began to talk.

Mary, he began, Mary. (He took my hand—he held my hand throughout.) Once I was just like you, once I was young, accomplished, a man respected and even loved. I had friends, I had a flourishing practice—I was a dentist, Mary—and the respect of my peers and neighbors. Why did I need to travel? What was there for me to see of the world that was worth putting everything at risk? I ask you, Mary, what did I need—why did I damn my soul? For curiosity, for wanderlust. For plain lust. I was without female companionship.

Therefore, I planned a vacation, a few weeks away from the grind, the drill. I had heard that Carpathia was beautiful—it was a part of the world I had never seen. Even the travel agent was surprised by my choice—and this was interesting to me. This made me feel that I was doing something outré, something remarkable.

I traveled alone, first by plane and then by train across that blighted landscape of crag and cloud. It seemed as if I had entered a dream—not a nightmare then, oh no, a dream—and I was carefree as I gazed out my compartment window at the darkling world going by. My final destination was a small village, G—, and as to why I chose this quaint község I cannot say. It was no more scientific than throwing a dart at a map, spinning a globe and stopping it with a single digit.

In G— I found a small inn, the kind of inn that Carpathia creates like milk. They are ubiquitous and nearly identical in any way that matters. The innkeeper there was named Anton Szerb, and Szerb had a daughter, a beautiful, mountain maiden named Erzsi. I did what any man would have done faced with such innocent comeliness, such lack of guile so far from home. I fell for her. (Here Larry paused for a sip of water—he sat slumped over, his gaze on his shoes for a long time. I did not think he would ever resume.)

Erzsi, he continued, was a mountain girl, born of spring water and chill air. Her skin was as white as Carrara marble and she smelled of cotton-grass. She smiled at me and I was hers, a suitor come from far away to die in her eyes. Soon we began taking walks together, farther and farther from hearth and home. Her father watched over us with something between consternation and pleasure—I do not think he quite believed I was real. I came from nowhere.

Finally, one afternoon as the gloaming began to blanket the hills and rills in grey, Erzsi and I lay down in the heather and made love. It was the most moving experience of my life, a love as physical as the winds yet as gentle as sleep. Erzsi moved onto me as if we had been lovers for centuries—I tell you, Man deserves not such divine passion.

(Here Larry broke off. He was near fainting and I took him home. I felt like it was the only thing to do—that my role was formed long before the tale began. That night Larry slept in my guest room—where once slept my son, gone ten summers. And in the morning, after coffee, a shower and a fresh suit of clothing, Larry began the story again. The morning sun seemed incongruous coming in my living room window, bathing Larry in gold.)

Erzsi and I continued to see each other, avoiding her father's over-protective eye as much as possible. Nights we would wander the lanes of the sleeping village or tread the silvery woodlands surrounding. And we made love often—like many lovers we felt as if we had originated something altogether unsullied and new, something startling. Erzsi, with moonlight on her downy limbs, appeared a creature from another century, from another world perhaps. She was so lovely I would weep. And, in turn, she loved me with a passion that seemed born of the night, born of the proximate atmosphere.

One night, after Erzsi snuck back into her father's home, I was feeling restless. I was awake in every extremity, animate with a nervous energy which may have just been love, only that. I felt as if I could walk forever, as if I could travel the tired old world and know its every contour.

The moon was full—the grass looked like crystal.

I entered a part of the forest I had never visited. It was dark though the moon was as large as Charon's ferry. Something led me on. Something from deep within the trees led me on. I could feel that there was life up ahead, and, in my enthusiastic state, I felt connected to anything living.

After some difficult travel, through gorse and bramble, I fell upon a small cottage, thatch-roofed and with thick baked-mud walls. It seemed deserted. No smoke emerged from the chimney, no light from any of its small, rectangular windows. I pushed the splintered wooden door open and it swept inward like a breeze. It was too dark to see properly—I could just make out a rough table and chairs, a small, charred chauffer. The table was set for dinner, a dinner that never occurred perhaps. I put my hand on the plates and crude silverware, groping like a blind man. Where was the small family who once lived here? The hut smelled of old food and dust.

Outside I heard something scrabbling in the dirt. It was a disturbing sound, for some reason. I was afraid suddenly, afraid to leave those dungy walls.

But the noise would not stop. Was it a spirit, something that wanted in? The door was open.

When I went outside the sound ceased. My head felt funny and when I turned, I saw the largest fowl I had ever seen, a pullet with a head like an anvil, and eyes that burned an obsidian fire. It's just a chicken, I told myself. However, it was the damnedest chicken I had ever seen. And it held me with its gaze, the way a snake-charmer holds the snake, or vice versa.

I crouched to be on its level. I do not know what I hoped to achieve except I was simultaneously alarmed and awed. I felt as if I were in the presence of an *élan vital* that went back centuries, an essence as ancient as the heavens, as old as the deep. I did not see the bird move forward but it did so with supernatural speed. It was a paroxysmal explosion of feathers and obdurate talon. The night seemed to explode—a red fire behind my eyes—and I blacked out. I blacked out so thoroughly that my dreams were of unseen worlds, of hells and pits of damnation that exist only in the subterranean mythos of man. The night was rife with lamentation. There were messages in the stars.

When I awoke, it was dawn and the small clearing outside the hut was as if swept and tidied by imps and pixies. The light from the sun was enchanting and the small dwelling at my feet seemed a fairy tale hut, made perhaps of spun jaggery and muscovado. I stood up slowly, yet I felt hale and hearty in every limb. I felt strong and light as if I could leave behind the tethers of terra firma.

Back inside the hut, now that I could see, I found many useful things. A pump that still spouted fresh spring water and a small sink. I stripped down to skin and splashed my sensitive body with water as chill as blight of dew. My body felt different, stronger, sinewy and powerful. I ran my hand over my dampened surface and relished the feel of my own flesh under my palm.

Over the small crude sink was a glazed mirror the size of a man's face. In that mirror I looked long and hard, recognizing myself but realizing a change there, an improvement perhaps to the map of my face. Something was clearer, some mystery revealed.

Then I saw the marks on my upper breast and chin, scratchings and cross-hatchings, as if I had been used to sharpen a small tool. In addition, a few puncture marks, as black as demon's dread and tender to the touch. Then I remembered the fowl.

The walk back to the tavern cleared my head and by the time I reached my room all thoughts of gloom and dread had dissipated. I dressed in a new suit of clothes and set off to walk the quaint streets of the town. G— was one of those small villages which proliferate in that part of Eastern Europe, towns that seem outside of time, as if the ravages and horrors of the twentieth century had not occurred, did not reach the contented populace here.

I stopped in at a small bistro—The Schtuppon Inn—and fortified myself with strong coffee and a Saleratus Muffin. Something perplexing occurred here. The waitress, a striking, ebon-haired woman, who spoke no English, backed away from my table, her eyes brutish. She gasped and retreated to the kitchen. Shortly, the owner came to my table. He was a round man with eyebrows like hayricks.

So sorry, he crooned. She not god girl, not god girl. She— cigány—cigány. I don't understand, I told him. He searched the air for the answer and then he beamed. Gypsy, he said enthusiastically, Gypsy!

Nevertheless, when I left, I was feeling chipper and the air outside was crisp and redolent of fall, a smell just this side of childhood, smoke and freshly cut wood.

As I walked the rough stone boulevards of G— I felt as one does right after a long illness, as if one were loosened from the planet's strictures. The sun seemed brighter, the way clearer. Then I heard my name called—and the voice was honeyed air.

It was Erzsi—she came running up breathless.

Where have you been, she asked me. Ah, Erzsi, my love, I answered. I have been to Albion, to Kur, to the Unruly Firmaments! She did not mind my japery, but she looked at me as if I were a thorny problem.

What is it, my sweet, I asked her. I don't know, she said, are you ok? I have never felt better, I said. Ok, she whispered. Can you come along with me? Of course, I told her.

She led me to an outlying back way, a row of houses that seemed almost painted against a stormy background, such brightly colored residences with the dark crags behind them. We stopped in at one. Erzsi explained to me that she had to see Professor Miles Markson, a friend of the family, and the retired Dean of Alternative Studies at the University of K—.

Professor Markson greeted us ebulliently. He had a face like a creature of lore, an inhabitant of the Land of Feathered Men (more on this), or perhaps a Wood Sprite.

After introductions, we settled into his cozy den, a room of books and dust and weight. There was a golden glow to the space, or so it seemed. An elderly Chinese woman, who smiled at us as if we were her most wonderful children, served us good strong tea and biscuits.

The conversation was lively—the professor had not lost some of his pedagogical impulses, and at times, I just sat back and listened to his learned speech. Erzsi was visibly pleased that I was so spellbound by her friend. She had come to pass on her good father's invitation to dinner. The two older men were sporting companions of long standing.

Eventually, I found myself speaking, talking about the impulse that led me to this obscure corner of the world. And, as the conversation warmed and tilted this way and that, I was nattering about the previous night and the strange hut and its malevolent hen. Professor Markson sat forward, his ears pricking with interest and, seemingly, concern. He gazed at me intently as I explained what happened. Erzsi appeared alarmed all of a sudden. Yet, I continued, like the Ancient Mariner, unburdening myself with my tale.

Finally, the professor spoke. This hen—how big did you say it was?

I told him that it seemed unnaturally large—and I chuckled at my own ostensible embellishment. He did not share my mirth but rather urged me into deeper description.

When I was done—after I explained that I had apparently

fainted—Professor Markson sat back in his chair and lit a ruminative bowl of frowzy tobacco. After an uncomfortable lag in the discourse, he smiled.

My boy, he said. Do you know anything about necromancy, especially animal spells? I admitted that I did not. In addition, do you know about the ancient connection between bird and man?

I said again no. So he launched into a dissertation on bird cults, bird spirits, bird Gorgons. The Greek Keres, The Welsh Gwrach y Rhibyn, or Washer of the Ford. The Hindu Garuda Bird. The Cockatrice, The Furies, the Children of Lir. Icarus.

And men, back and back, have conjured bird-gods to aid them.

These are principally men who dress as birds, yes? Just that? I asked eagerly.

He said, Oh yes! Well, not *just* dress as birds, like a child's make-believe. There are the Feathered Men, Aborigines, who envelop themselves with feathers from head to foot, to make themselves look like fowl, who can rise into the cosmos more easily. The Phoenix Myth, if you will. Then there are the countless types of masks, which, if one likes, can all be interpreted along these lines. Many of the masks have branches with several forks springing from them like antennae, a feathery effect, a bird-face. The modern act of tarring and feathering is perhaps sprung from this.

But possibly the Taoist Immortals—The Hsien are more germane. These individuals, so it is told, drank of The Elixir of Life and are often portrayed in art as Featheredmen! Immortality, son!

I smiled at his dynamism. He rose from his chair, pipe in hand.

He continued, as if compelled, as he ran a hand along the spines of his books. Consider, he said: a being who realized this spiritual transcendence through comprehension of the *Tao* was called a *hsien*, the same word used to illustrate angelic "feathered folk" with winged or feathered images appearing in Chou art of the period. The book of *Chuang-Tzu* pictures *hsien* as white-skinned, graceful and fragile superhuman beings. He paused, plucked a book from the shelves and found the passage he sought. "Professor Ed Schafer says this: 'These are divine persons, whose flesh and skin resemble ice and snow, soft and delicate like sequestered girl-children; they do not eat the five cereals; they suck the wind and drink the dew; they mount on clouds and vapors and drive the flying dragons—thus they rove beyond the four seas.'"

This is fascinating, Professor Markson, I said. However, really, what does it have to do with me? He looked me over with a medical eye. Nothing, my boy, don't worry about it. Chalk it up to an old man's logorrhea. A lot of knowledge is a dangerous thing, no?

Soon thereafter, we left the professor's house with hearty valedictions and promises of more visits anon.

Erzsi took my arm—I could not help thinking that it was with an equivalent combination of affection and concern. She kept looking at me with dewy eyes. Oh, how I loved her!

That evening we dined with Erzsi's father at the inn. It was a watershed event—the first time we had publicly acknowledged our relationship. And her father—albeit gruffly and in his studied, offhand manner—accepted me in his home as more than a paying guest.

After dinner, Erzsi and I took our accustomed stroll—though this time it was openly and with more outright affection. We visited our usual knolls and valleys, the warmth of our bodies like some diabolical admixture of chemicals. We made love with new vigor—I bit Erzsi so hard on the neck she startled—but did not quit our rhythm. Afterwards, there was a red and purple mark there—like a bloody paraph. I apologized for my *Schwärmerei*—and kissed her there numerous times.

When I went to bed that night I was restless—my blood was up—and the moonlight coming in through my small dormer window was as white as a gravestone. I finally threw the coverlet from me in disgust. My skin prickled; my heart beat fast.

I went out into the moonlight—it seemed to draw me as if I could travel up a beam into other worlds. This seems fancy, yet it was as distinct a feeling as I have ever felt in my life. The more I walked in the night the stronger I felt—really, I felt as if I could fly.

The rest of that evening is a black blaze—I fell off the edge of the world into Erebus and darkness. When I awoke, it was vivid day and I was lying prone on a small tumulus. There was blood on my mouth.

(Here Larry stopped. It had been a long, draining morning. Outside, a thunderstorm was gathering—the air was electric. Larry's eyes were world-weary. He lay his head down on the divan and fell into a swooning sleep.)

(By the time Larry began to stir, the storm had already passed— the air had that silvery quiver to it. He stretched and asked for strong coffee. After fortifying himself with this and some GORP he continued his strange narrative.)

There was blood on my mouth. A small smear in the corner, like a birthmark. And I tasted something dreadful: black earth, grave dirt. There was grit in my teeth. I sat up and my head was swimming. I did not know what day it was—it seemed I had slumbered for a week, or an hour. My limbs were sore from sleeping on the hard ground. I slowly made my way back to the village—the sun was an orange slur in the east.

I arrived before the inn just as a small cluster of townspeople was pushing through the streets, their faces twisted with grief and horror. They did not even see me—they had their sights set on the home of Constable Stern, the local *rendŏr*. His home was just around a small jackleg in the road from the inn. I watched in mute consternation as they rumbled around the corner. I felt begrimed—and somehow *guilty*.

When I attained my room, I looked at my face in the mirror and was aghast at what was there. A rough, stubbled face, not mine yet mine. The fuzz on my chin was white—nothing like my characteristic thick beard. And it rubbed off easily—I ran my thumb around my jaw and watched it flake away. There was also something odd about my eyes—they seemed smaller, blacker.

In addition, my clothing was a mess—small splatters of mud, ooze, and perhaps blood. And stuck to my shirt, like a postmodern painting, were feathery daubs, as if I had been lightly tarred and feathered. My thoughts went back to what Miles Markson had said. And I knew I had to see him—right away.

I cleaned myself up and, avoiding contact with Erzsi or her father, I slipped out and walked briskly to Professor Markson's. His cottage was dark—odd for mid-morning. I knocked tentatively and, when that produced no results, I rapped vigorously. After a considerable wait, Markson himself opened the door. He looked haggard.

His jaw was set when he spoke. Come in, he said, grimly. He looked at me with concern as I passed into the parlor. I hoped you might come today, he said.

We sat in the same highbacked chairs as last time. He fixed me with his gaze. My boy, he said, this is ghastly. What? I asked, in some alarm. He seemed almost angry with me.

You know, don't you? he continued. About Becca Lourdes? My expression told him that I did not. She's dead, son. Seemingly punctured to death. Her face was almost unrecognizable.

Horror stirred in my bowels. What kind of beast—I said. My entire body roiled—I wished to be detached from it. Somehow, this grisly business was connected to me.

My God, Professor Markson said. You don't know, do you? You really don't know. Larry, he laid a consoling hand on my forearm. There is talk of a birdman at large—a murderous fowl! Larry, do you remember anything about last night?

My head felt funny. I told him what I could.

This blackout, he said. I fear the worst, son. I fear you *are* the beast. He sat back in his chair, his face drained of color. When I heard the news, he said, barely above a whisper, I knew. I knew, Larry. It was that damned hen that pecked you. Son, you are a werehen!

I was physically ill. I had to remove myself to the facilities and evil bile spilled from me in hot streams. I felt like I had to urinate but I could not. I was sick, sick.

I returned to Professor Markson—I was as weak as a strand of rain.

Larry, he began. He had ruminated and, instantly, he was prepared for action. I think it would be best if you stayed here with me, he said. I have a guest room. Jun will fix it up for you. You must stay here where I can observe you—care for you—*restrain* you, if I must. He said this last phrase with particular fervor. And trimming your—eh, beak, may be in order.

Erzsi, I peeped.

I'll send for her, son. Now, do you need to lie down? I allowed as to how I did and he summoned Jun. The kindly, old woman looked at me with great sympathy and led me to the guest room. After fixing me up with a small daybed, she departed. I collapsed again into a sleep of turbid dreams—blood, feathers, darkness, *Schrecklichkeit*.

When I woke, it was early evening. I sat up feeling 100% better, durable in limb and trunk. Just then, the door opened and Erzsi stuck her head in. I thought I heard you stirring, she said. She was as lovely as peace after vicious battle. She came and laid her head on my chest—her hair smelled of hyacinths. I kissed her fresh mouth as if drinking from a sweet rill.

Erzsi and Professor Markson had formulated a plan, one designed to keep me from harm, from further misdeeds. What was my state of mind at this time? Dr. Kluckatt (I did not correct Larry here), I tell you, it was a capharnaum, a place of foul misalignment and dread. It was slowly dawning on me what had occurred, what foul sea-change had taken place in my body. It was like a spell, and like a spell, it was inexplicable, at least by all the laws of logic that govern our everyday lives. That I had become some kind of between-species creature seemed fantastic, yet that was what I had to accept—however beyond my former reason! Was it possible for evil to be visited upon Man in the form of some kind of possessed animal? This I had to agree was not only the possibility but also the probability. It was panic to an existential degree unprecedented: what I had to escape was myself, the cage of my own tabernacle, or body. I put myself entirely into Markson's self-assured hands, hands that he wrung all afternoon, while pacing up and down in his own parlor. Erzsi sat next to me, as if she were my once and future wife, her arm draped over my shoulder in the vein of a protective husbandry. She had earlier attempted a joke about my being henpecked. We both laughed with a cemetery cackle, a poor performance indeed.

The problem we face, Professor Markson said, is what to do when the transformation begins. My idea—if you will accept it, Larry—is to bind you. Physically prevent you from leaving your volary. Then, we will see if we can drain your body of the avinechemical toxin that has taken it over.

I nodded meekly. I only wanted to return to my daybed. My feeling of physical well-being—so evident only an hour before—had dissipated. I felt aching, scratchy, antsy. My left leg felt scaly. There was a distinct throbbing in the area of my prostate—I feared cancer, or some formerly unknown pullet disease. When I lay back down, I iterated my concerns to the kindly professor. He looked thoughtful and then sat next to me on the edge of the bed. Son, he said. I believe you might be trying to lay an egg. An inadvertent cluck came from my throat. The professor smiled as if in pain. Just take it easy, he said.

I was able to eat some leafy greens and some corn meal cakes that Jun fixed. Erzsi sat by me the whole long afternoon and early evening, sipping tea, smiling with her gentle eyes. Sleep, she said, brushing my hair off my forehead. Therefore, I did.

This evening was dissimilar—what fresh horror was I to expect each night?—I awoke and was fully mindful of an acute and excruciating metamorphosis taking place. The autumnal moon lit the room as if with hoar. My limbs fairly screamed with pain—my mind flashed extreme white light. I felt as if I were being turned inside out. Then it was all over in a burst.

My first reaction I felt through Erzsi. She stood so quickly she turned over the chair in which she was dozing. Her face was a rigor of alarm, her eyes wide like the hands of the dead. She let out an inadvertent gasp. It is one thing to understand what was about to happen—it was quite another to witness it in all its horrific beastliness.

My limbs were bound with heavy fabric and tied to the bed. I thrashed only once, recognizing my helplessness instantly. A mirror, I said, my voice clicking, my tongue clapping the top of my jaw, which felt unnaturally distended. Erzsi stood by in frozen fear—she clearly did not know what the right thing to do was. Professor Markson entered then—he started much as Erzsi had, but quickly gathered himself. Remarkable, he muttered as he hurried toward me. Mirror!—I repeated.

Markson nodded toward Erzsi, who found a hand mirror nearby. She passed it to Markson, who gripped my arm tightly. Larry—prepare yourself, he said, through grit teeth. He held the mirror a short distance from my face.

It was as corrupt as I had anticipated—horrid, vile! I was

a creature out of mythology, a manticore, a harpy, an opinicus! Theriomorph! Yet, in my revulsion was also the seed of calm—almost pride. I was venturing into uncharted waters—few humans knew what I knew. Few could even dream such a thing were possible. I was staring into the black eyes of a monstrous hen! And what eyes! Almost human though the center was as cinereous as pitch and there was no top lid. But, friend, the most astonishing, the most staggering change was in my jaw, which stood out a good four inches from my chin—and came to a sharp point! It was the dreadful melding of human and fowl—right there in my lower face! As rare as hen's teeth! Ha! I had a teethéd beak!

I lay back, my head teeming with ideas—some malevolent, some pitifully human. I was of two worlds and welcome in neither. Yet, I was powerful, and liberated! That I felt free though bound head and foot was evidence of my authority, which coursed through my distended body, down into my scaly toes. My transformation had ripped the clothing from me, so that under the covers I was all flesh and feather. The pressure in my crotch had disappeared and I reached down to discover something miraculous—my first egg! I lay in silent contentedness—my time was still to come. I would be free—to range about as I wished! To be top of the pecking order!

Erzsi still stood, her back to the wall. Her expression had been swept clean—she was spent, torn between love and terror. Poor Erzsi—it is for her I still weep. She could not get past my vileness—could not—but I get ahead of myself.

I spoke calmly to Markson and my beloved. I told them I was in pain but resigned to my new state, as a man who has died must resign himself to being incorporeal. I assured them that I was calm and in full possession of my faculties. I was peckish. I asked for water and some grain. Professor Markson instructed Jun to wait on me—to bring me whatever I needed. They had no idea what I needed. Who has seen inside the chicken's heart?

I sat up, sipped water, and swallowed some cereal. I smiled—though I had no idea what *that* could resemble. I tried to reach them through my eyes. All the time, see, I was calculating. I needed them to untie me. I needed to make it so.

And, gradually, as the night wore on, they grew soothed and more *laissez-faire*. We talked of many things—never touching really on what we would do, what our next step might be. Occasionally, the professor's brow wrinkled in dismay—he was intent on overthrowing this—this nightmare—this enchantment. He spoke of leeches, antitoxins. As one day bled into another, I stirred in my manacles and asked Markson if he could loosen them. He hesitated—glanced once at Erzsi who had been silent most of the evening— and then—blessed relief—he loosed the heavy material binding me. I thanked him and sat up straighter.

Then—Dear Doctor—I tore my shackles! Uhuru! Liberty! I was possessed of foul power. I fairly erupted from the bed—I swatted Markson with one of my massive arms as he moved toward me. Erzsi screamed and backed against the door—the door through which I had to abscond. I looked at her with hungry attention. She was not, at that moment, my beloved Erzsi—no!—she was an impediment. I moved toward her and struck her once, twice, three times about the face and neck with my beak. She screeched once more as blood burst from her chin—then fell back against the wall in syncope. I stood for a moment over her prostrate form—her swan's neck and lovely pallid breastbones were exposed where my actions had torn her garment. It was a queer pause—I was filled with concupiscence—yet I was a *female* chicken. Though the etymology is strange—I have learned since—the Old English word *henn*, which is akin to the OE *hana*, or rooster. At that moment, I felt like both, a hermaphrodite. I felt like the Cock of the Walk and I was torn—only momentarily!—only briefly!

I escaped from the professor's house and entered the argentine night of the sleeping town. All around me were new sounds—new sensations. The Carpathian night was *alive*! I heard the wings of the hawk overhead, the shy prattle of a female kestrel, the mumblings from the barnyard. I was stirred in my very blood—more alive than I had ever been. I had never felt so connected to the earth—or more unbound. I was beyond guilt or justice or sentiment. As I loped, my feet lifted from the ground—I could keep myself aloft for many seconds. I made good time—leaping through the deserted lanes and byways of G—. The yellowy glim through closed blinds drew me, soft voices in the public houses. It was as if the town were under the spell—not I.

I spent a long time utilizing my senses—enjoying the force of new sight—the vigor in my self-determination.

After an hour or more flitting here and there—enjoying the obscurity, the singular aloneness—I was drawn to some refuse near a tavern, discarded bits and pieces of foodstuff. In them I found grain and greens, as fresh as need be. I ate heartily. It was then that I encountered her.

She stepped out of the back door of the tavern. Presumably, she was a doxy, a Magdalene, finished for the night with the commerce of the flesh. She saw me there in the alley's dim illumination, a figure out of nightmare. She gasped and attempted to vault back inside and close the door. I was too quick. I struck her suddenly with my great pennon, felling her there in the doorway. I quickly closed the door and stood over her, now my prey.

Pity for her—she was still conscious—she looked at me with eyes that showed dread, awe, a horrid wonder. I brought my beastly avian face close to hers. I could feel her hot breath on my feathers—she was stunned into stillness.

She put one hand to her collar—a gesture of primness that

belied her trade. I pecked the back of that hand, striking deep into vein and bone. She sucked in her breath and pulled her hand to her mouth. I took the front of her dress in my beak and ripped it away. Her ample breasts spilled out into the air—I felt—what?—a pleasure beyond desire, a *need*.

Now her fear was more focused—something incomprehensible was about to happen. I saw her breasts there before me—the sweet flesh of meretricious duty—and I wanted to mar them—to destroy beauty and craving and want. I pecked downward hard, time and time again, opening spouts of fresh blood from bosom and nipple. Her sweet, warm flesh was as tender as fresh bread. Now, she squirmed, trying to crawl away. Yet, still no sound emerged from her. I pulled her back by the material of her dress, opening her to further revilement. I pecked the soft flesh of her belly—lower! She then put a hand to the side of my head—an almost tender gesture!—and took a handful of feathers in her desperate grip—and tore! I struck her once—hard!—in her neck and in a flash she was still. Her body gave up her soul to Holy Judgment.

In the distance, I heard a fieldfare, its plaintive nighttime *tchack*, *tchack* like a changeling's squall. I was reminded of my Hungarian friend, who signed her letters: *csòk csòk*, that is, with kisses. In this case, they seemed to me kisses of death.

I wandered now, drunk on murder. I stumbled; I was tired, bonedeep tired. I did not feel like flying— I only wanted sleep. Oblivion.

Around a bend in the lane I heard voices, soused rowdies. My first impulse was to flee. Then my blood answered and I stood in the middle of the street, Ozymandias. They came around the bend, preceded by their loud revelry. They stopped as if pole-axed. Jesus, one of them said. There were four of them, substantial lads, workers or sportsmen. What in the name of all that is holy are you? one asked, emboldened by inebriate.

I took one step toward them. They, as a group, stepped back.

I recognized the group leader—I had that kind of instinct. The pecking order is a flimsy and mercurial thing unless you have a bird's eye. I moved quickly toward him and pecked him once, sharply, in the middle of his forehead, right in his pineal gland, obliterating his inner perception and snuffing out his ruffian life.

In the end, three of them were killed. The one who survived is responsible for my capture, although initially his description of the events met with a great deal of skepticism. How they tracked me back to Professor Markson's is still a mystery to me. The next morning I woke up in the daybed in his guest room and there was Constable Stern with a set of manacles that would have held Houdini. Behind him Erzsi wept, inconsolable, and this still breaks my everloving heart. As I was led out, Miles Markson placed a warm hand on my shoulder and reassured me with his gentle ways. I spent two weeks in G—'s *fogda*, awaiting my fate.

It may seem strange now, but I did not again turn into a cockatrice while in captivity. I think, in retrospect, this may have been what they were waiting for. I do not know what held the bloody transformation in check. I only know that I sat in that fetid cell, a saddened man, a man who had lost the world, and possibly his own mortal soul.

After two weeks they set me free. The charges were too fantastic. The district judge was queried and it was his opinion that the whole tale was too incredible, too unbelievable. This is how they settled on deportation. I never saw Erzsi again.

They led me, shackled, to a train. At the airport, Constable Stern himself led me to the plane. Standing on the scarred and scoured tarmac, he looked at me as if I were Old Bendy himself. I hung my head and boarded.

(Here, Larry stopped. He asked for some food and then fell into one of those instantaneous sleeps he is capable of—the sleep of the dead.)

—Is that all he told you? Is that the tale's end?

—Not entirely. You know some of the details since his return to the States.

—Enlighten us.

—Of course. First, let us take care of the fee.

—The check has been cut. My assistant will present it to you right away.

—I'll see it now, thank you.

—Joe?

—Thank you. Now.

Larry began again the next morning. He had had an agitated night—the unburdening had awakened his own demons and he wrestled with them in his dreamland.

Once stateside, Larry began over pastry and coffee (like a fool I offered him eggs, only to see his brow knit in repulsion and anger), once stateside, I returned to my home, miserable, shattered, feeble, a wafting smell. I started to say toothless—yet I had a practice still. I returned to work and, for a while, everything was fine. My patients missed me, they said, and I suppose I had missed them, the routine, the work itself.

Then—it was one afternoon in November, a young woman came to me, a new patient. She was lovely, both blond and dark—I do not make it a habit to think of my patients in this way. But, there was something about her, about the way she carried herself, that was like a powerful drug. I knew immediately that I had to have this woman. It was the first emotion—the first mark of humanity—I had displayed since Erzsi. The young woman's name was Syrie Cossen (originally Cosanzeana) and she was receptive to my unprofessional advances.

That very evening we began to see each other. We were like two animals thrown together—we spent a large amount of time sniffing each other—circling, trying to ascertain what this was, what was happening. Syrie seemed wary of me—at first. Then, it all came out in the open the night of the blue moon.

Mary, in short, we changed together. We were both bird spirits, destined to meet, as inevitable as the unfolding of the lily bud to the sun. She told me her story—it was as fantastic as my own!—a real Bloody Bones and Rawhead tale—and we have been together ever since, contented, peaceful, open to amorous happiness. Neither of us returned to our murderous ways—her "episode" is still much discussed in the V— area in Hungary.

The rest you know.

—Fascinating.

—The rest we know. Larry ended up at Dr. Kluckatt's eventually, where he was diagnosed with Body Dismorphic Disorder—in essence, his beastly side was relegated to the darkened chambers of his mind. This is not to Dr. Kluckatt's discredit—really, what else could she diagnose?

—And no one would know any different had it not been for television?

—That is correct. We ended up booking Larry and Syrie on *Horrible Creatures Among Us!* on Fox. And the couple is as happy as Spirits cleansed, and rich as kings—and, really, they are that—the Royalty of an Ancient

Cult, as old as Sibylla, as deep as the River Jordan.

—Well, I think that will do it. Thank you for your time. We'll be out of your hair shortly.

—Not at all. And don't forget, Thursdays at 8 p.m. Eastern Standard Time.

"So we say there's no caffeine in our toothpaste."

"That's right."

"There is no caffeine in toothpaste."

"Right. We say that."

"But there's never been caffeine in our toothpaste."

"That's the pitch. 'Always caffeine free.'"

"There's never been—"

"Right."

"And people will think…"

"That other toothpastes maybe, just might, perhaps have just a little caffeine."

"Which they don't want."

"Not in their toothpaste."

The meeting went well. Alan felt the meeting went well. His boss, insecure and blustery, was the perfect boss. Alan spoke to him as if he were a child. His boss, Mr. Sentry, acted like a child. He was grateful like a child. Alan was his star employee. Alan could make the firm, put it in the picture.

Alan went home that night puffed up with pride. He could not wait to tell Jenna about his new campaign. It was a brainstorm, an epiphany.

"There is no caffeine in toothpaste."

"I know."

"So where's the revelation?"

"We say it. We say it like we invented it. We say it like it *is* a revelation."

"I don't get it."

"It'll sell. That's the bottom line."

"I hate the expression bottom line."

"Ok. I do too. What happens though is that the idea, the revelation, becomes the truth. It will become the truth with very little effort on our part."

"The truth."

"We're selling the truth."

"Good luck with that."

"Thank you."

"___"

"___"

"___"

"Do you think tonight?"

"Alan."

The next morning Alan was a bit deflated. He tried to cling to the original inspiration, what led him to the revelation. The truth. He tried to cling to the truth.

Mr. Sentry buzzed for him early. Alan took deep breaths. He was searching for the Alan of the day before. Before Jenna minimized him. Jenna did that. She was a minimizer.

"Alan, this is Spork from legal."

"Spork."

"Alan."

"Spork wants to hear the idea."

"Ok."

"Like you told me."

"We're selling the truth."

"Alan?"

"We're saying we have the truth. We're saying maybe some other unnamed people do not."

"The truth?"

"We sell that. We have it and it's for sale."

"I—"

"We're not, decidedly not, selling the truth."

"Yesterday you said—"

"Yesterday you brought me revelation."

"Toothpaste."

"Right."

"We're selling toothpaste."

"Now—"

"And our toothpaste is caffeine-free. Always caffeine-free."

"That's it, Alan."

"Huh."

"We're saying we care about health issues. Caffeine is bad. We're selling ourselves as caring."

"No caffeine."

"Right."

"That's good."

"Thank you."

"And cost-wise, removing the caffeine, is what?"

"Negligible."

"Better."

"Thank you."

"Alan, we have a go. I'm telling you, as of today, we have a go."

Alan went home again puffed up. He thought he had explained himself badly the previous evening. He needed Jenna to see the revelation. He needed his wife onboard. Jenna was not a minimizer. Jenna loved Alan. That was the truth. That was the truth that Alan was after. The truth of Jenna's love. Alan thought that if he just said it better, that was all, he just needed to say it right. He needed to sell Jenna and Jenna loved Alan. That was the bottom line.

The Stranger

"All things had opposites close by, every decision a reason against it, every animal an animal that destroys it."

—*Patricia Highsmith*

It started, like many stories, with a stranger appearing. We had just sat down to dinner, Eveline, the kids and me. Eveline had made up special a pot of organgrinder stew. Flint and Fletcher, my twins, were already elbow-deep in their bowls when there was a knock at the door. "Who could that be?" Eveline said. I rose, pulled the napkin out of my collar, and went to see. I crossed the living room and opened the door and there he was. I can't say I wasn't startled because I was and I don't startle easy. It was a bear, a Kodiak, I believe. He was dressed like my Uncle Julip. At first I thought it was Uncle Julip, who we hadn't seen in years. "Can I help you?" I said, because what else could I say? "Yes," the bear answered. "I was wondering if Eveline lives here." "Yes," I said without thinking. "I am an old friend of hers," the bear said. "From Eau Claire." "Come in," I said. "We were just about to—well, never mind. Have a seat. I'll get Eveline." When I went back to the kitchen the twins had finished dinner. They looked at me with curious smiles. As did my wife. "Ahem," I said. "There's someone to see you, Eveline," I said. "Well, Diggory, who is it?" Eveline rightly asked. "I didn't get his name. It's no one I've ever met before." Eveline looked at me as if I were slightly dizzy. "It's a bear," I said. The twins started to bolt from their chairs. They were not running away. They were running toward the living room and our guest. I stopped them with my arm and a stern visage. "A bear," Eveline said. It was neither a question nor a statement. It was somewhere in between. "A bear," I confirmed. Eveline rose slowly from her chair. She looked pale. She edged closer to the doorway and, holding onto the front of my shirt, she peered around my shoulder. She gasped. "Is it someone you know?" I asked. "No, no," she said, and began to sob. "I've never seen that bear before in my life." She collapsed against me and began to cry in earnest. I patted her and eventually set her back down in a chair. "Boys," I said, "You and your mother stay here." I returned to our guest. For a fleeting moment I thought again that it was Uncle Julip. "Hi," I said. "Can you tell me what this is about? My wife doesn't seem to know you. And, um, I didn't catch your name." The bear, who had been studying the spines on our bookshelves, turned and smiled a placatory smile. "I'm sorry," he said. "My name is Nessim." And here the bear laughed a short laugh. "When I knew your wife I wasn't a bear." "Ah," I said, though I didn't know what was made more comprehensible. Suddenly, my wife screamed from the kitchen, "Nessim!" and ran out to jump into the bear's outstretched arms. They held each other and rocked intimately for several minutes. I stood by, uneasy in my heart. Finally, my wife stepped back from the bear's embrace. "Diggory," she said. "You've heard me speak of Nessim. He and I were college sweethearts." She didn't say "sweethearts." She said "lovers." I didn't like the sound of it then anymore than I like typing it now. "Lovers." My wife and Nessim.

That evening was very uncomfortable. We all sat in the living room as if we had just come from a wedding or funeral. Nessim and Eveline talked non-stop, only occasionally inviting me into their conversation. The twins, after being assured that Uncle Julip had not come to visit, went to their room to play with their soldiers. I sat there like an ass as I watched my life leak away from me. I knew Eveline would leave with the bear, with Nessim. I knew as surely as I knew the twins were not mine. Eveline was pregnant when I met her and now I knew their father was a bear. Or had become a bear. I am still unclear about that part of the story. Nessim never did explain why he was now a Kodiak and Eveline was unaccountably incurious. I smiled here and there. I shifted in my seat. But I knew that at the end of the evening the bear would take my wife and children away from me and I would let them go without protest. Who wouldn't want a bear as a provider and lover? Who wouldn't choose a bear over a man? I didn't blame Eveline then and I don't blame her now. I know now that I am the stranger and that I have always been the stranger. Some nights I weep. I begin weeping when the sun sets and I go to sleep weeping. Other nights I am better, not quite so desperate, not quite so bereft. I still have my books and I still have my dog, Artegal. Sometimes Artegal looks at me as if he too wished he were elsewhere, some place rough and untamed, some place unsullied by the pale desires and halfhearted proclivities of the human race.

Chip

Sunday morning Chip didn't feel quite right. It wasn't anything he could pinpoint. It was a kind of head/chest/stomach/limbs/heart kind of peculiarity. Sitting at his desk with a cup of French Roast next to him he thought that it would be best if he took something, a medicament. Chip was conversant with many pills but he had already taken his daily dose of everything he owned. And it was only 11 a.m.! So, it was a bit of a dilemma. Then he saw, adjacent to his cup, a shiny dime. Just a shiny, 1945 Liberty dime. He picked it up and turned it round and round, watching it catch the light. It seemed numinous.

"This is *pillish*," Chip said aloud to no one.

And so he swallowed it with a judder of coffee. It went down hard. It passed that difficult passage in the throat which, occasionally, rejects intake. Then Chip imagined he could feel it working its metallic way down his plumbing. He imagined it reached his stomach and Chip could visualize it and immediately he began to feel better.

Later in the day Chip had a pristine sort of feeling. It was kind of silvery and fresh and minty. He had never had this feeling before. He decided, since he was unquestionably on the upswing, to call Ramona. Ramona loved Chip sometimes, a few times, on good days, and perhaps their good days could coincide, thought Chip.

"What is it, Meat?" Ramona answered.

"Ramona," Chip said, bright as a holy pyx, "What are you doing right now? I mean *right now*."

Ramona heard something brand-new in Chip but she was still

wary. Something new in Chip, however, could be a really good thing, thought Ramona.

"Knitting up the raveled sleeve of care," Ramona said. She tried not to invest her voice with anything lively, particularly hopefulness.

"I'm coming over," Chip made bold.

Ramona met Chip at the door. She was wearing only a sweatshirt, which said *Fuck Coprolalia* across its front, and panties because her heart was flinty. What did she care if she attracted Chip? There he stood, eyes atwinkle. She looked at Chip and cocked her head like a cur. There was something *novel* about him, something previously undetected. Perhaps it's just a good mix of chemicals, thought Ramona. She knew Chip's insides were one wild chemistry experiment after another. Still—this— today—seemed distinctive.

"Come in," she said, laconically, though she readjusted her sweatshirt a bit so that her small bosoms were more prominent.

"Beautiful, beautiful," Chip said, sitting on Ramona's couch. Ramona had put on the new album by The Crappy Saplings.

"What's up, Chiperoo?" Ramona asked and, almost involuntarily scooted herself nearer him on the leather couch.

"Ramona," Chip said, "I want us to see each other naked today. I want us to mate."

Ramona laughed despite herself. She face-palmed. She was amused. She also was a little turned on.

After a few moments of awkward silence, while Chip sat there grinning like scattered chaff, Ramona undressed. They made love softly, intensely, hotly and wetly, for a long time. Later, Ramona cooked some pork chops and mashed potatoes with toys in them (this was her code for anything added to staple dishes, in this case, scallions and skins). They watched a Zip Kadoodle film called *She Might Eat a Kitten,* and later they made love again until they were both so enervated they fell asleep, secured together like a key in a lock.

In the morning, they made love one more time and then Ramona got into a hot shower. When she emerged, rosy and naked, Chip was dressed, sitting on the bed, still wearing his mysterious smile.

"I have to go to work, alas," Ramona said. "Can you be here when I get off? What are you doing today?"

Chip was a writer which meant to Ramona, and a lot of other people, that he didn't really do much during the day. "Gathering moths, gathering moss" is the way Ramona put it, prior to yesterday. Now, if she was thinking about Chip qua writer (and she wasn't because she was thinking of Chip qua bedfellow) she was thinking that perhaps Chip was the finest writer she had ever known.

"I think," Chip said, after some consideration. "I think I will write the novel I have been talking about for years."

Ramona smiled a coltish support.

"But first I need to go by the bank and get myself a roll of dimes."

His Last Work

"What's it look like, Sarge?'

"Oh, suicide. It's suicide."

"Nasty, huh?"

"Yeah. You just getting here."

"Just got the call."

"Poor sap."

"Ever seen anything like it, Sarge?"

"Once."

"Another painter?"

"Oh, nah."

"You interested in painting, Sarge? You know this guy's work?"

"Nah."

"Hmp."

"You an artist, uh, McKinney?"

"Nah. Like it though. Spent a lot of time in art museums during school. And in Europe after the war. Seen the great ones."

"That so?"

"Yeah."

"This guy, this, uh, stiff here. He good?"

"Not great. Good. Derivative, they said. You know Soutine?"

"Saltine? Nah."

"Soutine. Chaim Soutine. French. Expressionist, but not dark like the Germans. Sensual. Brilliant colors. Lousy with color, Soutine was. This guy's got a lot of his vitality but none of his message."

"Huh."

"Also a bit Rouault. Georges Rouault."

"Another frog?"

"Yeah. Colorful too. Deeply religious. This poor sap was

religious, too. Shows up in his most recent canvases."

"Well, he's beyond earthly help now."

"Any idea why he did it?"

"Cunt trouble most likely. That's what gets most of them."

"Most of whom, Sarge?"

"Suicides. Some damn dame jacks him around, sleeps with his friends, talks about it. That kind of thing. Next thing you know there's a big vein open."

"Dame, huh?"

"Wouldn't doubt it."

"Lot of recent stuff here. Room fairly packed with freshly painted canvases. Looks like a flurry of activity near the end."

"Heard footsteps maybe."

"Could be. Like Pollock."

"Eh?"

"Jackson Pollock. Killed in a car accident, probably suicide, but worked like the devil was after him his last few months."

"This Pollock ever do anything like this?

"Well, ha, sort of."

"Pretty, huh?"

"Found him like this, did you? Stretched out on the canvas like this."

"Yep. Blood and brains all around him."

"Gesso still damp. Looks a bit like a sunrise around him, doesn't it?"

"Sunset more likely."

"His last work."

"Brilliant use of red, eh?"

"Yep. Like Calder, maybe."

Blue Positive

"Dawn, the slow unsheathing of a sword; then, the untempered effulgence of day, rapacious, brutal, striking away the merciful shadows, challenging the pygmy man to battle, daring him to look yet again upon his handiwork and pronounce it good. I sat there a long time—until it was not I who looked out at the city but the city that looked in at me."

—Jim Thompson

I have lived alone among bookshelves, an eidolon of a former man more vigorous, certainly more vigorous, and perhaps more intrepid about the bigger picture, the world at large, you might say. I have lived with the musty smell of pages on my fingers and the somewhat airy countenance of a dreamer, a man in cloudcuckooland, though, really, I am more grounded than most men, I boast. I think I can make that boast.

Every story like this story begins with a dame. This is my story that begins with a dame but I make no claims for its originality. Though I am a man composed of folios and phantasm, I often offer my services in a slightly more lucrative, more risqué, some might say a more *serious* occupation. I find lost people.

Usually the lost people don't want to be found. In Memphis, where I ply my strange vocation, there are many places to hide, places as dark as a thief's pocket, flash coves, buttocking shops and hot water doss houses. I am known in these places. I am respected in some, loathed in too many, welcome in few. Yet it is where I know to go. My name is Charlie Main.

I have a small office over Club Millar on Beale Street. The sign on my door says only "Charlie Main." I rely mostly on word of mouth business. Across the street from my office is the office of the recently deceased Mr. Honeywood Partridge, an extraordinary photographer: inside his office/gallery history crouches, gray and cold: the walls are festooned with iconic images of Dr. King, the Civil Rights marchers, Elvis, Sam Cooke. He was also, possibly, an FBI informer in the brutal conflicts of the 1960s. *C'est la guerre.* My associate, Anna Ford, says Mr. Partridge never pigeoned on anyone who didn't need pigeoning on. I don't care. But I do trust Anna the way an animal trainer trusts his luck. She's smart; she's got head-splatter to spare. She's as cunning as Becky Sharp. And she's made of fine parts which are put together well.

The dame, ahem, my new client, arrived one Friday morning just after I got to the office. My head was still full of *Laughter in the Dark*, the Nabokov novel I reluctantly left behind to assume my professional stance, one that required an office with my name on the door and an associate who is a wet dream's wet dream. Anna was gone that week. I was not sure where. She might have been working in disguise at one of the clubs, emporia of blues and blue tape. She did this occasionally because she said she could drum up business. I think she did it so she could take strangers home and show them the inside of her clothes. Anna liked, equally, the shine of bar lighting in a shot glass of whiskey (a glister of fish-hooks, she called it) and moral depravity. Hell, it wouldn't be wrong to say I loved her.

So, when a tentative knock arrived I shouted from behind my desk, "Come on in," in a voice meant to discourage the time-wasters, the feebs, the people whose fifteen-year-old tabby named Cuddles, was AWOL.

She entered with an air. The air smelled like honeysuckle. She looked like a well-made dresser with all the drawers full. She was about five foot nine in her bare feet (later), had hair the color of tobacco and the kind of mouth that makes men want to drink there. She had skin the color of the Bosco I drank in short pants. She smiled like a kitten. A kitten with teeth like filed steel.

"Mr. Main?" she said. Her voice was made of a parasite's silk.

It was a good enough way to begin.

"How can I help you?" I countered.

"I was told." She stopped. She looked around like an actress in a melodrama. I waited. I'd done this interview before.

"I was told you find missing people." She finished with a silvery period on the end of her statement. It could have been plate silver or something finer.

"I try. That is what I get paid for. Trying."

She looked at me with a school teacher's moue.

"I hear you're better than that." She let the tip of her tongue dot her eyes.

"Thank you, Ms....?"

"Himes. Greta Himes."

"Pleased to meet you, Ms. Himes. Sit."

She folded herself downward. It was worth watching.

"Do you know a piano player named Blue Positive?"

"Heard of him. Plays at Smith Wigglesworth's place, right?"

"Sometimes he does. He used to, I should say."

"Until?"

"About ten days ago. He never showed up. Mr. Wigglesworth called me a week ago to ask his whereabouts and I couldn't imagine. I hadn't seen him in all that time but that's not unusual. He was, is, a tomcat. I waited a few more days before coming to you."

"I see. And this piano man, what is he to you?"

"My lover, Mr. Main. Nothing more really. He and I sleep together when it's convenient."

"I appreciate your honesty. I'll give it a go. $500 a day plus expenses."

She didn't even hesitate. This began to interest me. She peeled off five c-notes and set them on my desk, right next to my baseball signed by Luis Aparicio.

"Gimme his addresses and friends' names and addresses and anything else you can think of and I'll get on it."

"I assumed everything was done online these days," she said, with a slight snark on the edge of her purr.

"If it were, you could find Mr. Blue," I said back. Not for the first time.

"You're right, of course." She stood and I almost asked her to do it a few more times. She had a body that was full of poetry and terror.

I gave her my card and she said she would email me everything she could think of that might help. I thanked her and then tried to memorize the music she made walking away.

*

Of course, I did go online to find out everything I could about Blue Positive. And about Greta Himes.

Blue Positive, age 43, had learned to play blues piano with some of the greats. He was precocious and was sitting in with Furry Lewis when Blue was only twelve. He played the Delta circuit for a while but, about five years ago, decided he wanted to settle down and he took a semi-permanent gig on Beale Street, where he became a popular attraction, both for his amazing left hand and his gold-toothed grin. He was playsome and randy (well-schooled in petticoats was Blue) and the stories of the beautiful women he bedded made me squirm. It had been a while. Where is Anna, I asked myself?

So, Blue was established, even cut some records on the Madjack Label, was nominated for a Handy Award two years ago. There the biographical trail stopped. I could find nothing about Blue Positive that wasn't dated over a year ago.

Greta Himes proved as appealing, perhaps more so. She was born with a silver spoon in her wanton mouth to a Collierville, Tennessee, family, whose residence there went back hundreds of years. The name Himes meant money, prestige, banking, big business and Cayman Island savings accounts. Greta's father, Grip Himes, married Cornelia Bryson in 1945. Cornelia was a singer and as black as Miles Davis. Needless to say, this caused great consternation in the Himes family, who were white as diatomaceous earth. They had two daughters, Camille, who went to Vassar and became a successful writer of murder mysteries, before her tragic death in a freak boating accident, and Greta, who became nothing much at all, except the rich, mulatto daughter of a prominent and powerful family.

These were fascinating histories. It was easy to see why Greta Himes gravitated toward Blue Positive and equally easy to see why Blue Positive wouldn't mind spending some of the Himes family money, and, presumably, spending some sack time with that supernal body.

So, why was he gone missing? It would seem he had landed in the lap of luxury. Who wouldn't want what he had?

I sat in front of the computer for another hour or so, randomly scrolling through pages about blues music, then pages about baseball, and then pages about Nabokov, and, in the end, pages with naked, attractive strangers rantum-scantum. That night I slept like a water-lily. I dreamed I was dead and seated at a dinner table with James Joyce, Brooks Robinson, Iris Murdoch and Greta Himes. Greta Himes was moving her fingers toward my tingling scrotum when the phone rang.

It was Greta Himes.

"I just sent you a list of names and addresses by email."

"What time is it?" I was having trouble distinguishing the dream Greta from the voice on the phone.

"Eight in the a.m., Bedhead," Greta said, with what I took for a coquettish lilt.

"Right. Thanks for the email. I'll go look."

"Can we meet for lunch?" Greta now asked. Something was pear-shaped in the way she was approaching this caper.

"Um, yes, sure" I said, like the sharp I am. "B. B. King's ok?"

"Noon. I'll be there," Greta said.

And at noon there she was, almost lambent in the darkened restaurant, when I strolled in, print-out in hand. The list she had sent was extensive indeed. I was surprised not to see Mayor Wharton's name, or Steve Cohen's. Or the Pope's.

"You look tired," she said, half-rising.

"I'm fine. I need more coffee. I've been going over the list. It lacks—*focus*."

"I know. Once I got started I could not stop."

We ate some lunch. I had a lot of coffee but it was Greta Himes who seemed jangled. She talked like an undammed river, mostly about inconsequential matters.

With dessert came this question: "Where do you wanna start?"

"I've an idea or two."

"Let's go then."

"Wait. Ms. Himes. Wait. I don't work with anyone." (I didn't want to go into the whole Anna Ford thing.) "Clients don't tag along."

"Oh." She seemed genuinely disappointed like a spoiled child who just lost her inheritance. This lasted for a couple beats. "Will you see me home then?"

Her home was off Parkway. It was the size of the Taj Mahal if the Taj Mahal were a rest stop. She invited me in and, damn it, I went. She was wearing this dress. It was made of butterfly wings. The sun shimmered through it. I am only human.

One of her domestics brought us coffee in the living room. It was a modest room. So is the Winter Palace. The couch on which we sat was the size of a small pasture, but softer.

After the manservant left us Greta Himes took off her shoes. There were her bare feet, dark like supple leather. They were the sexiest bare feet I'd ever seen. She tucked them under herself the way women do. I missed them immediately.

"Get comfortable," she said.

"What are we doing?" I asked. It was part of the training.

She looked at me like I had invented Swift-Peter, the mythical Cooper-Young beast that white merchants used to scare blacks out of the neighborhood. Her perfect face was squinched perfectly.

"You're funny," she said. She pulled her dress up over her knees, with a practiced nonchalance. Her thighs were bronze. I was defeated.

In her bedroom she undid my every button and catch slowly, both of us standing and swaying next to her vast bed. My knees were as weak as a bled calf's. When I was down to my hector protector she smiled at the bulge and touched it with the tip of her manicured pinkie. I imagine this is the classy way to approve a dick.

Then she let her dress fall. Then she undid her bra. Then she let her thin black panties slither down her magnificent gams. Her pubic hair, a glorious map of Tasmania, against her coffee-colored skin was as black as Alaskan sealskin.

She knelt and pulled my pistol out of its holster. She palmed it for a few agonizing minutes and then took it past her bright red lips into the warm pocket of her cheeks. Soon, I got the idea. Soon, we were in bed and she was sitting on me and riding me as if I were the Scrambler at the Mid-South Fair, (gone now, too). It was quite a performance. I was good. She was better. After it was over she mewed like a kitten.

"Find my Blue for me, Mr. Dick," she said, and tittered at her own joke.

"I aim to, Ms. Himes. I aim to start just as soon as I know my legs still work."

"You're funny," she said for the second time. "And please call me Greta."

*

I didn't understand what had happened but I didn't care. We both itched. I thought of it like that. And now I was back on the case, professional from the brim of my porkpie roofer to the aching culty-gun of my well-used body.

I started at the last place Blue Positive played, Smith Wigglesworth's. I knew Smith from the old days. We had gone to East High together. Smith played tight end. I played the fool. We were acquaintances back then and, since we both worked on Beale, we got together occasionally for lunch. By the time I got to his place they were unstacking chairs and cleaning glasses, getting ready for the evening's crowd. I was shown into Smith's office.

His athlete's body had gone to seed but, hell, we all weighed a bit more, and we all still thought we were as beautiful as teenagers. Smith wore a suit out of some material that looked like a cross between linen and tin foil. It gleamed.

"Charlie Main," Smith said, not rising and not taking his eyes off the computer screen in front of him. "Too late for lunch, my man. Did we have a lunch date today that I forgot?" Now he raised his Paul Newman eyes and brushed back his shoulder-length silver hair.

"No, this is business, Smith. We can do lunch another day."

"Mr. Serious. Tell me about it."

"I'm looking for Blue Positive."

"Who isn't?" he said, his eyes went back to the screen and then back to mine. Was he uncomfortable suddenly?

"Yes, but I am being paid to do it."

"Difference noted."

"You got any ideas?"

"You checked The Castle of Missing Men? Gamblers and drinkers go in but they do not come out." He couldn't resist a tight smile.

"You got any ideas?" Sometimes repeating questions works. I don't know why.

"Nah," he said as if he thought I might let him go at that.

"Come on, Smith. We understand each other. You know something."

"Not much, Chuck, not much." He was the only person who called me Chuck. I hated it.

"When did you see him last?"

"Last night he worked. Um, this is the 24th. Musta been July 14, 15."

"Anything special happen that night?"

Here Smith stopped. He pushed himself away from the computer. He leaned back in his leather desk chair.

"Maybe," he said. His eyes, the color of pulled pork, were doing that funny thing again. They were positively hiding something, trying to look inside their owner to see if he should spill.

"Smith," I said, letting the exasperation show.

"Big white guy came in. Big. I mean like Secret Service big. Looked like he could take you out while singing 'Rockin' Robin,' and never miss a beat. Like a walking wall. Solemn dude, asked my man

Petey where Blue was. Blue was on break and in the back. Big guy went back there as if he had permission from Hitler himself. In the back room I don't know what happened. The big white guy left after about five minutes, walked right by me, giving me the smartass grin, like he might enjoy eating my gonads for breakfast. That's it."

"Blue never came back out?"

"No, he came out, finished his set. Seemed a little shaky maybe, not much. Blue was an interior sorta guy, you know? He finished his set. But he never came back. I tried his apartment numerous times. Sent Petey around to see if he was at home. Petey said the place looked untouched but there was no Mr. Positive."

"Petey went in?"

"Well, heh-heh, yeah. He did. I gave him a little shiv, you know, a little skeleton key."

"Ok. Thanks, Smith. I get the picture."

"You need Blue's address?" Smith now said. He seemed relieved I was going.

"Got it," I called back over my shoulder.

Blue Positive lived in the Akimbo Arms, an apartment complex just off Beale, a stone's throw from FedEx Forum, the AA somehow surviving when they razed or gentrified everything within walking distance of the mammoth NBA mushroom.

As I ambled down the western end of Beale I passed the usual buskers and cackleberries, a bum-simple beggar, a Creole Conjurewoman. Ah, Beale, still the American Dream forced through a squeezebox and spat out, multihued and wet with dribble.

The guy who ran Akimbo Arms was a pipsqueak named Pipsqueak Martin. He used to be a mob marker but emphysema had slowed him down some.

"Charlie Main," he said, coming from around his desk to take my hand. "Hot enough for you?" I recognized this as a standard greeting in Memphis, something like "Howdy" for a Texan.

"Looking for Blue Positive," I told him straight out. I didn't really want chitchat with Pipsqueak Martin.

"That's a mystery, ain't it? Mystery inside of an enema, as they say. Ain't seen him, Charlie."

"Can I look around his apartment?"

"Sure," he said, after acting like he was thinking it over. "Let the po po see it, why not my old pal, Charlie Main? You're one upscale busy, my friend. You're one of the good guys. You know Pipsqueak's got the bull horrors."

"Law been here already?"

"Yeah, yesterday it was."

Pipsqueak let me in and then let me alone. I closed the door behind me and locked it. Blue's apartment was as neat as the altar of a church. Bed, dresser, computer, keyboards, stereo and the largest selection of jazz records I have ever seen. 33s and 78s. Like Crumb's house, all categorized and in original covers. Impressive. Of course all I wanted to do was look at his computer. I turned it on. Maybe he was careless with passwords. Maybe he didn't clear history. Maybe his screensaver said "*I have absquatulated to New Orleans.*" It was a prayer, really. Nothing is ever that easy.

The computer was clean or had been wiped clean. He used Google Chrome. That's about the extent of the information I got off it. If Anna were around, damn her, she could get me in. She never saw a hard drive she couldn't cozy up to.

I ran my hand underneath the desk surface and found fuckle. I stood and looked around the immaculate room. There is nothing for me here, I thought. I looked at his clothes closet. Hipster jazzman-wear. Nice stuff. Then I saw it. There was a military style jacket on a satin-padded hanger, the kind that was popular after Sergeant Pepper taught the band to play. I took it off its hanger and ran my hand over the brightly colored tunic. Tucked under one of the epaulettes, seemingly a part of the design, was a coral-pink flash drive about the size of a lot lizard's polished nail. I was about to try it in Blue's computer when Pipsqueak opened the door.

"How's it going, Charlie?" he said, sticking his weasel head inside.

I slipped the zip drive into my pants pocket.

"Nothing here," I said and brushed past him.

"Told you so," he said.

He hadn't but that didn't matter.

I made it to my office in record time. The door to Mr. Partridge's studio had a large sign in its window saying "Closed for Maintenance." I felt I had something vital in my pocket and when I pulled up the files on the zip I discovered I was right. I had something. Something good. Something I hated and wished I didn't have.

*

On the North side of Beale, closer to Big Muddy, there was a three-story, non-descript edifice. It held a real estate office, a lawyer's office and some charity connected to the Memphis Grizzlies. It also held a small office on the third floor, down a dim hallway, far away from the other businesses. On its door it said, in recently painted calligraphy, "Harris P. Kayshun, Accountant."

I opened the door without knocking. A woman who resembled the TV actress Kristin Chenoweth sprang from her chair. She was stuck somewhere between shock and indignation. It was clear people didn't just walk in to see Harris P. Kayshun. It was also clear that he was no accountant.

"Can I help you?" she practically snarled.

"Get Mr. Kayshun for me," I said. I tried to sound like Philip Marlowe. I was afraid of Harris P. Kayshun and for good reason. His connections had connections.

"He's not here. He's in St. Louis."

"He's here," I insisted. "Tell him it's Mr. Blue." I sat down in the room's only chair not behind her desk.

She appeared flustered for a moment and then she opened the door behind her desk and disappeared. I looked at the office. It was cheap, temporary, perfunctory. The pictures on the walls could have come from any Days Inn.

She returned. Her smile was as practiced as "Feelin' Alright."

"I don't know who you are but Mr. Kayshun said he had five minutes."

I let her have her attitude. I walked past her into the office of Harris. P. Kayshun. He was standing next to his desk. He wore a suit that cost more than my car. It was out of place in his shabby office. Even his desk was cheap. He was about six two and looked like he could handle himself. And me.

"Who are you, sir?" Harris spoke.

"A guy with some questions about Positive Blue."

"Positive…" he began.

"Can it," I said. "I am in possession of numerous emails and documents between you and Mr. Blue. They may very well put you in hot water. They may very well make a strong case for your going to jail."

I was partly bluffing. The computer files consisted of pages and pages of correspondence between Blue Positive and Harris P. Kayshun and they pointed toward some kind of nefarious deal (or deals) but they were not more specific than that. Kayshun was funneling a lot of bees and honey into Blue's accounts, especially right before the piano man disappeared.

The door opened. A man, who was made of whatever they make fireplugs out of, entered. He stood by the door. His silence was like suffocation. I tried to take a deep breath. I was playing a weak hand and, perhaps, playing it badly.

"You have nothing of the sort," Kayshun said. "What do you want, Mr....?"

"Main," I said. "Charlie Main."

"Private peon."

"That's right. Hired to find Blue Positive."

Kayshun sat down behind his desk. He nodded at the roughneck who went back outside. He played with a Shane Battier bobblehead on his desk. He took a deep breath and beamed like Barabbas.

"What you have, Mr. Main, Charlie, could embarrass me, it's true. It, however, is not the Pandora's box you think it is. I am willing to pay for its return, for good faith, you might say."

"How much?" Why not?

"Would 50,000 sound right?"

He was darling. He was real loveable.

"You know it sounds right," I said. "I'll take it. As long as the whereabouts of Blue Positive are thrown in to sweeten the pot."

He smiled a grim smile.

"Mr. Positive," he said almost dreamily. Almost the way a lover would say it.

"I can't," he said.

"Ok," I said, and started to rise.

"Mr. Main," he said quickly. "What will you do with Blue? Will you send him away?"

"I have no intention of doing anything with Mr. Blue except

telling my client where he is."

He seemed to think this over.

"Ok," he said.

*

I called Greta Himes. I told her I knew where her boyfriend was.

"Mr. Main," she cooed. "You are wonderful. I don't know how to repay you."

"Yes, you do," I said.

"Cheeky," she said in that voice that turned men into goats.

"I'll tell you where he is and I'll send you the bill."

"Mr. Business," she said. "Are you sure?"

I wasn't.

"Yes," I said.

And then I told her and then I sat behind my desk with $50,000 dollars in the locked drawer where I usually kept my blunt, and I created an invoice and emailed it to her. I sat back and tried to feel good about myself. It wouldn't happen. Something was wrong. I felt it in Kayshun's office and I felt it when I talked to Greta Himes.

I slept badly that night. And when I woke I still had a bad feeling in my gut.

I went to the office but I didn't want to see anyone.

Then the Creole Conjurewoman entered, a diddykay of colorful rags and trinkets. She was dusky and glittery at the same time, like a night when the clouds are torn newspaper and the moon a buttery nightlight.

"Hi," I said. "I'm closed."

She fixed me with her one eye that was not occluded by cloud.

"Open for a poor conjurewoman, Mr. Main?" she asked in a

voice like a giraffe's tongue.

"No, I, I'm not open, Ma'am. Sorry."

"Not even if I know who killed Blue Positive."

I involuntarily stood up. I wanted to hit her. I wanted to hit myself. My head swam. Her expression never changed. She looked like Bela Lugosi in *Bride of the Monster*. I sat back down. She sat on the chair on the other side of the desk and her back was so bent it looked as if she was about to teeter out of it.

"Wake you up, did it?"

"Please," I said. I don't know what I was asking.

"Not to worry, Mr. Main. You get to keep the 50,000."

"Who are you?" It was worth asking.

"Conjurewoman. You know me. All over. You've seen."

I hadn't but I played along.

"Blue Positive is dead?"

"As dead as Vladimir Nabokov," she said. She grinned like a wolf. She knew too much.

"How?"

"Shot through the heart. Twice. Both times through the heart. Nice clean kill, yes?"

"I don't understand. How did this happen?"

"You led her to him." Now she didn't seem so funny. Her voice dropped an octave. I imagined she could be mean as a nightmare given the chance.

I started to shake.

"G-Greta?" I said, weakly.

"Halfbreed bitch. Of course, Greta."

"But why?"

"Two reasons. Jealousy and she was paid to do it."

"She didn't need money," I said. I was playing with a blank deck.

"She was in a bad way. Her father was threatening to take the house, her car, her servants. He wanted her gone, out of Memphis. He was brokering a big deal and afraid having a mixed-race daughter might queer it. Kayshun somehow dealt himself into the deal."

"Kayshun?" But I knew. It had to come back to Kayshun.

"You had a part in this sordid affair, Mr. Main, but don't take it hard. It wasn't personal. You were used but it could have been someone else."

"I don't understand."

"Look," she said. Her voice did not seem as raspy. "Blue Positive was a gunsel. Hired talent. But he was also as gay as Liberace. And he was Kayshun's bum boy, as well as one of his operatives. You dig?"

"I don't know." I put my face in my hands.

"And Greta Himes?" I asked.

"She was really Blue's lover. She was mad for him, if a woman with the morals of a dingo can be mad for anyone. When Blue did a Judge Crater she genuinely wanted him back. She loved him—in her way."

"She knew Kayshun knew where he was?"

"That's right. She also knew he would never tell her. He wanted the boy for himself. We might give Mr. Kayshun at least that much credit. He loved Blue, too. Still, he was ready to do what he had to do, like the good Joe Bonanno he is. Blue became expendable when you started digging, in the service of that wildcat. How whimsical for Kayshun to use her as the instrument of Blue's demise."

"And the big deal?"

"I'm not sure. I think Kayshun might have cut out the father. He certainly made sure the daughter became his to utilize."

"Jesus," I said. "And I led her to Blue. I did it. His blood is on my hands."

"Don't feel so bad about it. Some folks need killing."

I looked up. Her gypsy voice was suddenly as smooth as Ruby Wilson's.

"What did Blue Positive do to need killing?"

"He killed Honeywood Partridge."

Now I stood up. My eyes popped. I was a cartoon gull. I didn't know anything about anything.

"Mr. Partridge died of a stroke."

"Complications from a stroke, yes. That's what they said."

"But—"

"He was killed before the FBI stuff leaked out. There are things in Mr. Partridge's file that could upset some official applecart."

"The Feds had him killed?"

"Who knows? But whoever was behind it paid Blue Positive to kill Mr. Partridge and make it look like a medical anomaly."

"And they got to Blue through Kayshun."

"Yes."

"Damn them all to hell. Let's go get Kayshun."

"Gone, brother. Gone like Jackie Brenston. Gone like Roscoe Gordon."

"Dead?'

"Oh no. Just—pfft. Disappeared."

"Fuck."

"Frustrating, isn't it? They did get Greta Himes though. Caught her on the scene, beautiful little silver beader still smoking."

"The Feds. The mob. Gunsel piano players. Deadly dames. What is going on?"

"Life, Baby, just life."

"I don't want any part of it."

The old crone put a hand over mine. Her hand was as soft as

cream. "Can't get away from life, Sugar."

I looked up into her eyes. Her eye.

"You slept with that mulatto, didn't you?" she said. It wasn't the conjurewoman's voice anymore. It was Anna Ford's.

I was through with histrionic surprise. I was as tired at Tiresias.

"Damn you, Anna," I said. This time I rose with righteous dudgeon.

She gave a graveyard chuckle and began dismantling her complex disguise. Soon, except for some greasepaint, some tacky maquillage and random streaks in her hair where the jasey had stuck, my associate sat before me, stripped to her underwear.

I sat back down. I was too dazed for rage.

"Oh, and I got you this." She reached into the conjurewoman's bag and pulled out a book wrapped in a plastic bag.

"It's a first of *Pale Fire*. Signed."

A book about as rare as, as we say, a John Calipari fan in Memphis.

"Jesus, Anna, this must have cost you a mint."

"We can afford it now," she said.

She stood up and walked around the desk. She unhooked her bra. Her breasts were as full as a vicar's wisdom. I thought I heard the music of the spheres but it might have been Howlin' Wolf.

For a while we forgot about the world. For a while we did things humans do to assuage loss and to express feelings too deep for words alone. For a while there never was a piano player named Blue Positive, nor a chocolaty temptress named Greta Himes.

Then I kissed Anna's hot mouth long and hard.

"You were here the whole time?"

"Right behind you, every step."

"You're amazing, Anna Ford."

"I know, Charlie Main."

"I didn't really sleep with her."

How good was her knowledge of the whole miserable kerfluffle?

"Sure, Bunky," she said. "Sure."

Barbra and Chuck Said We'd Like Each Other

—First dates, huh?

—Yes.

—Barbra and Chuck tell me you work at The Med.

—Yes.

—Ok.

—Sorry, yes, I work in Medical Records.

—I see.

—I see, as in, how boring? Or, I see, as in, I'm being polite but I have no idea what that is?

—Ha. The latter.

—Right.

—So, what is it?

—Not worth explaining really. Self explanatory, I guess.

—Ok.

—And you're—

—Oh, I assumed—never mind—I work for the newspaper.

—Delivery?

—Funny. No, I am a sports columnist.

—Oh, I don't follow sports much. Tennis.

—Yeah, we don't do much tennis.

—Oh, wait, I like poker!

—Poker is not a sport.

—But, your paper—

—I know. It makes me grind my teeth.

—What do you cover? Is cover the right word?

—Well, I do columns, that is commentary. You know, pithy observations about the state of the game, the age of the millionaire athlete, that sort of thing.

—Hm.

—Not up your alley.

—Oh, I don't know. That's it, I don't know. I've never really—

—It's ok. Read me tomorrow. Tomorrow the think piece is about whether the Grizzlies' recent trades made the team wiser and older or just older.

—Ok. A sports think piece.

—You're thinking oxymoron. For morons.

—No.

—Sorry. Boring you. Let's talk about, uh—

—Medical transcription.

—Ha, no. Let's see, do you read?

—Since I was 8.

—Books?

—Yes. Actually I'm a voracious reader. Definition of a reader: someone who is always in a book. You ask them what they're reading and they know—just like that.

—Good.

—You?

—I guess I'm a reader.

—And you're reading?

—Oh. *The Last Season*.

—I don't know that.

—Phil Jackson's book about the Lakers.

—Oh.

—Ok, what are you reading?

—Never mind.

—C'mon. Really. What are you reading?

—Susan Sontag's *The Volcano Lover*.

—Sounds hot.

—Funny.

—It's egghead literature.

—Not at all. She's a very good—plotter. Her novels have shape and—weight.

—Ok.

—We're not hitting common ground here, are we?

—Sure. No, it's ok. We don't have to love the same things.

—If what?

—If what?

—To be on a date? To like each other?

—Oh. Yeah. First date. I guess if Barbra and Chuck thought we'd hit it off we'd better.

—Ha. I know. Yeah.

—Have you eaten here before?

—Well—

—You have and it sucks?

—No, no. I ate here just last week.

—Oh.

—On another blind date. Sorry.

—Oh, damn. I'm sorry. This is awkward.

—Not really. Barbra—

—You bit your tongue. They tried someone else out first. I'm second string.

—I don't know what second string means but, well, it was someone Barbra worked with—you know, a librarian. So, the books and—

—A better fit probably. I suddenly feel deeply inadequate not to mention inappropriate and probably a few other ins if I were better with the language like I imagine your other blind date was—

—Slow down, Cowboy. It didn't work out. Obviously.

—So you're not here to weigh the pros and cons of each of us, to compare and contrast.

—No, not at all. It didn't work out.

—Because?

—First, I don't think he really liked me. And second I think he's gay.

—Really? Gay gay?

—Yeah, is there another kind? Almost gay?

—No, it's just—why did Barbra?

—I don't know. She doesn't know. I think he's in denial. Or in the proverbial closet. Maybe the library system frowns on alternative lifestyles.

—I wouldn't think so. Lot of gay librarians.

—Yeah, probably.

—I don't know. So, Barbra and Chuck are officially your procurers?

—Right. They feed me men as if I were a lion in the zoo. I am a man eater.

—I'm frightened.

—Be afraid. Be very afraid.

—Ha. Really, though. I feel, I don't know, I feel unable to compete. I think this situation is fraught with danger and possible disappointment and I don't know what all. Suddenly there are snares and snakes, pitfalls and pratfalls.

—

—What? You're looking at me the way Phil Jackson looks at Kobe Bryant.

—I'm thinking you're maybe a half empty kind of guy. You see a half-full glass—

—Sweetheart, you don't know. I see a full glass of water and I call it half-empty.

—Really?

—Everything diminishes. Everything dissipates. Nothing lasts.

—Things fall apart.

—More like things run out. Toilet paper, food, relationships.

—Wow.

—I know.

—So, this—this situation to you—is really already over. You've already failed?

—If this is a test, yes.

—Ok. Now we know.

—Forewarned is four-armed. Like Shiva.

—Is Shiva the one with four arms?

—I don't know.

—Sorry. I'm sounding like a librarian, right? Like a know-it-all.

—Oh. Hi. Yes, um, you go first. Saskia.

—Thanks. I'll have the fish.

—Me, too, the fish.

—Good.

—Saskia. I've just discovered I like to say your name.

—Many people do. It's an odd name, isn't it?

—Well, I don't know any others. Saskia. Where does it come from?

—Company my father works for.

—That's the name of the company?

—Yes. Art historians.

—A company of art historians? Doing what?

—Providing images—art for—heck, you know, I'm not sure I can explain it.

—That's ok.

—They license images. Jack.

—Ok.

—Right. What do your parents do, Jack? Are you from here, Jack?

—Born in Niagara Falls, New York. My father worked for E. I. DuPont and was transferred to Memphis when I was five. A sort of Southerner. My accent falls somewhere along the highway between New York and Tennessee. An Ohio accent maybe.

—And your mom?

—Does your mom work?

—She's a college professor.

—Huh.

—Why?

—Mine's a homemaker, through and through. Her generation.

—I think my parents are a little younger than yours.

—Probably. What does your mother teach?

—Russian studies.

—Huh.

—What were we saying— before the waiter—I had something—

—Shiva.

—No—oh, half empty. Are you really that downbeat or are you being ironic? This is the age of irony and sometimes I don't always get it. Not that I'm dense. It's—

—No, I wasn't being ironic. I don't think. I mean, really, I just think— well, that things are serious, that being serious is a, in a way, positive approach to the world.

—And if you're a half full kind of person? You're not taking things seriously enough?

—Well, I'm not judging, mind you.

—Aren't you? Aren't you saying that if you are light-hearted you're not paying attention?

—Yes. I am. I am saying that.

—Well, I'm lighthearted and well-informed.

—Then you're the exception.

—I don't really think so. I think that your ilk have your heads in the sand, not me. I think to see the world as nothing but shadows and cobwebs is really selling yourself and everyone else short. You can hate the problem and at least attempt to see a solution.

—But that's so empirical. It's like *Star Trek*. When all else fails short out the energy source and you conquer evil.

—I'm not sure—

—I'm saying—I'm saying that there are problems without solutions. There are ways in which things are just plain fucked up and we're better off seeing it for what it is.

—Ok.

—Sorry, language.

—No, you can say fucked up. I'm just—well, I'm not sure how to respond. This seems to be warp and woof for you. Deeply ingrained.

—I guess so. And this after 6 years of therapy.

—Six, huh?

—That's bad right? That's the test answer that fails me.

—Five years plus.

—What—

—I'm five years and counting.

—You're in therapy?

—Isn't everyone? I mean everyone except those twisted fucks who want to go into politics.

—Right.

—I've been seeing a therapist—well, I guess off and on—ever since my divorce.

—Divorce.

—Oh, sorry. I assumed Chuck had told you.

—Wow. You're so young.

—I'm only three years younger than you.

—So, you were married at ten?

—Well, 17.

—Oh, sheesh.

—Yeah.

—Pregnancy.

—Well, no. It was more like an arranged marriage.

—What—are your parents Hindu?

—No, but, well, ok, it was the son of my father's best friend. We grew up together. When he turned 18 his father wanted him to join the Marines. I kid you not. His father's best years were spent in the Marine Corps—and he was into that kind of discipline. He accepted nothing short of total acquiescence. Jip was not USMC material. Decidedly not. He wanted to teach high school English-—that was all he wanted to do.

—Jip?

—James Ingersoll Pratt.

—Ah.

—So, we concocted this plan to keep him in town so he could go to college. We drove up to Covington and were married in the County office there. Had a 2 hour honeymoon at a steak house on the way back.

—Wow. So, really you saved him.

—No, nothing so dramatic.

—And he went on to college—what happened that—

—He tried college. The secret of Jip—what I couldn't see because nobody could see it—was that he was not cut out for anything, Not the USMC or the U of M. It didn't matter. He only wanted to get high and—well—you know—

—Fuck.

—That too. But it's worse than that.

—Worse than fucking?

—No. He, well, there's no sugar coating it. He beat me.

—Aw, Christ.

—Yeah, good plan, eh?

—I'm so sorry. I—

—The fish!

—That's great.

—It looks wonderful. These garlic mashed potatoes—

—Right. What you had just last week.

—Right.

—Yours looks better than mine.

—It's the same—oh, half empty. You're joking.

—Actually no. Yours looks better than mine.

—Ok.

—Shall we eat? Can you eat and talk?

—Yes, yes I can.

—Ok. Oh, shit, I'm so sorry. You were actually physically abused.

—I was. Just like in the movies and books. I am a statistic. Women's shelter graduate.

—Not just.

—No, every unhappy family is not alike. He beat me in his own peculiar and idiosyncratic way.

—God.

—Sorry. What a downer.

—Yet you continue to think life is rosy. While I, who have had nothing more difficult than a job interview, piss and moan my time away.

—That's exactly what I was going to say.

—Really?

—No. I'm pulling your leg.

—Go ahead, kick the kid while he's down.

—Aren't you always down?

—No. I've given you the wrong impression. I'm sorry.

—Look, lets—if this has started badly, and I think you think it has, let's get it onto better footing. What say?

—Ok.

—So, let's think of something positive to say to each other?

—This fish is excellent.

—Thank you.

—Oh. Ha. No, let's see—

—I'll start. You're very handsome.

—Oh, jeez, thanks. I never get handsome. I get cute.

—Cute is ok. You're handsome. And sexy. Soulful eyes.

—No, now. Never have I been called sexy. Cute isn't sexy.

—Ok.

—Sorry. Um, you're lovely yourself.

—Thank you.

—Wait, that sounds trite like I'm only parroting. Let me see—you have wonderful eyes, too—are they gray?

—Yes, gray.

—And your lips are—look soft. And, um, you have great breasts.

—Ok. You don't have to travel south taking inventory.

—Sorry.

—No, I'm kidding. Thank you.

—It's just your body—well, you must keep in shape.

—Yes. I jog. I'm a jogger. I am one who jogs.

—Good for you.

—And the gym a couple times a week. So, at my age—

—You look great.

—For someone our age.

—No, no, for any age. Really. I'm impressed. I *used to* play basketball. Had a regular group of guys I played with on Wednesday nights. I actually, you know, ran around and sweated.

—Why don't you still?

—Knees. I have bad knees.

—Yeah, I read somewhere that the human knee was designed to only last 35 years or something like that.

—Mine did, almost exactly that. Bad knees came as a shock to me. Suddenly I was old.

—Not really old. You look great. You must eat well.

—Fish.

—Right!

—You—are you vegetarian?

—No. Well, I don't eat a lot of red meat. A few years ago—it was my therapist who said this: think about what's going in. I was apparently going on and on about what comes out—you know feeling like I was spitting out the wrong words, spiteful things, like epuration, uh like puke. Sorry. Not while we're eating, right?

—So, you concentrated on what goes in. You started dieting.

—Not in the sense of anything structured like carb-cutting. I started taking vitamins. Green tea.

—What is it with green tea?

—Anti-oxidants. I take anti-oxidants. Don't you.

—No. I'm just an oxidant waiting to happen.

—Ha ha hff—

—Oh, Jesus, ha—sorry—you've got food—

—Hff—oh, God—

—Wow, that's some laugh, that's some beautiful laugh.

—Heh heh. Sorry. Oh, God—

—You really laugh when you laugh.

—That was funny. You're funny.

—Thank you.

—I love funny. Funny is like the biggest turn on.

—Oh, really?

—Yes, yes it is. Funny is more aphrodisiacal than, say, hard abs or a law degree.

—Good for me then.

—Yes.

—So are you turned on now?

—Well.

—Sorry.

—No. Yes. Yes, I am turned on.

—Wow. Good. I think I am too.

—First dates.

—Rarely work.

—I know.

—You've been on many.

—No, not really. I was kidding you know about the sequential dating thing.

—Your laugh is—well, it's like wind chimes in a gale.

—Thank you.

—You put your whole body into it. Your whole lovely body.

—Oh.

—I'd like to make you laugh some more.

—I'd like that too.

—So. Where is this going?

—At least it's going.

—That's true.

—And shall we—be going?

—Yes, I think so. Your fish.

—I've had enough.

—Laugh for me again. Saskia.

—Be funny, Jack.

—Ok.

—Ok then.

—Saskia.

—Say it again. Say my name again.

Alan's Approach

Alan stepped from the shadows just as she was passing. He didn't mean for it to begin this way. He didn't mean to be in the shadows.

Perhaps Alan, poor gowk, was guilty of overthinking this whole thing. Perhaps what was called for was a more temperate approach, a card, sent anonymously, with a stamp affixed upside down, which Alan thought meant "sealed with a kiss."

No, not a kiss. It could not begin with even the suggestion of a kiss. Alan fretted. Late into the white nights he sat beneath his desk lamp and tried to focus. He pressed his fingers against his forehead as if he could force the insula to react.

He didn't mean to step from the shadows. She was so lovely. He saw her walking down the sidewalk just as carefree as a child at play, as if she were unaware that she was moonquakes and arrhythmia. She looked a bit like the actress Patsy Kensit.

Alan stepped from the shadows just as she was passing.

"I won't hurt you if you don't move," he said.

It was not what he had prepared. Alan was adlibbing.

Hypnotic Induction

"Soul is not only the 'still-point of Tao' where there is no more separation between 'this' and 'that,' it is also the presence of the unutterable within us."

James P. Carse

—Dr. O'Dyne?

—Call me Ann.

—Ann. Thanks for seeing me.

—This is what we do here.

—Thank you. Well, um, just thank you.

—Ok. What can I do for you, Mr. Galeen?

—Smoking. I have to quit.

—We can help you.

—Who is we?

—Sorry. It's just the way we phrase it here at the clinic. I. I can help you.

—Great. You use hypnosis, is that correct?

—That is the most efficient method, yes. We could also use EMDR.

—I saw something called Psychoshamanism. Is that—

—Fairy tale stuff. We're a bit more grounded here. Hypnosis—let's say that's what we do.

—A buddy told me it could take only one session.

—A myth.

—Ok. Do we start today?

—Sure. Lemme just ask you a few questions, get some background, put you at ease.

—I'm at ease.

—Of course. Mr. Galeen.

—Henry.

—Henry. You work, let me see, at a downtown bar?

—Sweety's, yes.

—As a—

—Manager.

—Ok. And you've been doing this kind of work for how long?

—I'm a bartender.

—Wha—

—I didn't want to get off on the wrong foot. I'm really just a glorified bartender. Night manager they let me say. I'm the bartender.

—Is there some shame associated with being just a bartender?

—No. No, I don't think so.

—Ok then.

—I used to be a drunk.

—Oh.

—Yes, I used to be a drunk. 11 months sober.

—That's wonderful. So, being a bartender—

—Is a refuge for many an ex-drunk.

—I didn't know that.

—Well, yes it's true. Many of us find that extra little bit of strength by being around what plagued us and not submitting.

—That's commendable.

—Not so much.

—Ok. And now—

—Like a lot of ex-drunks I smoke too much.

—I see.

—Now if I could lick cigarettes—

—You would be what?

—Clean. Really clean. A model citizen.

—You smile when you say that. Do you mean it ironically?

—No, well, partly. But, really, it's my last vice. Cigarettes. Coffin nails.

—Not many people just have one vice.

—I know. How about that?

—Why did you turn to cigarettes, Henry?

—Same reason as anybody. Well, any drunk. Something to suck on. Oral stimulation you might call it.

—Might I?

—I don't know.

—Right. Ok. Well, so, working in a bar, that lifestyle, how would you describe it?

—Um, late night. Lots of activity. Too much activity. An easy lifestyle to be seduced by.

—How so?

—Well, it's energizing. There are lots of things around to turn you on. Lights, music, women.

—I see.

—And lots of smoking.

—There's smoking allowed in, um, Sweety's?

—No, well there was until recently. No, not inside anymore.

—So you smoke on your breaks?

—Right.

—And women, you said. I assume you're single.

—Well, I'm sort of engaged.

—How sort of? Isn't it like being pregnant, there are no degrees to it?

—I guess so. Sandy is, well, she's really special. She doesn't care for the night life and that's a problem.

—I can see it would be.

—She works days. I work nights.

—And you are surrounded by should we say available women?

—Nightly. Right.

—And you have availed yourself of their seductive pleasures on occasion?

—Hey, this doesn't have anything to do with smoking. Can you just put me under and kill my nicotine craving?

—Yes. Ok. Is that the only craving you want killed?

—You're being judgmental, aren't you? Assuming I'm a birddog.

—No. I'm trying to establish what about your personality makes smoking so irresistible, so *necessary.*

—How do I know I can be hypnotized? Can anyone?

—Almost anyone. Not psychotics, not people with low IQ. Not people who do not want to be hypnotized. Do you fall into any of those categories?

—No, I don't think so. Ha, maybe low IQ.

—I doubt it.

—Ok. How do we do it?

—We'll lower the lights. I'll ask you to concentrate on a dot of light projected onto a small dark screen. Meanwhile I'll be playing a single monotonous note. Do these details help you?

—Help me? I don't know. You're the doctor.

—Right. Now, Henry, let's chat just a bit more. When would you say your worst cravings occur? Night, morning, at times of stress?

—Night. I guess. In the bar it's all I can do to serve drinks sometimes.

—Serve women drinks?

—You're hung up on this moralistic approach. Serve women, sure, anyone.

—I simply was asking if you found serving drinks to women especially troubling or disconcerting.

—No, I don't think so. Maybe.

—Ok.

—I mean, well, women are so free at night. They can be the straightest chick you know—Sunday School teachers—but in a bar, with their friends, it's like they are on another planet. The usual strictures are loosed. All inhibitions, all conventions are temporarily suspended. They dress provocatively, they flirt. It's hard—being, you know, engaged.

—Or even sort of engaged?

—Yes.

—Ok. One other thing. Sandy—does she smoke?

—Oh God no.

—Why so adamant?

—Sandy is, well, you know, straight.

—The Sunday School teacher type.

—She teaches Sunday School.

—I see.

—So, when we're, you know, married, I won't be around smoke, if that's what you're asking. Sandy wants me to quit more than I do.

—More than you do.

—A slip of the tongue. I do. I really want to quit.

—Ok.

—Ok.

—Let's just lower the lights. Get comfortable, Mr. Galeen. Henry.

—Ok.

*

—Now, Henry, you can hear me but you need not respond. Ok. You may respond but you need not.

—Yes.

—Very good. Now, I want you to place yourself somewhere else. The nicest, most relaxed place you can imagine. It might be the shore. It may be night. Moonlight on the water. You might be watching the calming lapping of the waves. You might be imagining yourself afloat on those waves, rocking with them. Everything is peaceful. Everything is calm. The moon seems to shine just for you. You are calm. All your cares, all your desires, all your attentions to the world, for now, are absent. They may still exist for you—but you have put them aside. You are only awake to the gentle sway of the water, the peaceful effortless rush of the blood in your own veins. Are you at peace?

—Yes.

—Very good. The world is far away. You are only yourself, alone, rocking with the world. You need nothing. You desire nothing.

—A cigarette.

—No, you don't desire a cigarette.

—I do.

—Relax. Let the waves carry you. You can ride the waves as if you are on a board, as if you *are* the board. It doesn't matter if the waves are big or small, you can ride them. You are so relaxed the waves are only part of your blood, the flow of your blood.

—Blood.

—Right.

—I want blood. A cigarette.

—Uh, Henry. You do not want a cigarette. You only want—

—Blood.

—I'm sorry.

—All I want is blood. I don't need a cigarette if I can have blood. Just a sip.

—Henry, I'm sure—

—Just one pretty neck. That waitress with the great tits. Trinka. She's always coming on to me. I want to suck.

—Her breasts. You want to suck her breasts. She is Mother—

—No, no, I want her neck. Her swan-like neck. So white, so smooth. To drink there.

—Henry. I'm not sure where this is going. This waitress—she is a problem for you? You who are trying to stay true to Sandy. She is temptation.

—She's always coming on to me.

—Ok.

—Rubbing up against me. If she knew. If she only knew.

—That you're engaged. That you are beyond temptation.

—That I would drink her blood. That I would bend her backwards, in a swoon, like a lover, exactly like a lover. I would tip her downy neck toward me and I would numb her with a kiss. She would at first think that I was making love to her. She would yield to it—can you see it? She is swooning toward me, she is offering her neck up to be loved. And I will attend to her like the gentlest lover—

—Henry.

—I would kiss her swan-like neck, gently, then more forcefully. She would moan as if I were her best lover. She would clasp her own breast. And in the moment that she gives herself up to me—that moment when she is sure I am her best lover—I would bite. I would lower my teeth into her flesh and—quickly, tenderly—she would think that she was in love—it must be love!—and I would begin to drink her sweet red blood. It would taste of iron and heat. It would taste of—eternity!

—Mr. Galeen. Where did this come from? I am waking you up now, I am releasing—um—

—Ann.

—Mr. Galeen.

—Ann, have you ever been made love to by eternity, by the endless wheeling of the stars, by the rotational tilt of the Earth itself? No—Ann—No—you don't know! Imagine I am leaning toward your neck—now!

—Mr. Galeen. When I count three and snap my fingers you will wake up. Do you hear me? One two three!

—Mm.

—You will wake now, Mr. Galeen.

—Mm.

—Mr. Galeen.

—Mm. Ann.

—Now, look at me. Open your eyes, Mr. Galeen. Open them, I say.

—What—mm, Ann. That was delicious.

—Ok, Mr. Galeen.

—What—did I do alright? I was really under, wasn't I?

—Mr. Galeen. I think. I think we should continue another time. If you'll make an appointment on your way out.

—Ann. Did I do something—what is it?

—Nothing, Mr. Galeen.

—Henry. I thought—

—Another time. We are out of time today. Now—

—Ann, did I—Ann. Look.

—Please, just leave. Please.

—Oh.

—Right—

—Oh.

—Mr.

—Mm, well. I'm sorry.

—Now if—

—Ann. I see. I need a cigarette. That's a bad sign.

—Mr—

—A bad sign. Ann. I'm sorry about this. I really am. I only wanted. Well, it's not important. Ann, I'm sorry about this. No—keep those lights off. Come here, Ann. Come. Now, you can see me. Now you can look into my eyes. Deeper, Ann. Look deeper. Yes, that's it. Ann. You're moving into my eyes. You're losing yourself, Ann. You're falling into me—keep looking right here, Ann. Everything is falling away. You have no more cares, nothing about the world matters to you now. You're already undoing your blouse, Ann. You're already offering yourself up. Undo those buttons, Ann. Yes, that's it—yes, Doctor, your breast is white—so pure. Open your blouse, Ann. Push your hair aside. Ahh, yes. Ann. You're losing yourself, Ann, leaving the world behind, the tired old world. You're leaving it all behind—for something better, Ann. Now—

Shadow Work

"Taking it in its deepest sense, the shadow is the invisible saurian tail that man still drags behind him. Carefully amputated, it becomes the healing serpent of the mysteries. Only monkeys parade with it."

—*Carl Gustave Jung*

Some say it started in Europe, like existentialism and psychotherapy. The truth is, however, that it was probably, initially, an American innovation because its contours were American: its swank exclusivity, its decadent solipsism. In the major metropolitan areas, New York City, Los Angeles, Chicago, Boston, it spread so quickly that it was as if it had always existed. In a matter of months, they were seen everywhere, in bright daylight on urban sidewalks, a vaporous dayglow, or evenings cast against grayish backgrounds by gentle streetlight or moon. Moonshadows were especially pleasing.

For Valerie, the issue was not whether she would have her shadow dyed—that was, as the young say, a no-brainer—it was whether to tell her twin, Vicki, about her plans. She and Vicki were close, don't get that wrong. And, being identical twins, the issue partly became whether their shadows should also be identical. They were not the sort of identical twins who dressed alike. At 20 they had eschewed all such frippery long ago. If Valerie opted for the magenta with iridescent gold highlights, which is what she was leaning toward, should Vicki then do likewise? Or, and here Valerie really balked as if reprimanded, should she consult with her twin before even scheduling the session? What if Vicki wanted the anodized purple? Or, gad, the new tie-dye?

In Memphis, where trends arrived on the last coach, there were already three parlors specializing in dyed shadows, two of which were also tattoo parlors (where the option had become *le dernier cri*, quickly), and one was a freestanding business in what used to be a 7/11: P. Cocky's. The tattoo parlors, Peter Pan's and Midtown Colours (they insisted on the superfluous *u* because it sounded *European*), were having a price war. P. Cocky's was a more elegant establishment and kept mum through the whole Shadow Color Wars. They were the tony top dog. Their reputation, already, was so solid that they did not feel the need to compete.

So, it was to P. Cocky's that Valerie went one day, the money in her purse hard-earned at her job as a mall security officer. She stood uncertainly in the doorway. The walls were papered with bright, blown-up photographs of happy people, trailed by shadows of every imaginable hue. The shadows, in the photos, seemed super-real, magnified and overly bright. The shadows Valerie had seen in real life were slightly plainer, though grand in their way. Some people swore their dyed shadows had changed their lives, made them more confident, in their relationships, in their business dealings. Some said, it was as if they were trailing light itself, instead of its obverse. Shadow envy was, suddenly, a bona fide social phenomenon. Valerie, still fighting inwardly with her devotion to her sister, left the shop, after picking up one of their eye-catching brochures.

The reason Valerie wanted the somewhat expensive procedure was the old story: she wanted to gain a young man's attention. The young man in question was named Tommy "Dago" Swell. He had gone to the same high school as the twins and had been the school's starting point guard on a team that went all the way to State. Coach Handbag said Dago was the best point guard he had coached since "Tiny" Barthelme. Dago was lean and muscular and wore his hair gassed straight back from his forehead. His tattoos were legendary, vistas previously unknown to the eyes of men. And Dago Swell was the first student at Ransom P. Stoddard High School to get his shadow done—it was a small scandal since shadow dyeing was an adults-only procedure at the time. But, because Dago looked 18 when he was 15 and 25 when he was 17 he passed easily. When he first came to school, highlighted, nonchalance belying a secret pride, his shadow was itself shadowed by a gaggle of underclassmen who had already worshiped Dago Swell as an athlete and now could revere him as a god. On the basketball court the varicolored shadow caused other problems. Occasionally flickering into view, a polychrome glint in peripheral vision, it was responsible for the team's increased steals record. But opposing players were afraid to point a finger, such was Dago's spiky reputation.

Valerie thought Dago just about the hottest male she had ever encountered. She thought he was the cats. She had been in love with him since ninth grade and when he got a job as a security guard at the mall alongside her she was fit to be tied. It had been assumed that Dago would attend the University of Memphis on a basketball scholarship but his grades were poor and, when it was suggested he go to junior college first, he gave up basketball, just like that. If his reputation suffered because of his change from baller to rent-a-cop, you couldn't tell it by Valerie. She still thought he was as sexy as a winter pear, one she longed to take a bite out of.

Vicki knew of her sister's moderate betrayal. Her twin ESP was more fully developed than Valerie's, to the point that Vicki occasionally listened in on her sister's private conversations simply by tilting her head toward the North and shutting one eye halfway. She heard Valerie tell her friend, Elspeth, that she had saved enough for a dye and was contemplating not telling Vicki. Elspeth answered with her own terse eloquence: "Whatever." Elspeth put herself above many of the world's more mundane proceedings. She feigned that she had seen it all. Vicki's own secret was that she was in love with Elspeth.

"Oh, you've had your shadow done," Valerie said the first day Dago came to work.

Dago gave her the look he reserved for boiled codfish.

"Years ago," he said, his fingers playing over his nightstick.

Valerie's face burned with shame. What a stupid thing to say! Did he know her? Did he realize that she was at Ransom P. Stoddard with him and hence would know before now about his infamous shadow? She wanted to die.

"I'm Valerie," she said.

Dago Swell looked into the middle distance. There he seemed to find a more interesting tête-à-tête and he slowly moved away, trailing behind him a candent bismuth-yellow and viridian eidolon. Valerie shrank. She became wee. She almost disappeared.

The next day Valerie returned to P. Cocky's with a fresh resolve. She didn't have to go to work until 8 p.m., and she was determined to show up with a brightly-hued shadow, one that would knock Dago Swell out of his hightops.

Her sister Vicki sat in their bedroom, the one they had shared since they were born, and tuned into her sister's erratic aura. It was flickering like a wounded thing and it was all Vicki could do to regulate its message. When she did she realized the degree of Valerie's disloyalty and she felt cheerless. She felt jilted and forsaken. She picked up the phone and dialed Elspeth's number.

"It's Vicki," Vicki said. "Valerie's sister."

"I know."

"What are you doing?" Vicki didn't know how to woo. That was clear.

"Hmph."

"Wanna—" and here Vicki drew a blank. What did she want to ask of Elspeth? To go get coffee? To catch a movie? She was suddenly up against it. Dating—it was a foreign concept.

"Where's Valerie?" Elspeth asked in the lacuna between words.

"She's—" Vicki burst into tears.

Elspeth waited a few moments and then, calmly, hung up.

Vicki dried her eyes. After letting the sobs dissipate she decided that she had done ok for a first foray. She felt—O mooncalf!—that she was on the righteous road to romance.

Meanwhile, Valerie was in the backroom of P. Cocky's, prone in their elegant leather chair, which looked like a cross between a barber's and a masseuse's. The dyer was a middle-aged man with a ponytail and only one tattoo, but that one tattoo was in the middle of his forehead and was an eye. "My pineal," he said. The dyer's name was Rip.

"Relax," Rip said. "It only hurts for a second. You wanna smoke to calm you down?"

"Grass?" Valerie asked, squinching up her face.

"Uh, no, that would be illegal," Rip said, but he didn't offer what the alternative was.

"No thanks," Valerie said. She couldn't stop her feet from dancing.

"Ok," Rip said. "Away we go."

When she got home that afternoon, Valerie felt a little nauseous. She sat in her car, in her parent's driveway, willing her stomach to go easy on her. After a few minutes she felt a little better. When she stepped from the car she saw it for the first time. Rip had said that the process takes anywhere from a half hour to an hour to take effect. So, emerging from her Toyota into the full blast of afternoon daylight, Valerie was able to behold the enormous change in her incorporeal self for the first time. She stepped away from the car. The shadow sprung out in front of her like a red carpet. Except it wasn't red. It was cobalt violet. With gold highlights! She had asked for magenta but Rip had talked her out of it. "Magenta—it's for tourists, tourists and receptionists. Not a serious color for shadows. I recommend the much subtler cobalt violet."

"Ok," Valerie said. "Can I still have gold highlights?"

Now, Valerie looked at her gold highlights. She loved her gold highlights! She twirled in the driveway like a child with a new dress. The air was ripe with Spring and Valerie was a kaleidoscope. Valerie was a dappled fairy castle! She spun until she was dizzy.

Vicki stood in the carport doorway behind the screen door. She watched her sister's self-centered dance. Vicki felt the tears coming again. But, she did not cry. Gradually, like the slow glow of an ember, Vicki began to feel extraordinarily happy. Her sister was beautiful. Valerie was like a glittery butterfly just emerged from her dun cocoon. A smile bloomed on Vicki's face, a smile that made the plain girl quite lovely suddenly.

Valerie stopped her caper and leaned against the Toyota for support. Then she saw Vicki behind the screen door and her heart stopped. Guilt flooded her. And Vicki, behind that metal scrim, looked as if she was installed in a black and white movie. Her silhouette was positively colorless, grey like a shallow sea. Valerie felt heartsick. And she knew she had to face her sister and tell her loving things and cuddle her and convince her that she too needed the dye job. She would tell Vicki that the only reason she did this was to be a guinea pig for the two of them. She wanted to show her sister that this was a selfless act, an act of bravery designed to brighten their lives. That was her tack. That was what she knew she must do.

But when she entered their home Vicki threw her arms around her sister and wept onto her shoulder.

"I'm so sorry," Valerie said.

"No," Vicki said, still snuffling into her neck. "You are the most beautiful thing I've ever seen."

"Oh, Vicki!" Valerie said. "Oh, my sister!"

"And Dago Swell is gonna eat you like cake," Vicki said.

That stopped the lovefest for a moment. How did Vicki know the secret of her twin's heart of hearts, the one secret Valerie held dearest? It was twin ESP, of course, Valerie realized; it was not the first time it had occurred between them. Vicki was fine-tuned. She was powerful.

The rest of the afternoon, the twins stayed in their room, casting Valerie's new shadow against each and every surface with the dazzling light from a gooseneck lamp. When their mother called them to the dinner table the twins emerged from their room, their arms locked, exchanging small kisses, petting each other as if they were new lovers. Their mother paused as she passed around the hamburger hash. Something was new. Something about her beloved daughters was brand new—and, somehow, as exciting as a spiritual awakening!

Valerie insisted Vicki go to the mall with her that evening. She didn't want to part from her twin now, now that their bond was re-established. Really, it was such a slight thing, their rift, so easily repaired.

"You can go to The Gap while we're there. I'll buy you something," Valerie said.

Vicki could only smile at her generous sister. Such love. On the way to the mall Valerie asked Vicki if she had thought about dyeing her shadow.

"It's really a good time to do it," she suggested. "Before, you know, everyone makes it trashy."

"If it's gonna be trashy, why do it?" Vicki countered, but with a smile.

"Well, the way I see it, is that we have the opportunity of being forerunners, and by making it beautiful *now*, we sort of set the ground rules, the groundwork, you know."

"I'll think about it," Vicki said. "Should we match?"

"Yes!" Valerie said. "Let's match!"

The twins entered the mall as if they were royalty come down into their kingdom for a visit, for a tour of all they governed. They shopped. They spent good money on good clothes and gaudy baubles. They were happy.

Vicki followed Valerie to work. There they ran into Dago Swell, who was just coming off duty. His uniform hugged him like a second skin. His nightstick was a dark dream-symbol.

"Hey Dago," Valerie said. She was showing her sister how easygoing it all was, this Dago thing. How blithe it was.

Dago Swell looked at the twins as if they were circus freaks, as if they were two-headed or had snake scales. Had he really never noticed them before, at Ransom P. Stoddard High? Perhaps not. He walked on clouds.

"Twins," he said, as if the word was a naming he could be proud of.

Vicki laughed. Valerie burned red, looked at her sister as if she had just burped in church.

"We're not twins," Vicki said, simpering. "We are the same person but occasionally it is called upon us—me— to travel to two places at once. It's a secret, so don't tell."

Dago Swell looked at this new girl, this mirror image of Valerie, Valerie—whom he had already dismissed in his mind, in his heart. She was an echo of her less interesting sister, a capricious echo.

"You got a mouth on you," Dago Swell said. "You giving me lip?"

Vicki smiled. Flirting with a man was easy because she had no emotional investment in it. It was sport. She looked at Valerie and

Valerie's stricken expression was like a tuning fork in her head. Yet Vicki found that betraying her sister was as uncomplicated a trick as a conjurer swallowing a poker. She uncovered a part of herself previously unidentified.

"You look like you could use some lip," Vicki said.

The air, the sweet mall air, crackled.

"I'm off work now," Dago Swell said. "You come have coffee with me. You want to come have coffee with me?"

Vicki allowed herself one quick glance at Valerie. Then she switched off her ESP and left the mall with Dago Swell.

Valerie burst into tears. And she cried the whole time she walked the mall that night. Before the place closed many salespeople saw the crying cop pass by and they shook their heads at the slight alteration in their otherwise tedious night selling perfume or books or pretzels or sex toys.

"Did you see the cop crying?"

"I did. Female cop, too."

"Yeah."

"Did you notice her shadow?"

"I didn't. She have her shadow done? Maybe that's why she's crying. I'm telling you that's messing with something that shouldn't be messed with, you know? Like DNA or something. That shadow work is tricky stuff. Hell, it made her cry."

And that was what the story became: the fable of a girl whose shadow job messed up her hormonal balance. That particular take on things caught on. It became, gradually, the truth.

All that night, after the mall closed, Valerie walked her rounds, sobbing, trailing her colorful shadow behind her like a spurned bride's train. The colors failed to glow. The shadow was inert, all but useless.

The next morning the breakfast table at Vicki's and Valerie's house was a place of inaudibly festering loneliness. Mother and Father ate alone, neither feeling it incumbent upon them to discuss their absent twins. The truth was that Valerie, alone, was in the bedroom. After coming in at 4:35 a.m., and seeing that Vicki had not come home at all, Valerie renewed her seemingly endless torrent of tears and never did collapse gratefully into the arms of Morpheus. After 8:30 a.m., when she was sure both her parents had departed, she dragged herself to the kitchen, fixed an indifferent cup of coffee, accompanied by a stale sticky bun, and sat with both foods in front of her and ate not and drank not and let the morning sun, coming in the window, smear her face and make tiny rainbows of her tears and she let the warmth enter her like a flu and she cursed her shadow and she cursed Dago Swell and, most of all, she cursed her foul, perfidious sister.

Vicki came home sometime later. She was chipper. She was animated. She was like a fresh apple, juicy and bright and full of sin. Valerie put on a brave face. That's what they call it: a brave face.

"Good morning, Sis," Vicki said, rummaging in the refrigerator. "Whatchoo eating?"

"Bun," Valerie said. She felt perhaps single syllable words would be ok.

"Where the hell is my kefir?" Vicki said.

Valerie concentrated on her coffee. If she took half-sips it would last twice as long.

Vicki sat with a cup of coffee and a box of shortbread cookies. She smiled at Valerie.

"Where?" Valerie said.

"Where was I?" Vicki stalled. "Well…first, no, not first. Here."

Vicki stood and placed herself against the light coming in the window. A versicolored shadow spilled over the breakfast table and onto Valerie's lap. It was shimmering like a trout freshly hooked. It did not match Valerie's at all. Worse, it outshone it. It was a deluxe job, with anodized mauve streaks. Valerie thought she was going to be sick. The shadow on her lap felt like glistening poison, as if it were leaking into her.

"Do you like it?' Vicki asked.

"How," Valerie tried. A beat or two of attenuated time stretched between the twins.

"How could you?" Valerie finished and then leapt from her seat and disappeared.

Vicki stood in the kitchen sunlight for a while, sipping her coffee and admiring her own dodgy shadow. It was a threshold day, a day when things formerly one way became forever another. Vicki decided that she was pleased that it was so.

Meanwhile, all over the planet Shadow Work became a hotly debated craze. Newer and more complex ways to dye shadows were invented practically daily. Some people, dragging around old uni-hued shadows, were suddenly cast as out-of-step, as if they were still watching Beta VCRs, or wearing the fashions of the year before. And, naturally, there sprang up movements which depicted Colored Shadows as dangerous, as Corrupt. One such movement was called Daltonism and its followers were as fanatical as Greenpeace zealots, though, honestly, they did not have that kind of moral weight behind them. Daltonists sprang up in every city, their meetings marked by a lot of bloviating and speechifying and much fun was poked at the Vainglorious Colored Shadow People. In Memphis a small chapter sprang up, meeting in the basement of First Congo Church. Enthusiasm didn't run very deep, however, and, after a few half-hearted gatherings, the group dissolved.

And so the twins grew apart. Where did the love go? The continental drift between them became cold and hard. They each thought the other a quisling.

"I don't know," Valerie lamented to Elspeth. "I think he's bad for her."

"Yah," Elspeth yawned. "But he'd a been good for you."

"No, I see that now," Valerie said. "I see how treacherous and shallow he is."

"Dago Swell is a piece of work," Elspeth said. Valerie didn't know if he was being praised or damned.

"Besides," Elspeth said. "I figured your sister for gay."

This gave Valerie pause.

"Why would you think that?" she asked.

"I thought she had the, you know, hots for me."

"You think everyone has the hots for you."

In a more conventional friendship this may have caused a serious breach.

"Yeah," Elspeth answered.

Time passed. Shadow Work became a part of the everyday. That is to say that it was amalgamated into the warp and woof of dailiness and, if thought about at all, it was with the attention afforded haircuts or spring wardrobes. Some people had shadows that were prettier than other people's shadows. Some people still had charcoal grey shadows, things which sometimes seemed quaint and sometimes seemed as beautiful as one of Dürer's engravings. A new appreciation was born for some of the old ways and many saw this as a good thing.

Meanwhile, the twins were so estranged that they rarely spoke. Vicki and Dago Swell got a place of their own and Valerie quit her job at the mall—how could she do otherwise? she couldn't abide seeing Dago every day—and began working for a small private detective agency. Alec "Fast" Lemon's Shadow Bureau. It was mostly repo work, or adultery cases. Valerie hated it. She grew morose and waspish. Her shadow, once a glorious appendage, seemed to fade and achromatize. She dragged it behind her like a tattered bathrobe. She probably shouldn't have been issued a gun but she was.

Vicki saw it coming. She was watching TV, eating Cheetos. Dago was asleep in the back room because lately he had been working the night shift. There was a tempering of the light, something at the edge of vision. At first Vicki thought it was just an anomaly of the TV reception. A sputter in her tangential vision. Then she realized that her shadow was bending unnaturally. It was moving, ever so slightly, *toward* the light. Her ears prickled, or perhaps her thumbs. She stood up just before she heard the shot.

In the backroom Dago Swell lay face down on the bed, a small, black puncture, deep as night, right in the center of his finespun foulard pajama top. Valerie stood at the foot of the bed, her face blank, her shadow a snapping shower of sparks. The room was unnaturally still as if the report of the gun had created a vacuum of silence and immobility. Very slowly, a shy creature emerging from its hole in the ground, a thick cord of bright red blood surfaced from Dago's new opening.

Vicki quietly moved near her sister. She took her hand. The twins stood there over the murdered body of Dago Swell and they held hands as if, against the indifference and gravity and approbation of the world, their united love was a safeguard, was ballast. And their shadows, their troublesome shadows, merged into one, pooling behind them on the hardwood floor, a colorful figuration, in fathomless hues like the wake of the helmsman's bark of yore, a final, vivid umbra.

From the Desk of Jojo Self

Resistentialism (ri-zis-TEN-shul-iz-um) noun
The theory that inanimate objects demonstrate hostile
behavior against us.

1.

Jojo Self's desk was piled with manuscripts, the weight of his collective literary world. He had written, as of today, 162 novels, all unpublished, most unsubmitted. The piles tottered over him like some paper Babel, or, sadly, like some paper twin towers, soon to fall. Still, he found a little cavern of space between them to write, to situate his computer. It was dark in this tunnel. It was dark and that's how Jojo Self liked it.

Jojo wrote long into the night most nights. He did this because he had no other life. He did this because writing about life was easier for him than living it. He was agoraphobic, if agoraphobic means he was too timid to mix it up with the rest of the population on Planet Earth, which as of this writing stood at 6,624,358,566 wandering souls.

Now, to say Jojo was writing about life is perhaps misleading. His stories mostly took place on invented planets with invented creatures that fought invented clashes mostly among themselves. Jojo wrote battle scenes because he loved action; he loved violence. He knew 15 synonyms for hit or strike. He knew 12 synonyms for wound. Jojo wrote violent scene after violent scene. It was better than sleeping because Jojo's dreams were full of concupiscence and he awoke from every troubled sleep lonelier than a dragon in a cave.

Jojo Self, partly because of these dreams, or in response to their ability to upset him, never wrote about sex. Oh, once, Princess Mandalooie, of the Planet Nfs-X, approached one of the Battle Ogres and dropped her top to bamboozle him, but Jojo covered her again quickly, and just as quickly moved back onto the battlefield.

So, Jojo Self wrote. He wrote and that was his life. Better than some, not quite up to snuff compared to others.

Then Jojo's manuscripts began to disappear.

He knew this because his cavern walls were not as precise. They were suddenly a little more loosely stacked, a little more haphazard. He felt their papery length and breadth and wondered what was missing. He began to grieve for his lost words before he even reconciled what exactly was missing. He checked his log, his list of works finished, and discovered there were 11 fewer manuscripts. How did this happen? No one ever entered his study save Jojo Self himself.

In anguish he began to search the drawers of his colossal desk and found that one was unaccountably stuck. It was the drawer that held work in progress. In addition to Jojo's 162 finished novels he normally had anywhere between 20 and 30 books that were fragmentary, unfinished, or ongoing. Some were no more than sketched ideas, stories about as long as the life of a wave.

As he pulled and pulled on the recalcitrant desk drawer a creepy feeling came over Jojo. It seemed to him that the desk, his antique gargantua of a desk, was *fighting back*. An absurd thought! But, there it was, suddenly in Jojo's heart, a new fear, a dread of confrontation with the physical universe. Jojo, who sought escape from the workaday world, was up against it. What could he do?

He stepped back into the room, ten paces backwards from the desk. The piled manuscripts looked like some modern art sculpture. The pages of the top manuscripts wafted slightly like tiny wings with the flux of a draught from the air conditioning vents.

Get a grip on yourself, Jojo told himself. Jesus God, a desk doesn't have consciousness. It was something out of one of his own stories. A leviathan desk, a freak, brutish desk!

Then, like something only seen out of the corner of his eye, Jojo could have sworn he saw one more manuscript disappear into the wood of the desktop. *Absorbed* into the wood of the desktop. He rubbed his inflamed eyes. Been working too hard, he thought. A desk doesn't swallow manuscripts, even if it does fight back.

He recounted. He counted an even 150 manuscripts. He was indeed down one more book.

Now, a real terror gripped him. He had to get a handle on this desk. He had to show it who was boss. First, he must clear its now treacherous plane. Take very damn novel off its surface and then he could possibly see what's what. That was his stratagem, his only stratagem.

He stood long in reflection. The day ticked by as he reflected.

One, two, three more manuscripts vanished.

"Oh, jeepers," Jojo said. "Oh, Jupiter's jockstrap!"

He practically sprang at the desk. He pulled manuscript after manuscript off and tossed them gently aside. They made a small slapdash snow fort next to the wall. Finally, he had the desk clear and he could scrutinize the surface circumspectly. It was wood, some kind of wood. It was an unbroken surface, as smooth as ice, dark ice. Jojo put a pensive hand to his chin and nearly chuckled at this unexpected turn of events. Was it some kind of benison? he wondered, the challenge of Calliope, or perhaps Melpomene? Was Jojo suddenly the center of his own tragedy? It was a writer's poser and hence he was proud of it. Though Jojo Self often felt like a writer—a lama in the lamasery of his own head—it never hurt to be reminded of his higher calling.

Since it was late in the day and Jojo was tired he decided to test the desk while he slept. He took a magazine, one about as thick as a sheaf of manuscript pages, and laid it on the desk's surface just to the right of his word processor. He patted it as if to say goodbye and went to bed where he dreamt furious aphrodisia dreams about women from high school, the ones mostly who had tormented him with derision and imagined putdowns. This was just the sort of night to tie Jojo up in knots and, sure enough, he woke the next morning feeling eviscerated, as out of place in the world as one of his aliens.

Having fixed himself coffee he approached his study with some trepidation, yet the trepidation was wedded to a new jangle of excitement, as if he were embarking on some exotic emprise. His eye went to the desk and he was almost pleased to see that the magazine was gone. The desktop was clear again.

Then he saw the magazine on the floor. It was some women's fashion thing called *Lucky*, delivered to his house by mistake, apparently meant for the long-legged blonde who rented half the duplex next door. Now, her copy of *Lucky* lay on Jojo's floor, a spurned offering. Jojo, coffee in one hand, bent to the magazine and picked it up. He held it in his hand, weighing it, looking for clues. Then he noticed the name of his neighbor. Had he really never noticed it before? It read Candy Marcrum. Jojo thought long and hard as to why that name set a small silvery bell tinkling in his head. Candy Marcrum, he said over and over. Of course, he finally glommed on to the truth, it was the name of a character in one of his early novels, *The Saturnian Age*.

Well, that's interesting, Jojo thought. He must have subconsciously seen her name once upon a time and threaded it into his story. Near as he could remember Candy Marcrum—the one in his novel—was a princess (women in Jojo's novels were princesses or queens or damsels in distress) on a moon of Saturn. On this moon women loved men unequivocally, just for being men, honoring them in their difficult lives. That's as much as Jojo could remember.

He shook off his reverie and returned to examine the desk. So, you only eat manuscripts. You're not only a papyrvore but a picky eater, Jojo said. There was only one thing to do. Jojo searched through his piles until he found one novel, *Ethel Paraben's Jaunt to Venus*, he thought dispensable, or as dispensable as any of them, and he ceremoniously placed it on the desktop. He stood back to watch vigilantly.

An anxious minute or two passed. Then, like a Hollywood special effect, the pile of paper seemed to sink straight into the solid surface of the desk. Spliff! it was gone! Now, nonplussed, Jojo sat down on the couch opposite his desk. He had to think this through. Nothing was coming to him. He looked at his lap. He was still holding the copy of *Lucky*. Almost as if controlled by unseen forces Jojo rose and decided to return the magazine to his leggy neighbor. It was an effort to effect change, *any change*, though not the change needed certainly in his study. But, reasoning that he could not return to writing, not today, he thought he could, perhaps, exit his house, walk the 136 steps to his neighbor's door and knock. It was quite a determination.

Jojo shuffled from his front door, across the grass, still damp with dew. He shuffled partly because he had little control over his motor skills and partly because he was wearing bedroom slippers. It never occurred to him that he hadn't dressed to go out. His head was full of midges. He wore a robe over his Star Wars pajamas. He made it all the way to Candy Marcrum's door, his heart pounding. The fear—the outside world terror—was close beside him. Stay behind me, Jojo prayed. He knocked.

After a moment Candy opened the door. Her lovely blond face squinched into a questioning grimace. She didn't offer a hello. Jojo almost ran for it.

"I got this mistake, by mistake," he said. His voice was dry as tinder, a wee spasm. He held the magazine out in front of him.

Candy took it warily from him. She looked it over. Finally she said, "This is 6 months old." She looked at the strange man in front of her. Her face offered no comfort, no way-in.

"Ok," Jojo said. He began to shuffle back home.

Candy Marcrum watched him for a second and then said, "Oh, you live next door. You're the writer!"

Jojo Self's heart turned over in its sleep. It punched the pillow a few times and resettled itself. Jojo Self's heart opened like an awakened flower.

"Yes," he said, without turning around.

"I'm Candy," she said.

Jojo Self turned slowly.

"I forgot to get dressed," he said.

"Yes," Candy Marcrum said back.

"I should go home now." But he didn't move. He wanted to look at Candy Marcrum as much as he wanted to fathom the mystery of the desk. She was a long cool drink of vitelline. Her legs—she was wearing buttercup yellow shorts—were tanned and as shapely as javelins.

"Ok," Jojo Self said, and he returned to his home. Once inside he willed his heart to act normally. He needed peace to work out his dilemma. He needed a cloudless coconut.

Countless times in Jojo Self's life he had turned to writing to stave off life-fear, to re-center himself. When the agoraphobic demon raised its ugly tentacled head Jojo often found solace in sentences. This is not uncommon among the writerly. So, now, with his manuscripts piled safely on the floor of his study, he decided to *not* solve the riddle of the hungry desktop. Instead, he fired up his Hewlett Packard and dove back into *Captain Wally Schmendrik's Voyage to Ataraxia*. He had reached the part where Captain Wally's storm troopers had penetrated the outer boundaries of the evil Dr. Diktat's ice-bound fortress. The action was running smoothly. Jojo's brain cells were firing smoothly and the problem of his disappearing manuscripts was forcefully exiled to the back burners.

Captain Wally entered the chamber where Dr. Diktat was known to hatch his evil schemes. He held his weapon at ready. His men had neutralized the Diktat guards. Suddenly, instead of the vile visage of the hunchbacked doctor, Captain Wally was confronted with the shapely form of a maiden barely old enough to vote back in Captain Wally's America. She wore only a see-through shift and her body moved like the celestial spheres. It was Diktat's niece, Cancrine, home from college, where she had a reputation as a bit of a runabout. Right now she looked at Captain Wally with lascivious hunger. Her eyes glistened with lust. She parted the simple folds of her shift. Her body shown like ambergris. Her pubic patch was a tangle of honey and soft coils. Her legs were as shapely as javelins.

Jojo Self pushed back from the desk. No, no, no, he said to himself. Is this my story? I don't write this way, Jojo Self said to himself. He moved cautiously back toward the screen and read what he had written. He stiffened in his pajamas and he was horrified. He got up from the desk and paced the room. Then he left, shutting the door. He sat in his living room and turned on the TV. He had not watched TV in years. There were people on the screen vying for some prize which eluded them and the sense of the show eluded Jojo. His mind was miles away. Not on a planet in a galaxy yet undiscovered, but here on Earth, stuck with Earth problems, Earth mysteries, Earth disorder, Earth discontent.

Some difficult days passed for Jojo Self. He did not enter his study. He watched TV shows which did not entertain him but only held his place like ludicrous, cosmic bookmarks. Jojo Self was spinning his wheels. He didn't know what to do next. Were it not for the inheritance checks he lived off and his grocery deliveries Jojo Self would have slid unceremoniously into destitution.

Then, about a fortnight later, there was a knock on Jojo Self's door. He answered it, assuming it was the grocery boy or another manuscript returned. Instead, standing there in a short skirt, surrounded by a surfeit of sunshine, was his neighbor Candy Marcrum.

"Hiya," she said.

"Hi," Jojo said, cinching the belt of his bathrobe.

"Not dressed again," Candy tried, with a quick laugh.

"Oh," Jojo said.

"Look, I brought you something. I felt bad about that day I didn't know who you were. One of the other neighbors, maybe you know Mrs. Glockomorra, down in 1954. Anyway, she told me you were a shut-in and I learned in this training seminar I took at the junior college that most shut ins crave books and, well, that's what I brought you, a book. I got it down at the bookstore." Candy smiled after this speech. And she proffered her gift, a new science fiction novel, its garish cover art just this side of amateurish.

Jojo Self looked at the book and his head swam. Suddenly he saw waves of psychedelic color, swirls of outer space debris and stardust. Pain punched behind his peepers. He had to steady himself on the door jamb. It was not the sight of the comely Ms. Marcrum which so flummoxed Jojo. It was not his proximity to those legs. It was not even the embarrassment of being seen once again in his pajamas at mid-day. No, what caused Jojo Self to temporarily lose his grip on Planet Earth was the book's title. It was *Princess Mandalooie of the Planet Nfs-X*. It was his title but it was not his name in the author's place on the garish dust jacket. No, the author's name, which was unfamiliar to Jojo, was Celery Moser.

Celery Moser.

"Are you ok, Mr. Self?" Candy Marcrum squeaked.

"Come in, come in," Jojo fairly shouted as he himself stumbled into a wingback chair. Candy Marcrum, sheepishly entered, closing the front door and taking her place opposite Jojo on the sprung couch. She sat primly, her perhaps inappropriate gift resting on her beautiful knees. She wished now that she could make it disappear. She had, inadvertently, upset her neighbor, the reclusive author, and she didn't know what to do to make it up, to make things right.

Jojo Self put his head in his hands. Then he raised his face to Candy's.

"May I see that?" he said, holding out his hand. Candy slipped the book into his hands.

Jojo stared at the cover. The artist's conception of Princess Mandalooie was spot-on. Jojo looked at the spine of the book. Doubledog. With its distinctive twin Border Collie logo. Whoever had perpetrated this theft had found a home at one of the largest publishers in America. He or she had had better luck than Jojo at placing his manuscript. Jojo could only imagine the 5 figure contract the picklock had garnered for work he (or she) had not done. A sourness bloomed in Jojo's gut. It didn't take too much cerebration to reckon how he had gotten the book. Jojo was sure it would turn out to be one of the missing manuscripts, one his desk had digested.

An awkward few minutes passed. Candy crossed and re-crossed her legs and each time Jojo's libido gained weight. But the book—*the damn book*—held most of his attention. He read it in various places. It was his story alright, right down to some grammatical errors and some jiggered plot elements. In all its artless glory it was Jojo's novel, now successfully published, but not under his name.

The face that he presented to Candy Marcrum held years of distress. It was a face going down a dark road. It was a face upon which was written the failure of Man, who once in The Garden reigned. It scared the bejesus out of Candy Marcrum. She felt responsible but she didn't know what for. How had she crushed her ascetic neighbor?

Cautiously, Candy moved toward Jojo Self and knelt next to his chair. She placed her hand on his knee. Jojo Self smelled like old tallow. He looked down into the comely face of Candy Marcrum and saw only his own failure, his own mistreatment, his own despair. Even her diamond-cut dimples seemed to him marks of the devil.

"Mr. Self," Candy said. "What did I do?"

"Jojo," Jojo said.

"Yes," Candy Marcrum said.

"Call me Jojo," Jojo said as if in a stupor.

"What happened? How can I help you?"

Had Jojo not relinquished his human credentials moments before this question would have raised many interested possibilities. Now, he could only shake his head.

"My desk," he said.

Candy Marcrum looked at him as if he had said, "My death." Or "My off ox." It made no sense to her.

"My desk ate this book," Jojo said, holding up Celery Moser's novel.

It was only getting worse for Candy Marcrum. She thought perhaps she had fallen down the rabbit hole.

"Your desk," she said.

"I know," Jojo answered.

"It eats—things?"

"Yes. Well, not just things. Books. Manuscripts."

"Uh huh."

"It eats them and then, apparently, gives them to other writers to publish."

"I see," Candy said, rising. Jojo assumed she was leaving now. He assumed that he had driven her away. Instead she rested her lovely haunch on the chair's arm and put a hand in Jojo's hair.

Jojo Self looked up into her face.

Candy was torn. She was nearly repelled by the unkempt writer, yet, something was happening to her, something mysterious. That was it. She thought she was face to face with the mysterious. This man, this *writer*, was tapped into something that was drawing Candy the way a flame draws air. She didn't meet many creative types, not in her line of work. Candy was a real estate agent. Her face could be seen on signs around their neighborhood and more than one young vandal had written obscene thought balloons coming out of her lovely blond head. Jojo could not know this since he did not leave his house. Candy was as much mystery to him as he was to her. All the humans out walking around, all 6,624,358,566 of them, were a mystery to Jojo.

"You need a shower," was all she could think of to say.

"I don't have a shower," Jojo Self said. He said it as if it were his worst failing.

Candy thought it was more nonsense-speak.

"Of course you have a shower," she said.

"Clawfoot tub," Jojo answered.

"Oh. Well, a warm bath. That would be good, wouldn't it? Make you feel all human again."

"Don't be nice to me," Jojo said. He didn't know where that came from. He wanted badly for her to be nice to him.

"Oh," Candy said, stung. She stood up.

Then the look on his face opened her heart one more time.

"I'm going to run you a hot bath and then I am going to leave and come back later. How's that?"

She didn't wait for an answer. She hustled upstairs, found the unclean bathroom, turned the taps to create a steaming hot soak, and hustled back downstairs. She resisted the urge to clean the bathroom.

"Ok," she said. "I'll be back."

As soon as the door was closed Jojo Self burst into tears.

Later, after a soak in a tub that was a little hotter than Jojo would have liked, he returned to his study. He stood and looked at that diabolical desk for a few minutes. He could think of nothing that he could do to work out the chthonic powers of the thing, to twig to its abracadabra. He was about to turn back to his TV when there came a timorous knock on the door.

Candy Marcrum re-entered Jojo Self's home with a renewed sense of purpose.

"Was your bath nice?" she asked, her voice light off a lake.

"Yes," Jojo said. "Listen," he continued. "I'm sorry. You're being awfully nice to me but you find me at a terrible time. I have been bewitched or something. I am not myself."

Of course Jojo thought, *myself* is not that great at the best of times. Myself is not a person in whom someone like Candy Marcrum would show much interest.

"Tell me what's going on," Candy Marcrum said.

Now, returned somewhat to human form, Jojo Self found himself unable to raise his eyes from Candy's remarkable legs. He sat there pretending to woolgather but really lusting after her in a profound way.

"Your legs," he said, almost involuntarily.

"Um," Candy said.

"They are perfect," Jojo said, slowly raising his gaze.

Candy Marcrum thought, oh no, here we go again. Men. Then Jojo Self added a line she had not heard before.

"They showed up in my new novel unbidden."

This was more nonsense, Candy thought.

"Mr. Self. Jojo. I want to help you through whatever this is. I claim no special ability but I cannot stand by and let a neighbor suffer, especially someone who cannot go out for himself. My mother suffered from agoraphobia. I know its ugly contours. I can help you. I can go out in the world for you. I can be your legs."

The mention of the word legs again brought a smile to Jojo Self's face. The smile made him almost attractive.

"Ok," Candy said. And she laughed.

After a minute Jojo said, "I fear there is no Earthly help for me, Candy." Saying her name gave Jojo a warm thrum under his breastbone. "This is beyond—well beyond human understanding. Let me run down for you what is happening."

And he told her the story of the disappearing manuscripts right up to the point where she brought him the book that was his and not his.

Candy sat stock still for a minute. She was digesting this implausible tale.

"Well," she said, slowly. "Then we must find this Celery Moser. We must go to Doubledog and demand they produce this charlatan."

Jojo looked like he was abruptly queasy.

"I mean, of course," she continued. "That I will go."

"Doubledog is in New York," Jojo said.

"Yes," Candy said. "I better get some time off."

Jojo Self smiled.

"Why are you being so kind to me?" he asked.

"Because you are stuck here. Because you are my neighbor. And because writers are important. They must be aided, supported. How we help the least of us, isn't that what any religion teaches us?"

These were solid good reasons. Jojo Self was, naturally, madly in love.

After Candy left Jojo approached his office with new self-assurance, almost a swagger to his step. He stood in front of his desk and appraised it as if it were a behemoth, or The Sphinx. I am not afraid of you, Jojo thought. I am not afraid.

The desk said nothing. It returned Jojo's gaze without flinching, without quailing.

Jojo flipped through his manuscripts. He found one that he was not particularly proud of, one called *Trouble with the Tottenhots*. He walked over to the desk, ran a hand over the smooth wood. Then he placed the manuscript there, a sacrifice. Take it, he thought.

A few minutes passed and nothing happened. Jojo scratched his whiskers. He placed his palm on top of the manuscript. Did it feel warm? A few more minutes passed.

Finally, Jojo took the manuscript off the desk. It felt queer somehow. He turned it over and the back couple of pages were dog-eared, as if they had been creased by an unseen hand. The desk actually rejected the book, Jojo thought. The desk was one tough-ass editor.

2.

Driving to New York City, Candy Marcrum had time to wonder at the turn of events which resulted in this mission. And she wondered why. Over and over she wondered why. It certainly wasn't an attraction, was it? Jojo Self was, well, too odd a bird for *that*. But, there was something going on…a *frisson* of positive energy which led to her involvement.

Traveling alone Candy kept a thermos of coffee on the seat next to her. Also a copy of one of Jojo Self's manuscripts, one that had not been eaten by the desk, of course.

The city was a super-scale board game, a crazy-quilt stratum with game pieces crowding for sky-space. Candy felt as if she were maneuvering her small car through a maze made up of plastic, and provisional, constructions. She knew something about how the grid was laid out but it didn't avert her from becoming lost. When she finally arrived at the address of the publisher she was sweaty and irritable. She stepped from her car into the redolent air and shook like a dog after a bath. The clarion taxi horns drove her indoors.

The revolving door admitted Candy to the lobby. The lobby was intimidating enough, stark yet bustling, full of recycled air and concatenation. Everyone knew what they were doing and where they were going except Candy. She took a deep breath, coughed, and strode to the guard dog at the receptionist's stall.

"Doubledog," Candy Marcrum said to the gnomic man behind the desk.

"Mm hmm," he said, glancing at Candy and returning to his newspaper.

"I want to see them," she said.

The little man looked up. He looked her over, not without a hint of ogle, and replied, "I don't care. Go ahead."

"Oh," Candy said. "Oh," she said, moving away.

There were many elevator doors. No waiting. She boarded one elevator, panicked momentarily, and deboarded. She checked the legend on the wall. Doubledog was on the 13th floor.

She reboarded and pushed 13.

The offices of Doubledog Publishing were lousy with dark wood. Everything seemed to be made of dark wood, including the little woman behind the desk who greeted Candy and whose ethnicity was cause for speculation. Her skin said one of the dark races. Her voice said Upper Crust Boston.

She also guarded the offices like Cerberus. Candy realized too late that she should have called for an appointment. She thought of it in the car on the drive North. By that time she had decided that an explanation by phone would be spurious and that, face to face, she could make her case better.

"Ms., um, Pettigoat," Candy said, eying the name on the desk-plate, after getting the must-have-an-appointment speech, "I have driven far to come here and present you with an ultimatum. If you would like that ultimatum to die here on your desk, if you want that responsibility, then just say so and I will open up like the gates of a dam."

It was a partially prepared speech.

Isabel Pettigoat looked Candy up and down.

"Sorry," she said, dismissively. She turned her attention back to her computer screen.

Candy stood there for a moment. She was stunned. She was stumped, but only temporarily. She never thought that this would be easy.

"Would you, could you, please give me the name of the man or woman in charge here?" Candy said. "Just give me his or her name and I will be on my way. The name of the person responsible for the theft of the manuscripts of Jojo Self."

She saw the swallow.

There could be no doubt about it. Isabel Pettigoat betrayed her knowledge of the subterfuge by a pause in her keystrokes, by a swallow, a single, dry, difficult swallow.

"I'm not sure I know what you mean," Ms. Pettigoat said, making a one quarter turn toward Candy. "Jojo Self?"

Candy now held the winning hand. She felt it.

"Uh huh," she said, slowly. She studied the receptionist's face. A drop of sweat the size of a pinhead appeared on one temple.

"You probably mean, heh, Mr. Newtix. Herman Newtix.

He, um, he is the chief editor here. I am sure, if Mr. Self submitted something, it went through proper channels, probably one of our junior editors, who, only if it merited especial attention, would pass it up to Mr. Newtix, or, well, to his office. Then—well, let's not discuss the whole process." Here a tight smile, a small attempt to win back the advantage. "Now, if you'll just give me Mr. Self's agent's name."

Candy studied her adversary.

"You are sure Jojo Self is a man?"

"Ach," Isabel Pettigoat said.

"I'll wait until Mr. Newtix can see me," Candy said. "Tell him it's about Mr. Self's *Princess Mandalooie of the Planet Nfs-X.*"

Isabel Pettigoat opened her mouth once. No words emerged. She shut it.

Candy took a seat in one of the plush chairs in the outer office. She picked up a copy of *Marie Claire*. She smiled her coolness toward Ms. Pettigoat, who was suddenly on the phone.

The waiting area felt like a medical waiting room and hence Candy thought briefly that she was going to see the doctor. A new doctor. Something was wrong with her. Was it going to be fatal? A book doctor. Would he prescribe more Russians, a little less chick lit?

As her mind played these games and bright, glossy ads sped by her thumbing fingers, time passed, glutinously. Then the ebon receptionist spoke as if from the grave.

"Mr. Newtix will see you now." She didn't look up.

"Thank you," Candy said.

The inner office she crossed into, if possible, exhibited even more dark wood than the outer offices. It was like entering a tree. And the gnome behind the large, dark desk was extending a chubby little hand, while smiling the smile of the troll under the bridge.

"Ms. Mackeral," the round, little man said. He was standing,

Candy determined. His body was round like a snowman's. His cheeks and neck were one continuous web of flesh. His color was rubicund as if all the blood was about to burst from the pores of his face.

"Marcrum," Candy said, taking the hand. It felt like a plush doll's hand.

"Sit, sit," Herman Newtix said.

Candy sat in front of the desk. It was an old desk, and the dark brown wood was polished to a vivid patina. Herman Newtix didn't so much commandeer the desk. It was more as if he was clinging to it to stay afloat. The desk was a good eleven times the size of the squatty, spherical publisher.

"Now, what's this all about?" Herman Newtix said. His smile seemed drawn on.

"*Princess Mandalooie of the Planet Nfs-X,*" Candy said, smoothly.

"Ah, one of our newest titles. We're very proud of it."

"That's fine, Mr. Newtix. That's very fine. Now, who wrote it?"

Herman Newtix hesitated and in his hesitation Candy saw a glimmer of hope. In his hesitation she saw the possibility of justice.

"I believe, let's see," he fumbled, dramatically, with some papers on his desk.

"Celery Moser?" Candy Marcrum asked.

Herman Newtix looked up brightly, as if this little problem had just resolved itself.

"Yes, yes that's the author's name. A bright, young talent. I predict good things for him. Great things!"

"Uh huh," Candy said. She let some tense moments tick by.

"Do you have a picture of, and an address for, Mr. Moser?" she asked.

"I think so," Herman Newtix said. Again, he went through the motions of moving papers around on his desk. He shuffled a stack. He put one stack on top of another stack. It was as if he were doing some light housecleaning while Candy waited.

"Mr. Newtix, enough pretense. The author of *Princess Mandalooie of the Planet Nfs-X* is Jojo Self. I believe you know this. I believe you are deliberately deceiving the public and me and, in the process, defrauding Mr. Self. Is there a Celery Moser?"

"Ms. Marcrum." Herman Newtix said. He cleared his throat. "I think perhaps I should get someone up here from legal. I believe you are accusing me of fraud, or plagiarism, or worse."

"Fine, Mr. Newtix. Get your lawyer. I know and you know that the novel was written by Jojo Self and stolen from him in a manner that is unclear. I further believe that you intend on stealing more of Mr. Self's stories, as more are missing."

"Folderol," Mr. Newtix said. "Poppycock. That is not the way Doubledog does business. We are an old and reputable firm." He turned to his computer screen and began to punch some keys.

And then it happened.

In the space that Herman Newtix had cleared a white blur appeared. Mr. Newtix did not see it before Candy did. The blur began to crystallize. Suddenly it was one sheet of typewritten paper. Then two, then dozens. A manuscript was forming there as speedily as a cloud streams rain. Herman Newtix turned quickly and slapped his hand down on top of the pages.

"Egad!" he said.

"Aha!" Candy said.

Herman Newtix seemed to want to crawl on top of the manuscript which had just materialized on his desk. If he could have he would have spread eagle on it and covered it with his butterball body. He looked up and his eyes were moist.

"Honest to God," Herman Newtix fairly exploded, "I didn't

want this to happen. I didn't understand it at first. It's the damn desk! It's some kind of black magic! It's some kind of devilry!"

Candy Marcrum knew she had the plump publisher over a barrel. She also knew that to press her advantage would not reflect well on her or on the man whom she was representing, Jojo Self. Candy smiled an indulgent smile.

"You must have known the books were not just yours to take," she said, softly.

"I didn't—I mean, at first, I didn't know what to think—I mean, it's not like someone was sending me the next John Grisham or the next Stephen King. These were genre books destined to be genre books. If you understand me."

Candy's perplexed face was his answer.

"Ok, look, I'm sorry, I'm not being clear. I bought this desk, see. I bought it at an antique's store on 6th Avenue. The owner said there were only two desks like it. I didn't understand but it was so big, so beautiful, and so cheap. The owner seemed happy to get rid of it and I was happy with the price I paid. Anyway, no sooner did I install the desk in my office than these manuscripts began to appear. All fairly crazy science fiction novels of questionable pedigree."

Candy made a moue.

"Now, now, no reflection on the author. But, I took it, I took the appearances as a sign. See, science fiction has not been what we're about here at Doubledog. We tend more toward the highbrow, the experimental, the oblique, the, well, difficult. Small sales, big reputation. I took these manuscripts as a sign that we would find some financial gold if we bent our usual policy and published these strange yarns."

"But surely," Candy said, heating up a bit, "You could see that they were someone else's books. Why invent an author for them when they already had an author?"

It was a good question, a poser really, and Herman Newtix was thoughtful for a moment.

"Celery Moser is not invented," he said, finally.

"Oh," Candy said.

"Celery Moser exists as surely as you and I," he said.

"Oh."

"I—I am Celery Moser," Herman Newtix said. "And I've always wanted to be a writer instead of a publisher."

Sandy was warming to the roly-poly publisher. She began to feel kindly toward him and she temporarily forgot that she was here to see fair dealing done, fair dealing for her new friend, Jojo Self. She approached Herman Newtix's side of the desk and put a consoling hand on his shoulder.

"You know you must do the right thing," she said. "No one is to blame here. No one is a bad guy."

"Yes. Yes, you're right," Herman Newtix/Celery Moser said. "You're right."

"So, what now?" Candy Marcrum said.

"Will you read my novel?" Celery/Herman asked.

3.

"So, then I said, 'Will your firm publish these science fiction novels under their proper author's name?'"

"Wow," Jojo Self said. He was resting a cup of coffee on his knee, staring into the pellucid eyes of Candy Marcrum. "You're my new hero."

"And, of course, he said, yes," Candy said. She scooted closer to Jojo. "Of course he said yes." She paused.

"I don't know how to repay you," Jojo said. But he did know.

Or at least he knew what was happening. He was not so far outside of human interaction that he didn't know what was happening.

And when Candy placed her mouth, soft as fire in dew, against his mouth, Jojo was taught how to love. He was a late bloomer but a fast learner.

It was only a month later that *Princess Mandalooie of the Planet Nfs-X* was re-released with the same striking cover art but with a different author's name, one the world had not seen before: Joe Self. And what followed, about once every six months, were more books in the series, later to be called *Joe Self's Planetary Adventure Series*. And his publisher, under the name Celery Moser, began his own series of adventures for young adults, the very profitable *The Bodgie Boys Adventures*.

United Artists released the first movie version of a Self adventure, *Commander Pomacious and the Metagalactic Ballroom*, starring Brad Pitt and Angelina Jolie. It was an international smash and it made its author a millionaire. More movies followed, soon as reliable a cash cow as the Bond films, or the Harry Potters.

Also, it should be noted, Jojo's books became less violent, such was Candy's gentle suasion. And his stuck drawer became unstuck. Inside he found the manuscripts that he couldn't finish or hadn't finished, for one reason or another, finished.

But, before all this success, Candy and Jojo lay in each other's arms after the first time they made love and they saw a future, not abounding with achievement and monetary comforts, but one of nurturing love and mutual support and erotic enthusiasm and the kind of companionship vouchsafed few humans, writers or not. And they saw little Selfs, too, two or three little Selfs, who carried Candy's lovely looks as lightly as a child carries a sack of Halloween treats. It was quite a vision.

"Oh, Jojo," Candy said. "What you were hiding. What was

under that bushel basket of yours."

"Candy, I had nothing before you," Jojo said.

"Sweet man. Sweet man to say that. It's not true but I love you for saying it."

"And I love you," Jojo said. "From a character in one of my novels to my bed, it's a very satisfying bit of legerdemain."

(When they made the movie of *The Saturnian Age* and cast Scarlett Johansson as Candy Marcrum, Candy was embarrassed. "Joe," she said, "Scarlett Johansson?" To which her husband replied, "Candy, come here and give me your body made of sugary cake.")

"And now, sweet, dear Joe Self," Candy said, in copulation's lambent afterglow, with limpid eyes—her eyes were limpid!—Candy said, "This new you, this published, confident, successful *new you* can venture out into the world. The doors are open. Together you and I can go out, anywhere, anywhere we please, oh, Joe, it'll be grand, won't it?"

"Oh no," Joe Self said. "Not that."

A Walk in the Woods

—It's nippier than I thought.

—It's nice. These woods.

—Yes.

—Reminds me of other woods, other walks.

—Whose woods these are I think I know.

—When younger, when we were younger.

—I remember.

—That was quite a walk.

—And quite a long time ago.

—You were so—impetuous.

—Youth.

—Not that you're less bold now.

—Well—

—I knelt in the grass before you. You leaned on a tree.

—I remember.

—A huge tree. A towering tree.

—Yes.

—A long time ago.

—Not so much.

—We were so young.

—How did we know? How—

—We didn't. We just went on. Life is—just going on.

—We've been through a lot, done everything.

—It seems so at times, doesn't it?

—How free we were. How natural.

—Is this a trail? I wonder. Is this a path?

—I think so. Not—

—There. It goes around there.

—Yes.

—Beautiful, though, isn't it? The woods.

—Yes.

—Good to be outdoors, alone again.

—After all this time, alone again.

—The children.

—Well.

—We wanted that. We did. That was what we did.

—Yes. A family.

—Yes.

—Time passes. Impetuosity wanes.

—Yes.

—You were so beautiful. I remember, the first time I saw your breasts.

—Gone now. I hate that childbirth does that.

—No, now.

—It's true. How can you—

—You are beautiful still. I didn't mean that.

—I know.

—Then.

—Yes. Have we done it all, do you think? I want to do something else.

—What—

—Something we haven't done.

—It's the woods. You're remembering.

—Yes.

—That was lovely. You kneeling in the leafrot.

—It was. Your dick.

—Come now.

—Your lovely dick. In my mouth.

—Yes.

—We could do that again. I would kneel here.

—Woman. You.

—I will. Do you want to? Do you want to stop a while?

—I do want to stop. Here.

—Yes. Sit.

—A fallen tree. How long ago?

—Right.

—If only to rest. Can't quite hike like I used to.

—No.

—You look lovely. The sun is in your hair. Your cheeks are flushed. Madonna.

—Sweet man.

—I need to pee.

—It's anywhere you want. Only nature out here.

—Damn prostate.

—Is it bothering you again?

—Not really. Not much.

—Are you going back to Dr.—

—Yes. I mean, I know I must.

—Yes.

—It's just—

—I know. Me too. I think I'm due.

—That scare that time. You had better.

—I know.

—Are you cold?

—Not much.

—You want my jacket? I told you to put on—

—No. I mean, thank you, I'm fine. The sun here is—

—Like honey. Your face.

—Yes. Sitting here is nice.

—It is.

—I could stay here. I could sleep right here, under this tree. I could.

—The woodland creatures would weave garlands for your hair.

—Let's take off our clothes.

—Grimalkin.

—I mean it.

—We'd freeze.

—We wouldn't, you know. The sun is quite nice.

—We're too old to be nudists. Too old.

—Ok.

—I still have to pee.

—Stand up and pee.

—Yes.

—Sweet—

—Yes.

—Wait—

—Yes—

—Let me hold it.

—What.

—Your dick. While you pee.

—For Godsake.

—No, really. I've never.

—Just because.

—I know.

—Well.

—Come here. Stand this way.

—Now, Grimalkin.

—Just you. How do you do it?

—It's fairly easy—just—

—Here. Take your trousers down more. There.

—Mm.

—Now. Do it. Pee while my hand is wrapped around it.

—Well—

—Just. Like this? Should I hold it like this?

—I'm not sure—

—What is it? Does this hurt?

—No, no. I'm not sure I can pee. With you.

—Really?

—Well, I'm not sure. I never could—you know—with someone else—

—Shy man.

—Yes.

—Here, how bout I just shake your balls a bit. That help?

—Not to pee—perhaps—

—Ok. Let's just be calm. Think about peeing. Water. Think about water.

—Yes. Is this important to you?

—It is. Suddenly it is.

—Ok.

—There, there. Calm. I am just rolling it in my fingers. There, there

—Mm.

—Go ahead, Darling. Take your time.

—Mm, just—

—Yes—

—I do—

—I know.

—I will—

—I know. You have to pee. I feel it.

—I do—I—

—Yes. There. Oh—oh—there we go. Mm, it feels so warm. Mm, yes, I
like the way it feels. Such a good stream, yes. Mm, that's my man—I like

how warm it is. Your dick thick and warm.

—Oh—mm—you're getting your hand in it—

—Yes, I want to. I want to feel your pee, yes. Keep peeing. God, you were so full. It feels funny—your dick is so warm—and it feels—kind of throbby—I like it—I want my hands covered with your pee—there— God—

—Oh. My sweet. That was quite a pee.

—Yes. Yes, are you finished now?

—Yes. I am. I think.

—May I hold it just a while longer? While my hand is still warm with your pee?

—Yes. My knees are weak.

—There, there.

—You're a funny woman.

—There. Now. Zip up.

—Yes. Thank you.

—That was—magnificent! I won't wash this hand for a while.

—You're a funny woman. My Grimalkin.

—We'd never done that before.

—Ok.

—A memorable day. Don't you think?

—I do. Yes. Thank you.

—Thank you, darling. You pee very nicely.

—Thank you.

—Now, that path. Where does it go from here?

—I don't—

—Is that it? Is that the path? Where do we go from here?

—I don't know. I don't have any idea.

Mystical Participation

"The primordial image, or archetype, is a figure—be it a daemon, a human being, or a process—that constantly recurs in the course of history and appears wherever creative fantasy is freely expressed."

Carl Gustave Jung

"My dear Jung, promise me never to abandon the sexual theory. . . . we must make a dogma of it, an unshakable bulwark."

Sigmund Freud

Gus called me up, a rare enough occurrence.

"I need you to come with me. I'm collecting," he began.

"Uh huh," I said. It was before coffee.

"Can you?"

"Sure. What are we collecting?"

"Unconsciousness."

"Right." I knew to give Gus enough rope. He went off on toots occasionally and it was best just to humor him.

"Of the entire race. Why I need your help."

"I guess you do," I said.

"Can you?"

"Sure, sure. When do you wanna start?"

"Right away, this morning if you can."

"Lemme get a few things done around here. About eleven?"

Gus allowed as how eleven would be ok. I didn't really have a lot to do, but I knew it was best to give Gus some time to reflect. On more than one occasion his initial enthusiasm for an idea waned after he'd had his morning bowel movement . . .

. . . "It's collective, not collected," my wife said.

"What?" I blinked.

"The joke doesn't work."

"Oh." She had stung me. While never my most enthusiastic cheerleader she normally gave me polite pass.

"The joke is your whole premise, hence the story doesn't work."

To be honest she had never been supportive of my little literary career (her diminutive), even after the novel. Sure, publicly, she had expressed glee. Ostensibly this was the best thing that had ever happened to me, us. She was the doting wife. The helpmate. Privately it was a different story. She wasn't hostile to my intentions—except when my "writing day" interfered with something she thought I should be doing. She was, and this hurts more, indifferent.

My name is James Royce. You probably remember my one afternoon in the sun, my academic novel, *Schooled Royal*. It made a small splash, the kind of splash that only happens in the shallow end. Kirkus called it "a good flirt." My friend, the Jewish novelist, Shlomo Einstein, said, "With a pitch-perfect sonata of voices recalling the experiments of Nicholson Baker and William Gaddis, *Schooled* is a bittersweet gospel for our time." My most oft-quoted blurb. Who can resist a good blurb?

But, it's been three years since *Schooled* was released and all I had accomplished was one short story in *Cranky* called "Notes Toward the Story," a do-it-yourself grabbag of story ideas that said more about its author's disarray than it did about experimental deconstruction. And I had a poem in *American Poetry Review*, a poem called "Strictly Blowjob," whose history is best not measured.

So, here I sit. Trying to make a story out of a joke, a joke my wife has informed me that worked about as well as an unreplenished stream. My eyes hurt—something behind them wasn't right. And my fingers felt stiff, perhaps because it was cold in our house, drafty. I tried . . .

. . . By the time I reached Gus's A-frame he was outside in the driveway leaning against his Pontiac.

"I guess you're ready to go," I said, grinning foolishly.

"C'mon," he said. Gus was intense—it was his defining principle. This intensity made him one of the best analysts in Zurich. Dr. Jung of Zurich—the Castor to Dr. Freud's Pollux. Or, better perhaps, the yin to his yang.

We took Gus's battered Pontiac into the city. He was an indifferent driver, indifferent to the ebb and flow of traffic, seemingly indifferent to the possibility of an injurious crash. He talked as he drove.

He concluded: "And that's where we need to begin, I believe, at the university, among the lithe limbs and torsos of the youthful. Where better to measure the consciousness of the race?"

"I'm with you, Gus," I said, around a half-masticated donut. "What's the process? I mean, you got like instruments, geigometers or whatnot?"

"Hm," he said, and his hesitation made me blanch. Another wild goose chase, I assumed.

Finally, he said, "We're fishing for archetypes. Ok? Now, archetypes, they have to be rooted out, like truffles. The unconscious needs to be plumbed as if it were a piece of ground full of elusive buried riches. What we use, in each case, will be determined by the individual. Ok?"

I could only say, Ok . . .

. . . It would help, my wife said, if you had some understanding of Jungian psychology. Wouldn't it? And, also, of Zurich. You can't set your story in Zurich in the early 1900s if you have no feel for the place. What's with the modern car, lingo, etc.?"

Clearly, I was going to have to stop showing my pages to my wife.

Now, for you out there unmarried, or perhaps married but oblivious to its various undulations and sea changes, I formulate this encomium: my wife is a wonderful wife. She is. Effie is a good woman, who, through years of living with a writer who is both abstracted and severe—if I may characterize myself in this way—has been driven into a certain blind alley of her customary personality, a blind alley which includes the desire to decimate my confidence as a creative person. Apparently.

"Well," I attempted, "the story is a, what?, experimental, possibly humorous, mock-CV. If you can see it that way—"

"Jim, sweet—" she cut me off. "Even so, one needs a *grounding* in subject matter. Take the time to do the research—if you want to parody something you need to know it inside and out. Know its strengths, weaknesses, places of vulnerability—"

"If you've been following my writing at all, over the past ten years, you would know I'm working in what I might call anti-research burlesque."

"Uh huh," she said, in that way of hers. An "uh huh" that transported more than its five letters and a space should be able to transport. Then she smiled a tight light smile. She turned her back to me and stepped into our closet to get dressed.

I could only stare after her. Her now denuded back, with its moles and strawberry marks, was a lovely thing to behold. The way it sloped down to begin her fine rear end never failed—even after all these years—to stir me.

"Effie," I said, weakly. I was disappearing . . .

. . . Gus swung the car onto campus. It was a bright, spring day, and all around us walked the beautiful children of modern Zurich. They were clearly the master race and I felt foolish for interrupting their glittering existence.

Gus was armed with only a notebook, a pen and his charming smile.

"This way," he said, as if it mattered.

He stopped the first lovely co-ed he came across, a young woman of indeterminate age—she could be 16 or 20—a young woman with hair made of pure light.

"Excuse me," he said.

She fixed us with a practiced hauteur.

"I'm conducting a scientific survey. Could I trouble you for a bit of your time?"

"Survey?" she said.

"Right. I just need to ask you a few questions and record what you say and we go from there."

"Sure," she said, a sparkling jewel to make Europe proud.

Her name was Joy Jacobi and she was majoring in Biology. Dr. Jung and I accompanied her to a room in the copious student center on campus, a semi-private room with tables and chairs. Dr. Jung seemed to know about these rooms beforehand—perhaps he had been conducting these experiments for years now.

Dr. Jung put the sweet co-ed through a labyrinth of questions, mostly about her dreams, which she remembered too clearly. I suspected she was entertaining us, spinning out exciting scenarios, to spice up the interview. Joy had a quick and creative mind.

"And I'm at an outdoor amphitheater, on stage. The audience is all men, sports stars and actors. And I'm naked—" here Joy touched the button of her shirt between her breasts. "And I'm enjoying being ogled—the men are clearly excited by my body. So I'm holding my breasts, offering them up, my nipples hard between my fingers. And the men, as one, take their stiff members out—and I'm looking at a crowd of beautiful erect phalluses—and my excitement grows until I'm touching my honeybox. Then one man mounts the stage—his large member in his hand . . .

. . . "Always with the sex," Effie says.

I had vowed not to show her anything else I'd written. But she had gone to the computer and pulled the file up uninvited.

"You turn every story toward sex."

"It's one of my themes, yes."

"It's not a theme, Jim. It's a prurient obsession. An author has a responsibility toward his characters, like a parent toward the child. It's literary rape is what it is."

"That's a little strong, isn't it? I write about sex because it's a major topic. It is the mystery inside us all. We have to investigate it. D. H. Lawrence said—"

"You aren't investigating, you're seducing your own creations. It's date rape!" Here she laughed. At least that.

"Thanks, dear," I said, with a bitter moue. I put the book I was reading—Goncharov's *The Same Old Story*—closer to may face, signaling that I was through talking. She had cut me again. I sulked in my Russian apologue.

I, James Royce, remembered a night from early in my marriage. Effie had taken longer than usual coming to bed. When she emerged from the bathroom she had on the most outrageously sexy outfit she had ever commandeered. Very brief panties—strings and a patch really—a bustier I think they call it—and cowboy boots! A laugh escaped before other ambitions took over.

"Ef-ffie," I had sputtered.

"You've sprung a leak, husband mine," she said.

"I've sprung more than that," I riposted, and pulled back the sheet to show her a knoll of appreciation.

"Mm, hm," she said. "I like. All that just for this——" and here she wiped a palm over her whole provocative tenement.

Then she had moved sinuously toward me—the memory is bittersweet in its singularity. I pulled my pajama bottoms aside and was revealed. She moved her whole erotic length against me, and, in the process, palmed my erection, a deft enough move.

As she began to pump it slowly, with a seemingly new genius, she whispered in my ear, "Don't write about *this*, asshole." . . .

. . . Gradually, our "interviews" took on the nature of a fever dream. It became clear to me that Dr. Jung had other things in mind than amassing the *collective* unconscious. Or he had become dangerously sidetracked.

"Ah, the slim, untouched bodies of youth, eh?" he allowed on the third morning of our collecting adventure. "A science beyond science, heh heh."

We began luring young co-eds to his dusty apartment. And once there it wasn't long before Dr. Jung had insinuated them out of their fashionable garments. Some of these young people seemed anxious to further scientific inquiry in whatever way necessary—such was Gus's reputation. Others—and I will relate the tale of one such minx—wanted the titillation of it. Thrillseekers, Dr. Jung labeled them.

It was with one such thrillseeker, on one sultry afternoon in sultry Zurich, that it came to a head, so to speak. Her name was Patty Bourgeois. She dressed like a hooker—or the approximation of a hooker for on-campus purposes. And she arrived at Gus's *appartement* smoking a cigarette, striding in with the confidence of unbroken youth.

"I hear we're studying things formerly hidden here, my good doctor," Patty said through a veil of smoke. Her cockiness did not bother Gus. He smiled like an adder.

"Yes, my dear," he simpered. "We're gonna enter the dream

world. Your dream world."

It was his standard patter, but with Patty it seemed iniquitous. I wanted no part of this—yet I could not leave. Was it loyalty, friendship? Was it pure animal desire? I lobbied for my better half to take over. My better half was on holiday. I was priapic, I admit. Animal, anima. What was at work, I half-heartedly grilled myself.

Patty Bourgeois was short work. She was eager to get to the good part.

"And in this dream, Patty, you desire these men?"

"Oh, yes, Doctor."

"Both of them—in this, what, strange, darkened cave?"

"Both, Doctor. And how."

Patty Bourgeois was playing a dangerous game. Yet, I wanted to go with her. God help me I did.

"Now Patty, we will act out this dream. Ok? We will strip down to your basic shadow self, yes? We will move from thinking, feeling, intuition to sensation. Are you with me?"

"Yes, Doctor, anything." Her trance-state was unconvincing.

"Show me, Patty, just what your dream is like. I want you to—"

Patty was already pulling her shirt over her head. I swallowed, an insensate assistant. She was naked before my saliva hit the floor. She had breasts like sea-swells, thighs crimson with heat.

"You are naked?"

"You're so *intuitive*, Doctor. I *love* that."

Dr. Jung smiled his demon smile.

"Tell us what these dream lovers do for you, Patty. Show us your dream."

Patty Bourgeois did not hesitate. Patty Bourgeois unbuckled Dr. Jung's pants and pulled his sizeable manhood out into the fusty air. Jung is hung, I couldn't help thinking.

"Aaah," Dr. Jung said. It was the most unmedical aah of his career.

As she began to fondle him in earnest and Gus began taking off his shirt, Patty's sensuous eyes met mine.

"Come here, Igor," she said. "Get behind me." . . .

. . . "Oh, for Christ's sake," Effie howled. "This is beyond the pale, even for you. You're sinking—willingly—into pornography. And your prose shows it. This is third-rate Cinemax coupling."

Goddamit. I had hidden the manuscript. Created a fictitious file called *Lyrical and Critical Essays*. She was uncanny in her ability to discover it.

"You're just jerking off," she continued. "I mean, this isn't for other eyes, right? You presumably are working on this between more serious projects."

I smiled my weak cat smile. The one I use when I want to hit someone.

"It's an experiment," I began.

"Right," she cut me off, her hand actually making a downward axe stroke. "The investigation to discover how horny you are." She laughed at least.

I could have countered that if I were horny the responsibility might be partly hers. I did not do it.

"Where is this going?" she softened.

I took the bait. She was playing good cop bad cop, playing both parts herself. She smiled encouragement.

"Um, I'm trying to steer it in the direction of—" I was cornered. I had no idea what to say. In truth the story had no plan. My stories never did. I began with a line and if it took me someplace the fishing was good. If it didn't I still got to sit in the sun by the river.

Perhaps this is what I should have told her.

"Let's make it simpler," Effie said. "I think I can help you with this.

What happens next—I mean, right here—what happens next? After 'Get behind me'."

"Um," I fumbled. "He gets behind her."

"Riding the train," Effie laughed, in playful mode.

"Yes," I laughed, too. I was trying to relax.

"So, they've got the threesome going, Dr. Jung, this surely buxom and nubile co-ed, and his assistant, who is a stand-in for you, right?"

"Yes," I said, warming, both to literary alchemy and fleshly pursuits.

"What does she say?" Effie asked, placing the pages down on my desk and seating herself on a hassock.

"What does she say?" I repeated Effie's query to stall for time. Could I write for a woman under a woman's scrutiny? Effie thought I was letting her fill in the blank.

"Oh, Igor, yes, like that. Hold me by the ass."

Gulp, I said. To myself.

"Ok," I said, " but she's got Jung's priapus in her mouth."

"Cock," Effie said.

"Cock," I parroted. "How can she talk?"

"She's talking around it, so to speak."

"Ok."

"Take it out and show it to me."

I was hard, readers, hard as a piece of the nether millstone. Just like that. It was not unusual for me to arouse myself writing—sometimes I think, partly, this is why I write. To animate myself. I reached for my zipper.

Effie laughed. "I was miming the co-ed," she snorted. She actually snorted. "Sorry, dear, I was saying, she could say to her rearward partner, 'take it out and show it to me'."

"Of course," I said, rezipping.

"But then again," Effie said. "Take it out and show me. Jim."

I looked long and thoughtfully at my wife. I wanted to understand what was going on. I wanted her to see me as the contemplative man I was. I also wanted to fuck her.

She put her hand over my crotch, giving with the limpid eyes. She kneaded me for a minute.

"This is exciting for you, isn't it?"

"Mm hm."

"I mean, this whole creation thing, this whole Godlike creation thing, where you control your characters like puppets, pornographic puppets. It's so Jungian, I see now. The literal dream and the symbolic dream, the sensation function, the anima, animus, the yin, yang. I see what you're doing, where you're going with this experiment. I think I can help you, would you like that? You know, there's more to you maybe than I imagined. Isn't that a funny thought after all the time we've been together? I think I haven't spent enough time admiring your mind, your mind's eye, your powers of castle-building. It's like a fever dream, isn't it? It is interesting, the nexus of literature and sex, titillation. I see why it gets you excited. This is like an epiphany! Making people up is sexy, it really is."

To my wife's credit, during this out-loud introspection, this aside, she never stopped stroking me. It was exegesis as foreplay. She did know where and how to touch me. And, my friends, she pulled me out, right there at my desk, with the blank page nearby, with my imagination fired, she pulled me out and very slowly, like the king's best concubine, lowered her wet mouth onto me. She had not sucked me in a decade. I was a teenager again. And she my new girlfriend, the one I'd always desired . . .

. . . "Christ," Patty said. "Goddammit."

"Umph," Jung said as his penis fell out of her mouth like a punctured balloon.

The three just stared at each other. Understanding this cosmic coitus interruptus was beyond them, beyond even the magisterial powers of Gustave Jung. It left them moony. It left them fish out of water. Suddenly the air had gone out of the story. With no conscious effort on their part everything just stopped, went south, stillborn like seed sown on rocky ground.

What happened? A failure of the imagination, a failure of nerve? The three were embarrassed, standing there in the all-in-all. Their faces were blank, so blank there is a yen to fill them in.

They are in hell, or perhaps in hell's *porte-cochere*, a limbo.

They are abandoned gods, spirits left to wander. Though they could not wander.

They could not even move.

Conjuration: A Fabliau

"a song is anything that can walk by itself."
    Bob Dylan

In the days when magic was plentiful and sacred (rather than the vice versa we know today) there lived near Beale Street in Memphis a man of extraordinary powers name of Beaureguard Rawhead. He was, as a conjureman, quite remarkable, but he wanted to be something else. He wanted to be a songwriter.

He had seen W.C. Handy as a youth and he had been thunderstruck. Suddenly all his magic was as if nullified. He wanted to conjure something as powerful, as universal as "St. Louis Blues," or "Mister Crump."

And as he grew older, and his fame as a powerful magicman grew, the need to produce just one memorable song grew, too, until it was an authoritative obsession. So, when the bluesman, Tiny Red, came to see Beaureguard about some business, he saw the chance for a right proper tit for tat.

Tiny Red was from Arkansaw by way of New Orleans by way of the Orient, which is to say Tiny was a grabbag of musical inventiveness. You know him best for "Silver Dollar Pantleg Blues" and "A Frothing of Delight" and for inventing the phrase, "Your world." But, in his day, Tiny was as hot as they come, as big as Big Bill. In his tiny way, of course.

Tiny came to Memphis that fateful fall to scout up some talent for a travellin' gig he was offered on the European continent. Most specifically he needed a second guitar and he heard tell of a Memphis bar rat name of Pete Holder played like the murmur of dreaming brooks. This was the word that he got.

He spent about a month on Beale scouting talent but he wasn't having any luck finding the elusive Mr. Holder. Some said they had just seen him, some said no he was in California. Some nights he was told he had just missed him. He's working at BingoBango, he was told, but no, when he got there he hadn't played there since last week.

But Tiny hadn't come to see Beaureguard Rawhead for no guitar player, no, naturally he came to see the conjureman for an affair of the heart. Seems Tiny had a major heartdeep crush on a dancer at one of the clubs, a woman with a rear like a Buick 6, comely like a pine bridge. Named Callie.

Tiny came, like so many before him, for a philter. He disbelieved in his own charm, in his personal ability to woo so fine a female, so he sought a charm outside of normal human makeup. A love potion.

Tiny knocked tentatively on Beauregard's tinplated door, anxious for thaumaturgy.

"Who?" Beau growled.

"Tiny Red Montgomery," Tiny swallowed. "From Arkansaw."

"Don't know ye," the answer.

"I need some help, sir."

"All God's children do."

"I was told you were the man to see bout this," Tiny said, a little bolder.

"Who said that?"

"Squiggly Robbins, for one. Bob Dobolina. Skincat Resin. All told."

"You music man?" Beau asked with a twinkle.

"That's right."

"Bluesman."

"Yeah. Yessir."

"You are welcome."

Tiny ducked entering the cramped quarters, dark as time. There was a jumble of material everywhere, tables piled with books and manuscripts, papers on top of an old upright piano, every surface obscured by knickknacks and gewgaws, objects seemingly floating in the air. One stooped, sidestepped, bent and shuffled to see the munificent wizard of Beale.

Who sat grinning in a burnished chair, a smile like a keyboard.

"Sit, sit," the old man gestured vaguely.

Tiny carefully pushed aside some papers and settled on an upturned crate.

The magicman fixed him with a milky eye.

"You know W.C. Handy?" he asked quickly.

Tiny hesitated. Know his music or know the man, he wondered. He had actually met the great man once in Montgomery, Alabama, in a dark club, shook his hand, even. This seemed like some kind of test.

"I play his supernal music in my act," he brought out, finally.

"Ahhh," Beau said. "I believe we can do some transacting."

The deal Beaureguard Rawhead laid out for the bluesman was simple but onerous. When he found out Tiny wanted a love potion (he coulda guessed, it was his main business) he allowed as to how he could grant him his every romantic wish in exchange for something a little less tangible. He wanted to be taught how to write a song.

Tiny rubbed his hand across his face, leaned back, leaned forward again. He blew out a bit of sour wind.

"I dunno," he began.

"No deal then."

"Mr. Rawhead, writin songs. I dunno, it can't be taught."

"You learned."

"No sir, I was born writin songs."

"Naw," Beau said and he grinned like a warden.

Tiny knew he was gonna agree to this, he just wanted the disclaimers up front.

"I can try it, sir. I can sure try it."

"Thas all I'm asking," Beaureguard said, standing up.

Tiny rose too. The two men shook hands. They agreed to start that very evening.

That evening the sunset in Memphis was red like the blood of Abraham, the river sucking up that color like a lamia, like a mother dog. There was an eeriness in the air, a tone underneath the everyday, like a buzz in the distance, like cicadas from another world.

Tiny showed up on time, as the bright, white day was giving way to vespertine purples. The old conjureman was eager to get started; he had cleared a space around his piano, like one might clear the ground to build a fire, or make a sacrifice.

Under his arm Tiny carried a sheaf of papers in a beatup folder, his songs. He spread those out on the piano keys and Beaureguard glanced at them perfunctorily.

"Don' need these," he said.

Tiny stared at him a second.

"Mr. Rawhead, lemme get started. You need to learn the musical notation. This the language of the music, the alphabet. Can't build no song without this."

"Don't want to build no song. Wan to..." and he stopped, seemingly to change his tack. "Awright. I see. Teach me this," he said, tapping the sheets.

They spent most of that evening going over basic notes and

melodies, Tiny using the out-of-tune piano to demonstrate the sound beneath the symbol.

It was 2 a.m. when he put his long arms above his head and stretched himself with a crackling of bones.

"That's about it for tonight, I guess."

"Don't know how to write no song, yet," said the old man petulantly.

"Takes some time, sir."

"Awright, awright."

A week passed this way. Small advances, stubborn setbacks. The two men at loggerheads, butting them.

After two weeks the men were more cordial, whiskey between them, good talk. They spoke of love, sex, the river. A bond formed like electricity and the lessons took on a new compeerage.

And progress was made in the manufacture of a song.

Who woulda believed it? Beau began to see the warp and woof of music, began to comprehend its sortilege, its special fluidity. Music spoke to him in his dreams and waking he spoke back. He began to hum around the house, tunes coming in like broken radio waves, indistinct at first, scattered. Gradually a cohesion commenced like his newfound fraternity with Tiny, some kind of coming together.

Secretly at first he began to cobble together a few lines, a phrase or two with accompanying melody. A song was perceived through the dim, a strain appearing in the murk. Beaureguard in private seclusion was writing a song, unsure about revealing it to his master, the man who gave him music.

For his part Tiny suspected the old man was onto something. A new lilt to his conversation emerged, a new lightness to his banter. And in his muddy eyes blue stars danced sometimes, tiny shots like sparks off an anvil. Magic commencing.

The party to celebrate the partnership of Tiny Red and his new guitar player (it was Andy Love due to the mysterious fact that Pete Holder never materialized) was held at the Club BingoBango on a mild Friday night in October. Word spread that there was to be an all night jam and a number of the great and near-great and never-to-be-great attended. At one sweat-retted point in the proceedings, there on the same modest stage sat in Mississippi Red, Alexander Jimspake, Styx Quetzelcoatl, Big Bill Broonzy, The Lonely Dog, Robert Jung, Jimmy the Snake, Ed Alexander, Pudding Puddinski the chanteuse, Roman Rebus, John Kills-Her (the Native American harp player), Squeaky Joint, Tuff Green, the Shawcross Brothers, Skeets Cameron and the Duchess herself. It was a callathump, a shivaree. A bombast. And it was the first time, historically speaking, that the word "bluesfest" had been used. It was coined that night. Write it down.

Long after midnight, the conversation a murmur of ghosts and drinking men, the air fuliginous, almost unremarked Beaureguard Rawhead slipped in through the back door. On the stage Styx and Peep-eye Harper were weaving a sleepy rondo, which sounded a little like "Back'em up Blues in D." Everyone was sorta half there and half woolgathering.

Beauregard slid up to the stage and took a seat at the 88s and looked at them with a kind of wonder and amusement and the other two musicians hesitated and the crowd sort of hummed and burbled and there was a few seconds of dusty silence.

Beauregard touched the first key with his left hand pointer and some other keys followed and before anyone could quite assemble their thoughts he started singing softly, almost to himself at first. The words were incomprehensible initially then took form and poured forth, Beauregard finding a voice as thick as annihilation, as sinuous as ice. Tiny rose slowly from his seat in the middle of the dim and din and hung there like a suspended orb. It was a minor miracle. It was better than he thought possible. The conjureman had a voice, a reason to sing.

And it was on that night that the now standard number, "Saprophytic Blues" was born.

Beaureguard had a minor singing and songwriting career, nothing matching the magic of that firstborn number (though The Latin Students had a minor hit with one of his songs, "They Bribe the Lazy Quadling" in the early fifties). His soul was at peace, however.

The other side of the bargain was, surprisingly, not as successfully achieved, even to making Beaureguard Rawhead cry out to his dark gods, "What good am I who cannot make the smallest world over?"

It wasn't that he gave Tiny Red a faulty philter, a no-motion potion. The elixir worked, oh yes.

Tiny took the small crystal bottle home with him and sprinkled it on his hairbrush as instructed. He lit the brush and it burned with a steady purple flame with a tiny red center like the back of a black widow as expected. But he never again saw Callie Pigeon, the woman he had so set his heart upon winning.

He went to the strip club to see her perform and was told she had disappeared. Poof, like a thought.

His heart ached and he knew an emptiness hitherto undiscovered, and he spent some lonely nights wandering Beale, in a trance-like funk.

He forgave the old conjureman, attaching no blame to the failure of the contract. He was sad but not bitter.

"I failed you, boy. I need to make it up to you," Beaureguard said, hangdogedly.

"It's okay, Beau. I'm okay."

"Man needs love, Tiny."

"It'll come."

"Let's go get us some Zombi Killers, drink ourselves outa the blues. What say?"

"I don' know, Beau. I don't feel right out on the street anymore. Something's wrong."

"What wrong?"

"Weirdness. Collywobbles. Somebody following me."

"Who do that?"

Tiny Red looked up at his friend. Tiny's eyes were deep sad, red-rimmed.

"Old woman. I look up. She everywhere I go. I dunno, she's okay, I guess. Kinda pretty. But, I don' need nobody following me, you follow?"

"Right."

The two men sat in stony silence for a few moments, the love between them like a cat. The air was tinny, faraway music somewhere.

"I get rid of that woman," Beaureguard spoke. "I make you a potion. By the way, Brother, I saw Pete Holder today."

The Day the Change Came for James

—Hey, Honey, where are you? I've got news, good news.

—What—what is it, James?

—I've decided not to be afraid anymore, not to be neurotic.

—What—what do you mean?

—I was at the office today and I thought, *I am not neurotic*. Why have I been living that way?

—Just like that.

—Well.

—James—you can't—

—Gloria, go with me. Listen to me. This is important.

—You just decided—

—Mostly. I suddenly—well, just felt good and. Suddenly—listen, I mean, there's a new secretary. 25. Real cute, great butt. Short skirts. And always real nice to me.

—Uh huh.

—And I thought, you know, when I was younger, I would have just approached her and told her what I think. Like that day I showed up on Wendy Whatsername's front porch. Didn't know me from Adam. And I said, Hi, this is kinda crazy but I think you are so beautiful and I want us to try out a relationship.

—You did that?

—Yes, yes, Surely I've told you. But I felt that old courage again, that surge of bold energy and confidence. I want that feeling again, that coolness. That self-assurance. It's been missing, Gloria. It's been missing too long.

—Because of this secretary with the great ass.

—Well, no, no, not entirely. I thought about you and the kids. You deserve better. You deserve the good me, the one before the great troubling. I want you to know *that* man, not the one I have been for the past ten years, the one who sometimes can't go to work simply because it involves leaving home, the one who can't grocery shop or fly in an airplane or get stuck in a crowd. I am not that guy anymore. That drip. I am the Ur-James, the one who first courted you. What do you think?

—Well—

—Remember when your sister said that thing, that she didn't understand the agoraphobia, the burden of it. She said she was just too busy to worry all the time and that maybe I just needed to stop thinking about myself and start living. Remember she said that?

—Yes. You hated her for saying it.

—Yes, I did.

—You called it bushwa. I called it bushwa. It is bushwa. James—the doctor said—

—I know what the doctor said. I know I thought your sister an insensitive philistine, especially for saying you were "an enabler" and that she would never do that for her spouse. Enabler. A word she read in some pop-psych book. And like she can even keep a husband.

—But—

—Right. Sorry. Off-track. I was thinking. Maybe it is just an illusion. Maybe it is like I am hypnotized by myself. Self-hypnotized. And I can just say, No more. Or: Now wait a minute. Demon, get thee behind me. Just *say* it and by saying it make it so. What do you think?

—Well, James, I hardly know what to say. I mean, well, we've compromised, sure, but this is the life we've built. We are comfortable in our cocoon if that's not overstating things. We don't really miss parties, crowds—

—But, Sweetie, don't you just want to bust out, to cry to the populace that life is real, that life is all around us? Don't you want to howl from the roof sometimes?

—The roof.

—Metaphorically. No—no—wait—really, from the roof. I am going to climb up there and howl. I am going to climb up on the roof and make my declaration to the world.

—No, James, really, the kids—

—They'll love it. They will love their new dad. They haven't met the man. He is going to be the Uber-father!

—James, don't—James—

*

—Well, that went well, didn't it?

—But, Gloria, it did. In a way, it surely did.

—James, Mrs. Turra called the cops.

—I know, I know. I'll go talk to Mrs. Turra. I'll just tell her it's the new me. I'll tell her I won't need to get on the roof very often.

—James. The police came to our house.

—Just to talk me down, Honey. You know. They were very nice. I told them—

—James, you didn't—

—I told them about my new life. Or about how I was reclaiming my old life. That I was no longer phobic. That I was pulling myself up by my bootstraps. That I was saying, James, buck up, you little weasel. Dare to eat a peach! Life, man, life!

—You said that to the police officer.

—A version of it, yes.

—And he let you go back into the house.

—He handed me a card, a shrink's card.

—Of course he did.

—But, isn't that great, Gloria? Isn't that rich in irony? I've been crazy for ten years but now, saner than sane, I am told to see a shrink! Isn't that rich?

—James, the kids—

—I know, I know—I'll go talk to them.

—Don't—

—Gloria, this is good. I can explain.

*

—How did that go?

—I think they got it. Or sort of.

—Janie didn't understand.

—Not entirely, no. She asked if we were getting divorced.

—Mm.

—Well, it's ok. She'll get it.

—Frank?

—He asked me if there was another woman. He sorta didn't get it either.

—Another woman.

—Yes.

—And you told him?

—I tried to explain about the new secretary's great butt. I think I might have gone off the rails there.

—No doubt.

—You're laughing.

—Well, James, I mean—well, hell, ok, it's a little nuts, but I haven't seen you giddy in a long time. It rather undoes me—it rather *pleases* me.

—I know! I know! That's the point. This is me. I used to be giddy!

—Ok, James.

—So, now, whew. I need to sit down. I feel a little dizzy.

—You climbed too high.

—Yes. No. I'm just—dizzy.

—Sit down. I'll get you a drink.

—Yes. A drink.

—Sit down.

—I will, yes. Thanks. Honey, come here, take my hand.

—Of course, James. I am here.

—Just hold my hand. I got so—dizzy.

—I know.

—I—I want to tell you something.

—Of course.

—I want to fuck the new secretary.

—I know, James. I know you do.

—I mean—she's so young, so full of life. She's like a fresh plum.

—I can see her.

—And that butt. It is, so— Perfect.

—Yes, James.

—I want her.

—Ok, James.

—Do you—is this how people feel? Is this normal? Do people walk around wanting each other and fearless and full of seed and life and passion? Do you, Gloria? Do you walk around like that?

—I do, James. Sometimes.

—And you want to fuck men you don't even know.

—Of course.

—It's—dizzying. It's—I don't know.

—I know. It's scary, really. Other people.

—Yes. Exactly. Other people are scary.

—Just sit here.

—Yes, I will. I'll just sit here for a while and then I will get up and look at things again.

—That's a good idea.

—I'll just sit here. I'll relax. And then I'll—reassess.

—That's right, baby.

—I feel so funny, Sweet. I feel—I don't know—*empty*.

—Of course, James. Just sit.

—Yes. Just be still.

—Yes.

—Just sit and reassess and later, later will come, and I will think about what I want to be. I want to be something, Honey.

—Of course, James.

—I won't fuck the secretary.

—I know, James.

—And you—you—

—Just sit here, my husband.

—Yes.

—I'll get you a drink.

—Thank you, Honey. It's all—

—Yes.

—It's just—

—I know.

—So—

—Yes.

—So—dark. It's getting dark in here, Gloria.

—I know, James. Let it come.

—Yes. Let the darkness come. That's the ticket. Thank you. I'll just sit here.

—Yes.

—And let the darkness come.

—Yes.

—Let it come now.

The History of the Memphis 4-H Group
Part One: The Biographies

"But many artists are that way. They're not sure of existing, not even the greatest. So they look for proofs; they judge and condemn. That strengthens them; it's a beginning of existence. They're so lonely!"
—*Albert Camus*

"We came together out of, you know, intellectual horniness."
—*Cord Wetrim*

THE MEMPHIS FOUR-H GROUP

The personae:

Buxton Wales (1953—) painter and poet

Bud Dronetie (1954—) blues singer, songwriter

Dani Veerruss (1955—1992) essayist

Cord Wetrim (1956—) painter

Pinter Monk (1960—) poet, priest

Fret Kessler (1961—) bookstore owner, publisher

Pringle Stokes (1955—) professor of philosophy

Cara Bedwell (1965—) dancer, filmmaker

Peter Natural (1965—) novelist

Huddy Brass (1950—) poet

Norman Claycher (1954—) professor of history

Elmer Marks (1949—) novelist, singer/songwriter

Herd Mankern (1957—) sculptor

Nan Devine (1960—2010) dancer, novelist

Buxton Wales (1953—) **painter and poet**, born 1953 in Yazoo, Mississippi, moved to Memphis when he was five and his father (Grantland Wales, architect and designer of the famed Hot Sizzlin' Barbecue Restaurant in Ingomar, MS) was called on to design the new wing of the Higbee School for Young Ladies. Buxton was a poor student and a worse sport, though he excelled in athletics. He was known more for his on-field meltdowns than his scoring prowess. A kindly art teacher at Nicholas Blackwell High School saw something in the merciless schoolboy and, under her tutelage, his artistic side blossomed. He began painting in imitation of Richard Diebenkorn and Chuck Jones. He had his first show at the Millington Naval Base Stephen Decatur Gallery when he was only 17. Later, he became one of the city's most celebrated oil painters. Of his work, arts writer Fredric Koeppel, writing in *The Commercial Appeal*, said, "He could have been Larry Rivers but he was too cantankerous." The reasons he quit are still argued about. Some say one mean-spirited review did it. Some say his wife at the time, Lise Teetcrock, the writer, didn't understand his paintings ("Daubs," she called him) and wanted him to write verse, which he did, beginning in the early 1990s. His first collection, *Gimme Dat Harp Boys*, was a Yale Younger Poets Selection for 1993. His second, *Horrid Music*, drew comparisons to Robert Lowell. His association with the **Memphis 4-H Group**, as they came to be called, was both a burgeoning and a disenchantment. Known for his acid wit he alienated many of his better friends, including the writers Peter Natural and Pinter Monk. An argument over what the 4 H's stood for led to his estrangement from the group. In 2008, Pinter Monk said, "Buxton was the heart and soul of our group, until he became the fundament of it. Still, I miss him and would rank him as a poet with the best the city has ever seen." When reminded that Buxton Wales was still alive, Monk said, "I thought he died during his ego transplant."

Bud Dronetie (1954—) **blues singer, songwriter**, born in Memphis, in 1954. Bud, who later became the only African-American member of the **Memphis 4-H Group**, started singing at Olivet Baptist Church when he was only 5. His mother, a strict disciplinarian and a gospel singer of some note (one album, *Jesus, Wait Up a Sec*, 1963) raised him by herself. Bud's father died in a railroad accident before Bud was born. Bud went to Melrose High School but dropped out after his sophomore year. He was drinking and smoking a lot of marijuana at the time and did a short stretch in Juvenile Detention. (Judge Turner said about Bud, "He was a nice boy, a polite boy, but he was as restless as a cat.") In his early 20s Bud was working steadily in various clubs in Memphis, North Mississippi, and West Memphis, Arkansas. Bud began writing quite young (an early song, which Bud never recorded, "Sandra, I am Almost Finished" was later recorded by Robert Cray.) Bud wrote the blues standard "Furbelow," ("She ain't much on top, but she's plenty of furbelow"), "Swing Time Handy," "The Seduction Shirt," and his biggest hit, "Grace Kelly Basement Blues," all before he was 25. His comeback album of blues standards, *Down Here on the Graveyard Shift*, won a Blues Music Award and a Grammy in 1991. In 2000 he was inducted into the Blues Hall of Fame in Memphis. He met Elmer Marks in 1982 and through him the other members of the **Memphis 4-H Group**. At their regular Saturday night confabs at the P&H Café, Bud was often called upon to sing impromptu. Wanda Wilson, owner of the nightspot, loved Bud like a son and often stood him to drinks and even paid his rent a few times. Money went through Bud like a dose of salts. In 2011 it was rumored that Shark Tooth Records was compiling a career-spanning box set, to be called *I Have Some Beautiful Rejections*.

Dani Veerruss (1955—1992) essayist, a home birth in Bolivar, Tennessee, in 1955, only daughter of the singer Julip Yield (Fat Possum Records) and noted botanist Tony "Baldy" Veerruss. Dani was homeschooled till she was 17 and remained in her parents' home until she was 23, when she met Herd Mankern and followed him to Memphis. He was unhappily married at the time. In 1990 Dani and Herd were married in the Unitarian Church by the River and produced one child, a son, Veer ("Very"). Dani was the light and heat around which the **Memphis 4-H Group** gravitated, and her late night suppers for the artists and their extended families were famous. "She was a better person than me," Herd said at her funeral. In her 30s she began writing essays on everything from women's rights to hair boiling to cheese to sports, especially zorbing. She was called the "female John McPhee." Her essay, "Hitler: The Dark Side," drew comparisons to Hannah Arendt, was featured in *The Best Essays of 1985,* and is still much discussed in Holocaust Studies. She published one slim volume of essays, *Thanksgiving in the Bughouse* (William Morrow, 1987). At the P&H she was as famous for her impromptu tabletop readings as for her gossamer gowns and outrageously shapely legs. It was rumored that she was, at one time, carrying Pringle Stokes' child, and that the abortion almost dispatched her and additionally almost splintered the group. Dani Veerruss was killed in a car accident at Hollywood and Poplar when her VW Bug was broadsided by a van full of drunken Scientologists. Mayor Willie Herenton, a friend of Baldy Veerruss from college, spoke at her funeral. He said, "She could have succeeded at anything she put her hand to, with the possible exception of running against me for Mayor."

Cord Wetrim (1956—) painter, born in the Lauderdale Housing Projects, the son of Anglo Wetrim, a furrier, and Abigail "Abbie"

Ellinger Hunt, a former Cotton Carnival Queen. Cord went to Central High School where he studied under legendary high school art teacher, Bill Hicks. Hicks called Wetrim, "the best nonrepresentational representational psychic automatism painter I ever taught." Wetrim turned down a scholarship to Memphis College of Art, opting instead to study in Paris with famed Dadaist Rash Pan. While there he met the comedienne Nash Timid, and they had a brief affair. Cord returned to Memphis for the wedding of his old high school running buddy, Herd Mankern, and decided to stay. He started teaching at the College of Art in 1992 and is there today. He married Aspasia Norfleet, the actress, in 1994. He has shown at the Brooks Museum and the Pig and Whistle Gallery in Memphis, but it was his major show at MOMA in 2000, which cemented his international reputation. His series of paintings based on the gestation periods of different ungulates, *Polyphyletics for the Single Gal*, are in the permanent collection of the Hirshhorn Museum in Washington, DC. His *I Love You Keely Smith* is in the San Francisco Museum of Modern Art, and his *Bozo in Scenic Hills* is owned by The Dixon Gallery in Memphis. Of the **4-H Group**, Wetrim says, "Well, it was never a group really, never really a collective or *gesellschaft*. It was more a coffee klatch. We were all too individualistic to cohere. Only Huddy wanted us to be a band. And he was like the Pete Best of the group." It was Wetrim who said that one of the H's in 4-H stood for whatever the H in P&H stood for.

Pinter Monk (1960—) poet, priest, born in the back of his parents' van on a road trip from California to Florida. They said they were looking for Ponce de Leon's fountain of youth. When Pinter's parturition forced them to pull over near the Memphis-Arkansas Bridge they settled in Memphis and lived there until their untimely death in 1965 in a tragic exploding bong accident. Pinter was raised at the Baptist Children's

Home in Ellendale, TN. He attended Bartlett High School (lettering in baseball and graduating with a dual major of Earth Science and Ecumenical Scatology.) He never went to college but did study under Memphis State poets John Nail and Gordon Osing, mostly over beers at The Toast and the P&H. It was through his times in these watering holes that he hooked up with Buxton Wales and the rest of the group. His first book, *Satori on the Bridge*, was published by the University of Arkansas Press in 1988. He followed that with two more collections, *Sometimes a Man Stands up During Supper* (1992) and *The Two-Prostitute Race* (1998) and then *Burning Tracy Prow's Letters: New and Selected Poems* (Viking Press, 2003), which was shortlisted for The National Book Award. It was soon after this publication that he had a very public and passionate affair with Nan Devine, leading to his renouncing, not only **The Memphis 4-H Group**, but women, "odes and epodes," and the secular world. He entered The Brotherhood of St. Prosdocus Mission, in San Luis Obispo, California, and has not been heard from since. (It must be mentioned here that a poem entitled "Meditation on a Thurible," which appeared in Antaeus in 2008, under the name "Willa Magpie," was rumored to be actually Monk's). His books, however, remain in print and continue to sell to that small, passionate group of readers who follow the **4-H Group**, as well as similar poets like Ward Abel and Alp Bilge. "He ended up taking his name all too literally," said Memphis writer, John Fergus Ryan. "It's our loss."

Fret Kessler (1961—) bookstore owner, publisher. Born in Geevil, Mississippi. His family were cotton farmers and they moved to Memphis in the late 70s with enough money to retire. Fret's father bought a small independent bookstore in Poplar Plaza because they wanted to do something relaxing in their waning years. Fret grew up in the bookstore and fell in love with reading and, more importantly for his later development, with the book as object. His younger brother James "Kes" also worked in the store briefly, before marrying the choreographer, Bran Noah Hunt, who was actress Cybill Shepherd's cousin. After high school Fret worked with the Toof Company and later with book artist, Dolph Smith, learning the ins and outs of producing handmade books. "He was the virtuoso of the Vandercook," Smith said of him. Fret's father died in an automobile accident in 1989 and his mother followed shortly from "grief and laxatives." Fret took over the bookstore, renamed it City Nights, and proceeded to publish, under the name Kessler Press, the works of poets, both local and national. He published early books by Gordon Osing, Bill Page and Kenneth Beaudoin. He also published important work by nationally-known poets like James Tate, Marvin Bell, C. K. Williams, and the poet/occultist and Alastair Crowley devotee, Jase Girly. He also worked with the **4-H Group** on their joint publications. Their first collection, *Killed at the Bazaar in a Previous Life*, with writings by the whole group and illustrations by Buxton Wales, Cord Wetrim and Nan Devine, sold out of its limited first edition in one month. Copies on online book sites like Alibris and Bookinder now fetch prices in the thousands. The bookstore became a completely antiquarian business in 2003, run by Fret's wife, the poet, Canada Ambush. The press is still publishing. Its most recent list included books by Babs Ungar, Ed Sanders, Mandy Bush and Under Pierson. Fret says "the four aitches stand for Hurt Hot Healthy and Horny." Canada said, "No, the fourth is for Haints.

Pringle Stokes (1955—) **professor of philosophy**, born in Unlasting, Utah. His parents were Mormons but Pringle left home early, spent some time in San Francisco, and then at 14 met the modal realist philosopher, David Kellogg Lewis. Lewis saw something special in the precocious teen and inculcated him in the philosophy of Australia as well as metaphysics and logic. Pringle stayed at UCLA when his mentor moved to Princeton, eventually graduating Magna Cum Laude at the age of 20. He published his first book a year later, a repudiation of the American Philosophical Association, called *W(h)ole Watchers: A Game Theoretical Prorogation*. He fell in love in 1980 with the novelist and photographer June Baretime (her 2007 novel, *A Short Introduction to the Neighborhood*, is purportedly about the **4-H Group**) and followed her to Memphis, where she replaced Walsh Lobar Smell in the English Department at Rhodes College. The couple started Rhodes' radical left-wing group, Quidnunc. It was there that Baretime befriended Peter Natural (they had a brief affair in 1999) which led them to the **4-H Group**. Stokes began teaching in the Philosophy Department at the University of Memphis, where he became head of the department. He teaches there still. Stokes published many influential books, including *It's Getting Hard to be Someone: a Memoir, She and He in a Swivet*, and *What Happens Next: Counterfactuals and Grigs*. He wrote an affectionate biography and critical study of Lewis, *My Cicero*, which was praised in some corners and called eisegesis in others. He said, "Everything I know, if we really know what we know, I got from Kellogg Lewis and Mr. Peabody."

Cara Bedwell (1965—) **dancer, filmmaker**. Cara Bedwell was born Caraway Weed Bedwell, in Memphis, to Boyd Bedwell, a gay theater director, and Suzy Spiller, a taxidermist. Cara began dancing in the annual Nutcracker Ballet put on by Memphis Ballet, when she was 5. In high school she danced the lead in the ballet *There's a Hole in my Beckett*, based on a short story by Memphis writer, John Pritchard. In college she was spotted by Alvin Ailey, who was in Memphis to have a sinus drained. Cara went to New York and danced there for many years. She also began to study film, after appearing in a Bow Wow Wow video. She worked with Woody Allen (the nymphomaniac character Hermia, in Allen's later film, *A Day When Nothing Else Worked*, was purportedly based on Cara) for a while and released her first film, *Mount the Ass*, independently, but was offered a job with Fox Pictures, which she turned down to return to Memphis. She worked with Truck Tankersley on *Floor Monkeys*, the underground smash, and then released *Memphis Movie*, with Fine Line Features, with Hope Davis and Dan Yumont. It made her name. According to IMDB: "Bedwell was Named among *Fade-In Magazine's* '100 People in Hollywood You Need to Know' in 2005." Though openly gay she had affairs with many Memphis musicians, writers and artists, both male and female, including Jackpot McRey, Zink Snooks, Buddy Gardner and Nan Devine. It was through Nan she met the other members of the **Memphis 4-H Group**. Her affair with Bud Dronetie produced a son, Foghorn, in 1997. Once, at the P&H, on a Thespian Thursday, Cara did a striptease on top of a table, removing everything except her Ida Lupino tattoo. "God, she had great tits," Nan Devine said of her.

Peter Natural (1965—) **novelist**, born in Queneau, Arkansas, to Recoil "Mister" Natural, a house painter, and Lide Orange, a housewife. The family moved to Memphis in 1980 and Peter was enrolled at Central High School. His academic career is hazy and the records lost in a mysterious fire. It seems he attended the College of Art for one semester and then quit to open a restaurant with Catfish Smith, a friend from MCA. That enterprise lasted less than a year. Peter went on the road for a while, as a roadie for the Memphis pop-soul group, The Cairo Proctors. It was while he was working with them that he met Bud Dronetie. Bud and Peter formed a group, briefly, with Amy Lavere on bass. That group was called Pecksniffian. After going bust in the music industry, Natural, starving and suicidal, took a handful of pills one night. It turned out to be a weak amphetamine and the end result was that he was awake for 92 hours straight. It was during these high strung hours that Natural wrote his first novel, *Vertiginous Waves of Murmuring Need*. It was published by New Directions and nominated for the PEN/Faulkner Award. His second, *This Way We Sleep*, got mixed reviews but was a best seller, and did make the Cleveland Dispatch list of best novels of the year (1996). Natural began teaching at Rhodes College in 1997, met June Baretime, and became a part of the **Memphis 4-H Group**. He had a falling out with Buxton Wales (the two got into a physical tussle one night at the P&H) and quit the group briefly, before being lured back by Nan Devine. Peter and Nan never married but produced twin children, Inger and Lark, in 2002. Natural's last novel was called *Memphis, City of Regicide*. "Nan's death marked the end of me as a writer and a man," Natural said. He has not written since.

Huddy Brass (1950—) poet. Born in Bolivar, Tennessee, son of a cleaning woman, Melusina Brass, and a traveling salesman for university presses, who disappeared sometime during Melusina's pregnancy. Huddy was an exceptional student and began classes at Memphis State when he was only 15. He graduated from there and went on to do his MFA at Iowa. His dissertation, *T. S. Eliot Midst the Sodbusters*, became his first book. Collections of poetry followed: *The Dotage of a Fairy Story Hero* (1970), *This Curtailed Life* (1973), *In Zabriskie Point* (1978), *Life in and Out of the Sty* (1986), *The History of Sequential Monogamy* (1995). He was awarded a chair at Memphis State. He retired from there in 1999. The general consensus on his work is that he could have been the next John Berryman if not for his drug abuse. He and Bud Dronetie smoked a lot of grass but Huddy in due course moved higher up the drug chain. Bud Dronetie tells of one particular night of debauchery: "Huddy was a hophead and a ladies man. One night over at Cara's, Huddy took his hostess atop the dining room table while the party went on around them. Later that evening, on a combination of psychotherapeutics and Chocks vitamins, Huddy sat naked in one corner, saying over and over, "I am the original Lumpy Rutherford." He was given to such gnomic pronouncements. A few years older than other members of the **Memphis 4-H Group**, he was the elder statesman of the alliance, much as William Burroughs had been for the Beats. He continues to publish a book every few years. His latest, *The Agoraphobe's Pandiculations* (2009), won Brass his first Pulitzer Prize. Huddy contends that one of the H's in 4-H is for Huddy.

Norman Claycher (1954—) **professor of history**. Was born in East Park Lane, Philadelphia, the son of noted professor of Hebrew at Gratz College, Herbert "Swamp" Claycher, and Sookie Everingham, an ecdysiast. Norman was an exceptional student but got his girlfriend, Enny Johnson, pregnant and married her in 1972. The couple moved to Memphis where Norman took a job teaching in the city school system. Meanwhile he was writing a book about the Rosenbergs and the Marx brothers (*Jews Just Trying to Get By: A Syntactic Approach*, Basic Books, 1980), which won the Linguistics and History Prize from MIT. He was given an honorary doctorate at Memphis State and has taught there ever since. He received the Zelig Harris Chair in 1990. He continued to produce books every seven years or so. *Morphophonemics in the Works of Howard Zinn and Robert E. Howard* was an alternate in the History Book Club in 2002, *The Dancing Plague: Calamitous Ergot Poisoning or Just Good Fun*, won the Albert J. Beveridge Prize in 2007. Meanwhile his wife, Enny, began an affair with Dunque Wetrim, Cort's brother. This caused a strain, briefly, in the **Memphis 4-H Group**, which Norman had joined by invitation in 1994. He was the only member of the group given a formal invitation to join. Norman and Enny's daughter, Eldritch, whose beauty was remarked upon by the poet James Royce, in his poem "Eldritch among the Igmo Set," also had an affair with Herd Mankern. Mankern was 50 and Eldritch 28. Norman was told when he joined the group that one of the H's was for "History." Later, he would say, "Well, they sorta hoodwinked me on that one. The closest any of those ivory tower cognoscente ever got to History was watching *A Man for all Seasons.*"

Elmer Marks (1959—) **novelist, singer/songwriter**. Born in Ripley, Tennessee. His family was so impoverished they lived for an entire year on potatoes and Fizzies. Elmer's father was a farmer but he drank better than he tilled. His mother, Kissy Ripedunn, was once a debutante in Memphis, and fell into moods of black depression when Elmer was small. Elmer moved to Memphis when he was 16, living with his Aunt Rose Ripedunn, school teacher and private tutor in math and science. She doted on the boy and Elmer graduated from East High School with honors. He attended Yale, then Harvard, then Princeton, never actually earning a degree. He moved to Nashville in 1975 and tried to make it as a country music singer and songwriter. He wrote "The Face of Jesus in my Soup" for Dolly Parton, and "Midnight Hankering" for Nanci Griffith. He relocated to Memphis after hearing Bud Dronetie on American Bandstand. He moved in with Dronetie and the two lived together for many years, some say platonically and some say not. Elmer moved toward the nascent punk scene in the 80s, playing at The Hole and later, The Antenna. Marks had a mid-major hit "Ozma's Prisoner," with his band, Herbicidal Sawdust (later Titanic Nausea), in 1984. At the get-togethers of the **Memphis 4-H Group**, Elmer often sat in brooding silence while the drollery and wit flew around him like shrapnel. He and Bud fought like Kilkenny cats. "Elmer was the quiet one," Cara Bedwell said. "He told me once that he hoped folks would mistake his silence for depth instead of ignorance. He and Bud, I don't know. They didn't seem right for each other. They tell me they were a couple but I hardly believe it. I know Elmer and Huddy's sister had a thing for a while. She was in

Titanic Nausea and maybe it was just that band thing. They didn't really fit together either. Elmer was a fey fellow." Cord Wetrim's large-scale nude, "Get Up, Jeune Premier," hanging in Brooks Art Museum, is said to be of Elmer Marks.

Herd Mankern (1957—) **sculptor**, born in Lawnton, Mississippi. Mankern's parents were Irish Travelers and hence, the family moved around a lot. Herd did time as a teenager for shoplifting and assault with a kitchen utensil, in this case a lemon zester. He quit school when he was 14 but began to make mud sculptures during the long evenings in camp with his extended family. Soon, they were selling his sculptures and from then on Herd Mankern went straight. One night he met a woman in a bar who sang country and western and lived in Nashville. Ramona Clawhuck was a red-haired siren, who had slept with most of the music industry in Nashville. She latched onto Herd and some said he seemed bewitched by her, literally witched. He became friends with her brother, the Nashville TV personality/songwriter Alec Clawhuck, who is first cousin to Memphis painter, Cord Wetrim. Soon, the Mankerns had joined the **Memphis 4-H Group** and Herd was one of its most vociferous members. He was a natural talker. It is said that many of his stories ended up in Peter Natural's and Elmer Mark's novels. Coaxed to write his own story he stayed up one night with a case of Mountain Dew and a butcher roll and attempted to write his own *On the Road*. The result has never seen the light of day. Unfortunately, Mankern became addicted to uppers and was in and out of rehab. Herd, like Peter Taylor for Lowell and Berryman, was the rock of the group, the one with a strong shoulder and bail money. Mankern began working in Plexiglas in the 90s and he enjoyed a brief vogue, selling pieces to Neil Young, Kareem Abdul-Jabbar, and Karen Valentine. He never really made much money as an artist and spent many nights cadging off friends for cigarette money and Taco Bell bean burritos. Ramona left him in 1990 and moved to Montana with a mysterious man, whom some people said was Thomas McGuane's brother. Herd and Dani Veerruss were married a week later, and then Dani died in 1992. "Mankern was a sort of sad clown," said Hannah Sayle, arts writer for *The Memphis Flyer*. "He could have been great but was easily distracted. Still, his "Maya Deren in a Darkened Sea Shell," in double-knit polyester (now in the private collection of the William Eggleston family), in my opinion, ranks with the best work of Alina Szapocznikow and Starkey Kind."

Nan Devine (1960—2009) **dancer, novelist**. Born Janette Angela Devine, in Memphis. Her father was Andrew Devine, bank manager and patron of the arts, and her mother, Angela Singer, of the sewing machine Singers. Nan began dancing at a very young age and by the time she was in her late teens she was celebrated nationally. She originated the role of Cathy/Patty in Gregor Melville's jazz opera, *The Patty Duke Show*. She danced nude for the premiere of Pope Kale Lewis's opera *The Collective Submission*, at the Rio de Janeiro *Theatro Municipal*. She went to Germany in search of the last living "Isadorable," Alexandra Karina, who was then 90 years old. She lived with her for a while, then moved to Russia and joined the Communist Party. She came back to Memphis to dance the role of Sharilyn in the opera *Après Richard Brautigan*, and decided to stay home to nurse her mother who was then suffering from Alzheimer's. She helped found the avant-garde Memphis dance troupe, Motion like a Stone. She began writing novels in 1999 and turned out one every two years until her death, including *Take the Last Train to Clarksdale* (Knopf, 1999), *Thanatopsis, Kiss my Ass* (Viking, 2001) (PEN/Faulkner winner) and *The Judge's Narcolepsy* (Algonquin, 2006) (Lila Wallace-Reader's Digest Writer's Award). She had a generous nature and was said to be the Mother-spirit of the **Memphis 4-H Group**. "She was so beautiful men and women both would rend their own privates in tribute to her," Buxton says. And he adds, "One of the H's is for "Hoochie," Pinter Monk's pet name for Nan's pudenda." She was loved by Memphis novelist Ernest Vest, architect Cherry Chouinard, as well as the Historian of the Pinch, novelist Shlomo Einstein, and had twin children with Peter Natural. "She was the best of us," Pinter Monk said. Nan Devine died in 2009 of complications from a blood clot in her lung. Her funeral lasted three days and the procession of cars following her casket was said to be 25 miles long. "When she died, *we* died," said Buxton Wells.

COREY MESLER is the author of the preceding account. He and his wife own Burke's Book Store in Memphis, Tennessee. He knew the members of the 4-H Group and discusses them at greater length in his autobiography, *My Medicine Is Making Me Sick* (Bottomless Books, 2009).

Aftermath

Right after the crash Ralph went around talking about it as if he were the ancient mariner. "The guy came out of nowhere," is a phrase I remember from numerous renditions. It was soon reported that there was trouble at home, his still young wife was spotted at Arby's with Jack Diamond from the church choir. Later Ralph would say he could have predicted it all, the dirty affair, the acrimony, the loss of his self-respect and then his job. Ralph really went downhill. "The only thing I didn't see coming," Ralph was saying, "was that goddamned Plymouth."

The Plot to Kidnap Stonehenge

1

Randolph—Good morning, Sir.

Merlin—Morning? Hmph, is it?

Randolph—Indeed, Sir.

Merlin—Breakfast then.

Randolph—Yes, Sir. Soft-boiled quail eggs, dry toast, a banger.

Merlin—Quite.

Randolph—I'll let you eat in peace.

Merlin—Wait, Randolph. Mm, this quail's egg…um, tell me, what's on the agenda today?

Randolph—Full day, as usual. Perhaps moreso than yesterday or tomorrow, as the case may be.

Merlin—This living backwards.

Randolph—Yes, Sir.

Merlin—What's up first?

Randolph—Let's see (rattling pages)…9 a.m., the King's mandolin lesson.

Merlin—Poor Wart. He's horrible, of course. Well, that shouldn't take long. He gets frustrated quickly, smashes instrument and we have to send for another. Ok. Then?

Randolph—You have an eleven o'clock with Mordred, Sir.

Merlin—Oh, hell. That little eelshit.

Randolph—Yes, Sir.

Merlin—Do you have any idea what that's about?

Randolph—No, Sir. No idea. He seemed quite hot to see you.

Merlin—Of course, he did. Why doesn't he take this up with Wart, er, Arthur? I'm not the fucking king.

Randolph—No, Sir.

Merlin—He's afraid of Arthur, of course.

Randolph—So it seems.

Merlin—Well, see if we can wiggle out of that one, eh?

Randolph—Um, yes, Sir.

Merlin—Problem?

Randolph—Mr. Mordred, Sir. He can be so unpleasant.

Merlin—Oh, fie and damnation. All right.

Randolph—Yes, Sir.

Merlin—What else? Give me something to look forward to today, Randolph. Mm, this banger is especially succulent.

Randolph—There's Guinevere at 1, Sir.

Merlin—Ah.

Randolph—Yes, Sir.

Merlin—She is one spicy little queen, isn't she, Randolph?

Randolph—I've heard tell, Sir.

Merlin—A regular nymphomaniac.

Randolph—I cannot speak so plain, of course.

Merlin—Just between us, eh? Randolph? Have you ever seen a better ass?

Randolph—(blushing) No, Sir. No, I haven't.

Merlin—She fucks like a wild animal, Randolph.

Randolph—Indeed, Sir?

Merlin—Gets on you and moves that great behind around. Ah.

Randolph—Yes, Sir.

Merlin—Well, that's something to look forward to anyway. Lancelot must be away?

Randolph—No, Sir. He's about.

Merlin—And she still wants Old Merlin, eh? That little minx.

Randolph—Yes, Sir.

2

Merlin—Come in, Mordred. How are things in Cornwall?

Mordred—(bowing) Quite satisfactory, Merlin. Rain, lots of rain.

Merlin—What is one to do, eh? Everyone talks about the weather—

Mordred—Of course, you could do something about it.

Merlin—You sweet-talk.

Mordred—Not at all.

Merlin—So, what's on your nefarious, little mind this morning? Why so passionate to see Old Merlin?

Mordred—Off the record?

Merlin—If you wish.

Mordred—I have a plan. A monumental plan. Something that will make Camelot great.

Merlin—Camelot is already great.

Mordred—Well, the word on the street (here, Mordred lays a finger beside his nose) is that the whole Round Table idea is old hat. There's talk of the Queen's concupiscence. Many say Arthur isn't the King he used to be.

Merlin—Blasphemy.

Mordred—Yet, there it is. Covetousness, perhaps, but the word on the street...

Merlin—Right, right. What is this plan?

Mordred—Well. (Mordred moves slightly closer while Merlin unconsciously moves slightly away.) Perhaps you've heard of the Irish Giants?

Merlin—So.

Mordred—They're Giants. And they live in Ireland.

Merlin—Get on with it.

Mordred—Well, word has it that they have built something. Something miraculous, full of marvel and portent.

Merlin—The clock thing.

Mordred—(after a pause) Perhaps. A clock? Perhaps.

Merlin—An astrological clock.

Mordred—You continue to impress.

Merlin—I hear things.

Mordred—This is no ordinary clock. It is mammoth, built of bluestone and hand-carved sarsen-rock. And it stands a full ten men high, with lintels weighing 5 tons.

Merlin—Indeed. Well, there are wonders in the world. What has this to do with us, Mordred? (Merlin is impatient thinking of the afternoon tryst with the Queen.)

Mordred—We can make it ours.

Merlin—(Surprisingly taken aback) Ours? Well, that wouldn't sit well with the fucking Giants, would it?

Mordred—They wouldn't know what hit them. You spirit it away. Whoosh! You can do it, Merlin, only you can do it.

Merlin (hand to chin, rubbing furiously)—As much as it pains me to say this, I'm interested in what you propose, Mordred.

Mordred—Thank you, Sir. It will be greater, more mystifying than your Cerne Abbas Giant.

Merlin—A good jape, that.

Mordred—That it is.

Merlin—Fucking Giants, eh? What?

Mordred—Exactly.

Merlin—Where would we put the damn thing?

Mordred—Well, there's this nice space on Salisbury Plain. Lots of ground, slight promontory, nice long path for an entranceway. Some shrubbery.

Merlin—Salisbury, yes. Yes, that might work.

Mordred—Thank you, Sir.

Merlin—What's in it for you, Mordred?

Mordred—The pride of Camelot.

Merlin—Don't bullshit a bullshitter.

Mordred—Well, I *would* want a finder's fee.

Merlin—Ah.

3

Merlin—My Queen.

Guinevere—Are we alone?

Merlin—Quite, my Queen.

Guinevere—Ok, drop the "My Queen" crap and undo that robe.

Merlin—You little minx. (He opens his voluminous gown.) Where is Lancelot?

Guinevere—Jealousy doesn't become you, my Naked Necromancer.

Merlin—It's only that, well, never mind.

Guinevere—Never mind, indeed. That's quite a stout birch-branch, you've got there, Magician.

Merlin—You've never complained before. Unclothe thyself, my dear.

Guinevere—Make yourself young first.

Merlin—Oh, stuff and incense. Here then.

Guinevere—Yipes. I love those pecs, my Lothario. (She slips out of her silks.)

Merlin—And you turn around and let me see it. The Royal Rear.

Guinevere—You rascally conjurer. (She turns and bends slightly at the waist.) Here 'tis.

Merlin—Holy cats, My Queen. That is a formidable fundament.

Guinevere—And that is a thick staff. Is it legerdemain or tribute to my pallid backside?

Merlin—Ah, Guin. It's all for you, my pretty. As round as Norval's shield, as white as Albion moonlight, as alabastrine as the cliffs of Dover.

Guinevere—Flatterer. Bring that bludgeon here.

Afterwards

Guinevere—Ah, Merlin, no one quite fucks like an archimage.

Merlin—You're not bad yourself, Toots.

Guinevere—That part where you turned briefly into a bull.

Merlin—Unintentional.

Guinevere—Inspired.

Merlin—Thank you.

Guinevere—Now, my horny magus. What is this I hear about a granite moon-mirror?

Merlin—Bah! Are there no secrets in Camelot?

4

Randolph—Good morning, Sir.

Merlin—Morning? Mmmph. What day is it?

Randolph—Thursday.

Merlin—Thursday. (He shakes his hoary head.) What happened to Friday?

Randolph—You slept through it, Sir.

Merlin—Indeed. It's very confusing.

Randolph—It is. You were powerful tired, my Lord.

Merlin—Indeed, I was.

Randolph—Well, anyway, Sir. Light schedule today.

Merlin—Fine, fine.

Randolph—The King at 10. He wants to congratulate you on the piece of art you erected on Salisbury Plain.

Merlin—It's *not* a fucking piece of art.

Randolph—Yes, Sir.

Merlin—It's a timepiece. An astrological wonderment—oh, never mind. If you have to explain magic it loses its, its…

Randolph—Luster, Sir?

Merlin—Precisely.

Randolph—At any rate, it is the talk of the town, Sir.

Merlin—Well and good.

Randolph—Mordred is taking credit left and right for it, of course.

Merlin—I'm going to turn that turncoat into a stoat.

Randolph—Quite right, Sir.

Merlin—After all is said and done, we have it now, don't we? It's ours. It's Britain's.

Randolph—Rightfully so, Sir.

Merlin—Can't help feeling a little guilty over the Irish though.

Randolph—Send them some rainbows, Sir.

Merlin—Randolph, you have a keen grasp of International Politics.

Randolph—Yes, Sir. Thank you, Sir.

Merlin—And it's popular, eh?

Randolph—Quite. I hear the tourist trade is up 37% in just one week. There's talk of an inn, a roadway, and a couple of food stands.

Merlin—Good, good. An unequivocal hit, then.

Randolph—Ye-es.

Merlin—You seem hesitant.

Randolph—There was a suggestion about the entranceway, lining it with topiary in the shapes of the Twelve.

Merlin—Inappropriate.

Randolph—Yes, and, well the name, Sir?

Merlin—Yes.

Randolph—Some people want to call it something else. Woodhenge was such a bust, there's talk that we need a catchier moniker for this one.

Merlin—Hm. I'll think on it, Randolph.

Randolph—Quite right, Sir.

Merlin—Anything else?

Randolph—I hesitate to mention it, Sir.

Merlin—Randolph.

Randolph—Well, the blood sacrifices, Sir. Some people are taking exception to them.

Merlin—Nitpickers.

Randolph—Yes, Sir. There's also talk about Avebury wanting one, too.

Merlin—Imitation is the sincerest form, eh, Randolph?

Randolph—Quite, Sir.

Merlin—(striking his forehead) The Giant's Dance!

Randolph—Sir?

Merlin—For the name.

Randolph—Ah. Quite euphonious.

Merlin—Oh, and Randolph, is the Queen about?

Randolph—Yes, Sir.

Merlin—Can we squeeze her in before the King?

Randolph—(allowing himself a small smile) I believe so, Sir.

Merlin—Tell her I am ready to show her the Bull again.

Randolph—The Bull, sir?

Merlin—She'll understand. The Bull, Randolph.

Randolph—Yes, sir.

Waiting for the Train

We, in the village, prepare for the next train with a reverence some folks might call devout. We pack and unpack our luggage and when we pass each other on the sidewalks we ask questions about the packing. "Are you through, Suzette?" "Did you pack evening wear, Mr. Carmincross?" "Should I bring two swimming suits?" Ronco and I have matching bags as big as hassocks. Ronco keeps his by his side of our bed because he says he gets most of his inspiration at night. It's not uncommon for him to get back up two or three times to put something into his bag or to take something out. I restrain myself. My bag is in the closet, open, its contents as neat as a library. Some years, if the weather is bad, the talk turns to railroad lines, how much snow would queer the train's arrival, or delay it further. We who have lived in the village all our lives know that the train will come when it comes. Our lives are based on faith. Henson, the oldest man in the village, says he thinks there was a train in his childhood but he's not sure. This cheers us. We are comforted with our foreknowledge; when the train comes we will be ready. Old Henson is the blithest man in the village.

Publisher

"That was commonly believed to be a function of great literature: antidote to suffering through depiction of our common fate."

—*Philip Roth*

1.

I am a whore and a pimp. This may seem preposterous to you, but I assure you, though self-knowledge has not always been my strong suit, here I am neither exaggerating for shock value nor confessing for pity.

I came from good schools with a lot riding on me, the aspirations of my own ambition, duly inflated by well-intentioned professors and administrators, the hopes and dreams of my hard-working but underachieving parents, the burnout of my older brother, who was both smarter and more industrious. These are onerous pressures, each, and collectively, quite oppressive. I was promise and capacity. I was Golden Boy. It was assumed I would make it, in the vague sense that expression is intended, but mostly this: procure a big bundle of money while doing meritorious things.

Oh, I started out with high hopes. With my degree in English Lit tucked, metaphorically, under my arm (my area of specialty was 20th century British Literature) I headed to New York City—where else?— with the aim to get a job in publishing, figuring, naively, on walking into an assistant editorship at Knopf or Henry Holt or Farrar, Straus & Giroux. Figuring, I guess, they were hungry for a bright young man who had digested a lot of writing and practically passed metaphors and similes with his flatulence. You've guessed by my tone by now that the doors were not exactly swinging open for me. Oh, everyone was nice enough—egad those publishing houses are filled with beautiful young 24 year old women fresh from college, firm jawed, severe, the kind of women who look you right in the eye until you look away no matter how unchallenging your last remark was—and I even had a few promising interviews. I actually met Roger Giroux—he must be 104—though it was in the corridor of the building where FS&G resides and our conversation was brief, chatty, meaningless. He was, at that particular moment, concerned about some television show which had just aired (I gathered from his somewhat disjointed commentary) and which offended him deeply by its depiction of J. D. Salinger as a nasty old man. To be honest I'm not sure Mr. Giroux knew to whom he was talking or ever registered a single comment I made.

So, to pay the rent for my pitiable one room apartment (New Yorkers settle for so little in the way of comfort, the city itself, supposedly, redressing the imbalance by its sizzle) I took up a job—where else?—in a bookstore in the Village, a squatty, dark, dank little dungeon where used books mixed with a random, arbitrary sampling of some of the newer offerings by our contemporary geniuses. If this all sounds rather bitter, rather sour grape flavored, I plead guilty. I enjoyed spending my time in the bookstore—more often than not, rearranging Trollope, Iris Murdoch, the Powyses or John Fowles, *ad infinitum*, one week alphabetizing their subsections by title, one week placing the books chronologically. And, if this was just idle make-work, the owner, Pat Trevelyn, a corpulent, ex-hippie who only wanted to make enough money to feed his cat and keep himself in marijuana, never questioned a single move I made. Nor did he recognize any of them.

So, the time went by, weeks and months. New York became a heavy yoke around my neck and my letters back home were full of book-talk, most of which I garnered from the eccentric clientele which frequented The Book Inglenook (a clumsy appellative which one can only imagine was designed to avoid the clichéd Book Nook) or from the sagacious pages of *The New York Times Book Review* and *The New York Review of Books*. It didn't take too many ramen noodle meals to make me realize what a failure I was and I was on the verge of bailing out—running back to Saskatoon with my paper stuffed suitcase—when an ad in the back of the NYTBR caught my attention.

It said: *Editor wanted. Small press. Benefits. Rapid advancement*, and a phone number.

I called—of course I called—and got the ubiquitous answering machine and it wasn't until the next day when I returned home from the BI that a return message lit up the red-eye on my own machine. Its message, delivered in a smooth, slightly nasal but very proper voice said, "Mr. Brackett, thank you for answering our ad. If you could appear at our offices tomorrow morning at 9 a.m. we could talk further about this employment opportunity. Please bring a current resume." And he gave the address. An address, which I was unfamiliar with, though I knew it was squirreled away among some claustrophobic uptown nondescript buildings, and, indeed, it turned out to be absurdly difficult to find. One had to wend one's way through trash-strewn alleyways, up some unpromising exterior stairways, down some darkened corridors to finally arrive. I expected the Minotaur at any moment. It was almost as if it were consciously concealed.

The small white sign with black lettering on the door said, "Ardent Publishing, James Quillmeier, Publisher."

I gave the hollow plywood door a light knock while opening it enough to poke my head in. My first sight was a wall decorated entirely with oversize blow-ups of book jackets, presumably some of the firm's successes (though I had heard of none of them). Rotating my head a few degrees east I found a smiling visage which was bright as a blister and seemed to single-handedly hold back the room's fuscous gloom. The face belonged, it turned out, to Ardent's loyal secretary, Sherri Hoving, and it was a face which was to turn up in my dreams for years to come, a face like an iceberg refracting light, with a gaze like a baby uses to gaze upon another baby. She was a brunette with skin like sealskin and she seemed to be both dark and light simultaneously. But, before I get ahead of the story, before I wax idyllic and burn my candle at both ends, leaving little suspense for your delectation, allow me to proceed into the cluttered and claustrophobic offices of Ardent Publishing.

"Mr. Brackett?" the face tinkled.

"Yes, I have..."

"Yes, I know. Mr. Quillmeier is expecting you. At the moment he is on the phone to Tokyo but he'll be with you momentarily, I'm sure."

"Thank you," I said and backed, self-consciously, into an old-fashioned armchair that was shoved against one wall.

The face beamed at me. I tried to beam back but my smile felt phony and I imagined I might have looked like Dr. Sardonicus. I tried to relax.

"Can I get you anything?" she asked after a few sunny moments.

"Nothing, thank you."

"Oh. By the way, I'm Sherri Hoving. Sherri. Sort of the grunt around here, do a little of everything, nothing of any real consequence."

This turned out to be so far from the truth—Sherri (short for Sherrifa, of all things) Hoving kept Ardent Publishing together with ingenuity, spit and rubber bands, and, if not for her devotion and sapient governorship, this small concern would not stay afloat. It didn't take me long to learn this, and other necessary, hard-to-swallow truths.

I bided my time in their cramped waiting room, feeling as if I were being kept waiting only for show, but enjoying the view of Ms. Hoving's immaculate bare legs under her desk. Every few minutes—you could set your watch by it—she raised her freckled face toward me and smiled.

When I finally was ushered into Mr. Quillmeier's presence I found myself in an office not much larger than the waiting room, papers on every surface, the walls decorated with more book jacket blowups (*Mr. Anthony's Reproductive Organs, Flowers and Petals, The Scamp's Dog*) and along every wall stacks of books, about a hundred copies of each title.

Quillmeier was a piece of work himself. As round as a turnip with a mustache which appeared to be stuck on with sweat, he punched out a chubby fingered hand and gave mine one quick pump.

"Sit down, Mr. Brackett," he said, gesturing toward the only other chair in the room, pushed up uncomfortably close to the edge of his worn old desk.

"Thank you," I said, already formulating escape plans. This was certainly low-end publishing. How desperate was I to work in that rarefied atmosphere of disseminating literature to the great unwashed?

"Your resume," Quillmeier spurted.

I fumbled in my cardboard briefcase, which I tried to keep partially concealed between my knees. I pulled out a copy of my freshly printed resume and in so doing wrinkled it. I began an apology and a quick search for a second copy but Quillmeier snatched the proffered first copy from my sweating hand.

"Fine, fine," he said. He read it the way a child reads a history book. His concentration appeared to cause him pain as his face squinched, his left arm shot out involuntarily in spasm; he squirmed in his seat. It was an uncomfortable ten minutes before another word was spoken. I thought, flowers *and* petals?

"Starts at 20 a year," Quillmeier said, finally.

I hardly knew what to say. That was the interview?

"I hardly know what to say," I offered.

"Take it or leave it," Quillmeier said with a not unfriendly, but somehow greasy smile.

"Can I sleep on it?" I asked, sheepishly.

"Nnn," he said, settling back into his well-broken in chair. I thought I was almost dismissed. I thought to Mr. Quillmeier I was already a former applicant.

"No," I said. "No, I don't have to sleep on it. I'd be proud to work for Ardent," I said. I don't know where it came from.

"Fine, fine," Quillmeier said, rising ever so slightly from his seat and giving my hand one more fat pump. "Monday at 9, then?"

"Yes, surely," I said, backing out of his office.

In the anteroom Sherri Hoving was standing next to her desk, the whole, dark, willowy length of her, presented to view. She wore a smile that said *I knew you would get the job.*

A momentary queasiness overtook me. Sherri Hoving took a step toward me and put her arms around me, the way an aunt might hug a troubled nephew. I placed a tentative hand on the sweet, slick material over her lower back. Here was warmth, succor. Everything was going to be all right.

When I stepped out into the big city sunshine elation welled up inside me and I said to the lizard which lives inside us all, "I have a job in *publishing*."

When I left Ardent it was still only 10:30 a.m. I first went to the bookstore and told Pat that I had found another job and would work out the remainder of the week if that was what he wanted. It was Thursday. It wasn't much notice. But Pat looked at me through his herbal haze and smiled a beatific smile and said, "Blessings on you, Brackett. Go out there and find the best damn authors you can. Make them write books that will shake the foundations of our constipated society. Draw from them their best work. Draw from them the words inside themselves that they are unaware of, words which lay dormant like an illness of rage. Publish, Brackett. Do good."

Well, I was somewhat taken aback. Part of me knew I wasn't exactly indispensable to The Book Inglenook, but I didn't expect such a divine sanction, such a heartfelt fare-thee-well.

"Well, damn, Pat," I said. "I will try to live up to your expectations. I will do my damnedest."

"I know you will, Brackett. Which publishing house has the good fortune to have picked up your worthy services, if I may ask?"

I hesitated. A foreboding came between us.

"Uh, a small concern. You might not know them. Little house called Ardent." I started to throw off a couple of their titles as if I had heard of them prior to my visit to their Lilliputian offices but Pat's expression was one of consternation, dismay, perhaps qualmishness.

"Ardent," he said like a book dropped on a dusty floor. He looked down at his desk in embarrassment.

"What's wrong?"

"Nothing. Nothing, Brackett. I thought, you know."

"I don't," I assured him.

"Well, it's just that they're a, a vanity house."

The words hit me in the solar plexus. The dreaded words hit me like being told "Can we just be friends?"

"Shit," I said.

"I'm sorry," Pat said. "Rain on the parade, that's me. Look, go there. Get started. Do the best you can and look for greener pastures. It won't be bad. It *is* publishing. Sort of."

I carried that "sort of" around with me for the next couple of weeks. After leaving Pat (he said, go ahead, he really didn't need British Fiction re-alphabetized again) I treated myself to a real deli sandwich and an egg cream. I felt very New Yorkish, though that "sort of" sat in my stomach heavier than the sauerkraut on my Ruben. I called my parents that evening and told them I got a job in publishing and tried to make it sound lively, consequential, promising. I think it worked. My parents wouldn't know Alfred Knopf from Cima Academic & Language Media.

I wouldn't have thought it possible that they had room for me in the offices of Ardent Publishing, but when I went in that Monday morning, my cheap case stuck self-importantly under my armpit, they had cleared a corner of the anteroom (I can't imagine what was there before—I had no memory of a filing cabinet or couch or potted plant). There now was an old oak desk, the surface of which was as bare as a stone. Sherri Hoving gestured toward it like Vanna White toward a new SUV and I returned her friendly smile. We were roommates.

"Wow," I said. "My own desk. It looks so pristine, so uninhabited. It appears ready to transact some majestic and transformative legerdemain. I hardly know how to become worthy of it."

"Well," Sherri said and bent her—have I already said willowy?—five foot nine frame over her own desk and fetched from there a stack of what I immediately recognized as manuscripts. There were a dozen or so of them. They were printed on various qualities of paper. Most at least were typewritten, if not composed on a word processor and printed in dot matrix or laser jet, but there were a couple copied out in long hand on hundreds and hundreds of legal pad sheets, neatly stapled together. I sighed.

"Yep," Sherri Hoving said, relinquishing the burden to her new co-worker, the sap. She practically washed her hands in Pilate's bowl.

I weighed them in my hands for comic effect, as if in so doing I could determine their value.

Sherri Hoving laughed. It was the sound of snowflakes falling on a harp. I was enchanted. I suddenly knew something new: Sherri Hoving enchanted me.

"Read them. Write up a page of synopsis and critique for the boss and then type a letter of acceptance to the author," she said, and was betrayed by a slight blush.

I wavered. "We accept them all?" I asked, though my pride was already an area of deep despoliation.

She opened a drawer in her desk and produced a fistful of checks.

"Fifteen checks. Fifteen manuscripts," she smiled, sheepishly. "We accept them all."

I sighed, set down the stack on my desk, set myself down in the chair at my desk, which suddenly threatened to throw me around a bit, spinning like a dervish, its ancient spring so loose and disconnected. This bit of pratfall, perhaps, erased the tension of the moment.

Sherri tinkled again, again like the music of a harp, and I smiled a big, goofy grin.

"Welcome to the fast lane," she said and laughed again.

"I'm here to do my best," I said, a little too earnestly. And, then because that felt awkward I compounded the awkwardness. "Would you have dinner with me tonight?"

It was a complete surprise when to my unexpected question she barked out a quick *yes*, and was herself embarrassed by her enthusiasm.

So, my stint at Ardent Publishing began with mixed blessings. Sherri Hoving moved like a springborn fairy around that tiny room and every time she did my heart played the anvil chorus. And, meanwhile, I amused or depressed myself with the worst prose ever committed to paper. Ever, beginning with the Egyptians. It was mixed blessings all right.

That night I arrived at Sherri Hoving's apartment in one of the nicer buildings in the same area of uptown where Ardent was also housed. She answered my buzz and when I found her on the third floor she was standing in the doorway to her apartment. She was wearing a sleeveless, short black dress, which set birds loose in me. Her long, bare legs were lightly tanned and sprayed gently with freckles, as were her delicious and pronounced shoulders. Her knees were brown biscuits. Her limbs were exquisite.

"Hello," she said, and I thought I detected a slight purr.

"Hello," I answered back. We moved into her rooms that were shockingly well-appointed. How much was she making at Ardent? Tasteful doesn't begin to describe how divinely laid out her apartment was. Interior decoration to me had always meant, "Where do I put the bookcase?" But, here, well, here was art.

"This is lovely," I said. And even though that sounded a tad fey the sincerity won the point.

"Thank you," she said.

We stood awkwardly near each other for a moment and I was about to ask for a restaurant recommendation when she stepped into my personal space and put her mouth against mine. The kiss—warm as life and moist enough to make its prolonged hold unbearably exciting— lasted until she turned her cheek slightly and exhaled as if she were overwhelmed.

"I've been wanting to do that since the first day you walked through the door at Ardent," she said.

"You haven't been alone," I said. It was almost right.

"Kiss me again," she said. I did.

That evening we spent on her plush, off-white couch, our tongues intertwined like the caduceus. And, while the making-out (forgive the seventh grade terminology) was erotic and moist and stimulating, it went no further. Oh, at one point, I believe, I cupped her small, bird-belly breast and she sighed and we kissed and kissed some more. I remember thinking, we have all the time in the world. We never did eat and I left around 2 a.m., my head spinning, my mouth refreshed as if I had drunk at Tantalus' pool, and my heart full of love, oh overflowing love, for Sherrifa Hoving.

Over the ensuing months I was responsible for publishing numerous books under the Ardent imprint. My name appeared on them all as editor, though, in truth, my only addition to the stream which is literature, was to make subjects and verbs agree (sometimes when they stubbornly seemed unwilling to, fighting like Kilkenny cats), clean up any language which strayed from the somewhat rocky path which is English grammar, take out the names of famous people in far-fetched tales of sexual misconducts (to stave off lawsuits, obviously) and substitute names of my own invention. This was at least creative and, at times, diverting. For instance, for John Kennedy I substituted Matt Chinoi, Snake Charmer. I replaced a particularly ugly reference to Calista Flockhart with the ridiculous name Sysipha Van Grubelhoffer. I turned Johnny Carson into Mungo Park. Etc. It was the only thing that made me feel as if I were not scooping up hot dung with my own well-trained hands and flinging it out the window onto the passersby below.

Some of the titles that left our offices with my name printed in garish Franklin Gothic on the copyright page were: *The Battle of the Bulge as Witnessed by Me and Tom Rasking* by Lt. Col. Gerald "Flip" Craig, *Senior Citizens are Sexy, Too* by Jenny Vookles (that Jenny rankled, for a woman in her 80s), *Liposuction and You* by Dr. Vance Partridge, *Diddy-Wah-Diddy* by Resole McRey (surely a pseudonym—I wonder what *he* was hiding), *Tambourines, Pig-whistles and Daisies in Gun Barrels:*

A Nomocanon of Poems by Camel Jeremy Eros, *Huckleberry Finn, Racist* by Janet Grimace, *Love Gained, Lost and Regained* by Anonymous (hmm), *Southern Jewism and the Delta: A Prototype* by Shlomo Einstein, *I Fought the Gulf War by my Own Damn Self* by Larry "Renegade" Yates, and on and on.

And, in truth, some of these dogs sold. I imagine what happens is the author's hometown bookstore, some mom and pop place called Book Land, or The Book Rack, orders a couple hundred for a signing, and the author's friends and family feel obliged to come and actually purchase a copy. At least our books are inexpensive, comparatively. But, of course, we can afford to be. We are totally subsidized up front. And our author's contracts, well, I can't even discuss them. They are the special province of J. Quillmeier and J. Quillmeier alone. Who, by the way, is rarely in the office, the official statement being that he is having lunch with a client, or meeting with Japanese businessmen about overseas rights, or somesuch nonsense. But, those contracts, which are kept in locked files in his office, are as secret as the recipe for Coca-Cola. Very fishy, but I suspect our authors, for whom we promise to work very hard, pumping product out to the media-drenched society which awaits such drivel—we send out a single press release to a select group of bookstores and trade publications, total cost about $43— our poor deluded authors, I suspect never have made a penny from their Ardent contracts. This is just supposition on my part, but it is not without some basis in evidence. But, that's another story and not this one, and, to be honest, what the hell do I care? These schnooks knew they were buying their way into authordom. What did they expect? Had they ever seen an Ardent title on the bestseller lists? Had an Ardent author ever been on Oprah? No, they knew the pond they were fishing in was stocked and the catch was a cheat and they knew that in the end even the water in that pond would prove to be a sham, like the water under Casanova's boat in Fellini's film. I didn't care. Sorry.

The absence of the boss in the incommodious space of Ardent Publishing made for a sexual tension between Sherri and me, a delicious, daily sexual tension. Many days we spent with our respective tongues in each other's mouths, hands wandering the curvy landscapes that are the human body, heat rising like fervor from the Devil's kitchen. But, beyond experiencing how lovely Ms. Hoving felt through her midsection, or where her hip gently swayed into her tender thighs, or circumnavigating the sweet meat of her upper arms, and down her choice lower back which effortlessly tipped into her incredible hindquarters, and all this mostly through whatever silken material covered her winsome body that day, nothing else happened between us. Every time the caloric vigor rose to danger levels—she could feel my need through the front of her brief skirts I am quite sure—we swayed away, we danced into a joking middle ground where there was only close friendship, companionship, *flirting*. It was frustrating, of course. About equally as frustrating as wading through those irksome manuscripts, feeling myself dipped in bad prose as if in machine oil, or a particularly adhesive oleo.

Meanwhile, Sherri was the most professional secretary/jackie-of-all-trades I'd ever witnessed or worked with. She literally did everything for Ardent, from mailing out the many letters of acceptances, to keeping the books (and cashing those mendacious checks), to acting as go-between between the elusive Mr. Quillmeier and *anyone* else. I composed my own letters of acceptance (oh, sorry lies! oh, loathsome soft-soap!) and for that, and for my 200 word synopses, I called myself an editor. I collected a paycheck that allowed me to live in the hub of the publishing industry, the city which never sleeps.

It was around my one year anniversary at Ardent (my parents in their frequent phone calls and letters were fond of repeating to me the gloating and inflated remarks they made to their septuagenarian friends about their big-shot son), after a particularly dispiriting evening at Sherri's (we had actually unzipped a couple of pieces of clothing, almost touching various body parts through only one sheer layer of undergarment) I arrived about thirty minutes late to the office.

"Hey, Hotshot," Sherri said, a shy, almost frightened smile tempting the corners of her syrupy mouth.

"Hey, Sherri," I dropped.

"You okay? You look a little bedraggled. Maybe bed-raggled, eh?"

This was sexy banter to her, I suddenly realized. She thought what we had done the previous evening was highly erotic, would garner a couple of x's at least. Were there really young women this innocent living in New York City? The notion seemed ludicrous and I admit I was a bit cross.

"Not raggled enough, perhaps, lover?" I practically snarled.

Her face retreated like a beaten cur. She turned to her desk and made a show of shuffling around in the papers there. She turned with a snap and held out a slim stack of telltale, ecru 8 ½ by 11 envelopes.

I groaned.

"Mail's here already," she said, throwing a slight lilt into her speech, a pitiful attempt to cajole me into our old style.

"Thanks," I said and took the stack as if it were a flattened and exenterated piece of roadkill.

I sat at my desk and stared at the return addresses for many minutes, stalling, trying to gather what wits I had left. The work came from all over. America was awash in wannabe writers. There was Abe Peters, Lincoln, Nebraska; Rory Canseco, Wind River, Wyoming; Lauralyn

"Laurie" Enos, Fidelity, Georgia; Lamar Negri, Page, Washington (a writer's town, surely!); Kenny the Snake Girardi, Somerville, Tennessee. It was all so—debilitating. I was tired just holding these monstrosities. I punched them aside, dismissively. I couldn't do it. Not that day. Maybe never again.

I don't know what caught my attention, what about the envelope made it stick out—maybe it simple *stuck out*, lay uncovered in the cast aside heap. The envelope itself was smudged, as if handled by a car mechanic. Were it evidence in a police investigation the culprits prints were readable with a naked eye—there was no need to send these babies to the lab in Washington. And the return address said, simply, "City." Presumably, this meant this labor of love came from somewhere within the confines of our sprawling megalopolis. It was addressed "Ardent Publishing. Fiction Editor." And our address. Written in blurry pencil, as if from inside an aquarium. It was a wonder it made it to us, so indecipherable was the penmanship, so childlike the scrabble.

It was an exotic enough piece of communication that I slit it open right away. The yellow ledger-pad paper tumbled out as if enchanted, as if the pieces of foolscap were fey genii released from their bottle. They made a mad pile on my desk, papers from hell, or some suburb of hell reserved for the work of the crazed, for the products of contaminated minds. They scared me somehow, covered as they were with that same penciled scrawl, which seemed alive on the page, like some particularly loathsome form of insectivore, one which found its way into your bedclothes at night, one which entered your body through the soles of your feet and lodged someplace vital and vulnerable, slowly poisoning you, slowly fusing or liquefying your entire inner self. They were chthonic.

Yet, I could not look away.

The topsheet bore what I imagined was the title, flung across the head, above where the lines began, like on a school report. And the title was *Anima*, certainly a broad enough topic, I thought. And in more crabbed alphabetiforms, as if it pained the poor soul to pin his name on the page, as if, indeed, by pinning it there he may have trapped himself, below the larger title, it said: by Jim Nozoufist. And, of course, there amid the detritus which was his book lay his check, which I barely registered except to notice it was at least made out in ballpoint to Ardent Publishing, Publisher.

Ridiculous, I thought. Ridiculous title, absurd nom-de-plume. Who was this wise guy kidding? And, somewhere in the middle of my nonsensical fear, a small anger grew, a misplaced anger at this ridiculous Jim Nozoufist and his unsanitary manuscript. How dare he! I huffed. I sat back hard in my chair, which once again tilted dangerously, like a rolling log over a chasm. Sherri looked around hopefully with a can-I-help look on her exquisite, colorful face. I scowled back.

After a moment I picked up page one of *Anima* and began to read. I read the first sentence with a self-righteous mad on. I read the second sentence with a prickle like fever at the back of my neck. I read the third sentence, a sculpted piece of prose mastery worthy only of some pixilated offspring of Beckett and Virginia Woolf, with a growing sense of disbelief. Oh, my lares and penates!

An hour passed. Two. Somewhere beyond the periphery of my mindfulness I was cognizant of a sulking Sherri who went about her work, left for lunch, returned. It was four o'clock in the afternoon when I threw down the pages I still had in my hand and craned my stiff neck heavenward. It was unbelievable. It was preposterous. I looked guiltily around me, as if I had smuggled some plutonium and was squirreling it away in my desk drawer, or as if I had just inherited the secrets of eternal life and did not want to share them with anyone. Not even my sweetheart, not even my parents. Sherri turned inquisitively toward me but my face must have seemed deranged, goggle-eyed, for she crinkled up her nose and widened her beautiful mahogany blinkers and turned back to her own work. I took a series of deep breaths and leaned back precipitously in my chair. What was first an inkling of something *other* had become a faith in something grand. I had on my desk a masterpiece. A piece of the puzzle, the missing pieces perhaps in the puzzle of world literature. Or, so I felt initially.

No. It was stronger than that. I was sure. This was *it*. This was *the real thing*. And I was an editor at a dog-assed, corrupt publishing concern that would take this precious cargo and jettison it upon the world like another book of grandma's poetry, like another memoir of "My most memorable character." I surged with power, but it was a power checked, a light under a bushel, a light obliterated and trapped under a sleazy, perplexing bushel. But my metaphors run away. I had to think. I had to clear my mind and figure out *what to do*.

I gathered the pages together and stuffed them back into their envelope (they didn't want to fit, as if once oxygen had reached them they had expanded, full of life, or as if they would not be imprisoned again, ever again). I made a quick, rude excuse to Sherri, rushed past her and went immediately home.

I must keep *Anima* with me at all times. I must never let it out of my sight. These were my thoughts.

And I must find Jim Nozoufist. And tell him—what? That he was a genius, that he had written the most important novel since Joyce reconfigured things. Needless to say, I re-read the book in its entirety that night—it took me until the wee hours—and it only reinforced my opinion. This was the book that the literary world had been waiting for. It was an answer to questions we didn't even dare ask, questions we didn't know needed asking. And I owned it. *Anima* was mine.

2.

The address listed for the author of *Anima* was in a tony part of Manhattan, a part, quite honestly, where I rarely ventured, high rises where the word penthouse was tossed around lightly, where the recirculated air was ripe with the scent of freshly minted cash. Was it possible this adept was worth more than the entire publishing concern on which he was pinning his literary aspirations? Why didn't the joker just publish the book himself, certainly a time-honored way of appearing in print, and just slightly more expensive than turning over blood money to Ardent?

After some initial wrangling with a taciturn doorman, who insisted there was no one living in Two Towers by the name of Jim Nozoufist, a call was made to the apartment number written as the return address on the soiled envelope I had clenched under my jacket. (I had spent the earliest hours of the morning at Kinko's making a copy of *Anima*, which now resided in the locked drawer of my desk in my apartment.) Some muted conversation was made into the phone, while I stood by like a miscreant pupil, some description given of the personage wishing admittance I imagined, and after hanging up, the doorman simply opened the inner door without apology or even assent. I walked past him, hiking up my dignity, looking into his dead eyes as I walked unnecessarily close to him and into Two Towers.

The elevator stopped on the thirteenth floor and I bobbed down the thickly carpeted corridor to Apartment 1307 and lightly rapped on the door. After a few sweaty moments—was there another gauntlet to run before admittance?—the door opened and an astoundingly beautiful woman in her mid to late 50s stood there glittering like a prize. Her jewelry glittered, her dress glittered, her teeth glittered, even her décolletage, sprinkled with some kind of glitter makeup, glittered. She was smiling to beat the band.

"Mr. Brackett?" she twinkled.

"Yes," I said, transfixed by her. "Call me Todd." I was so nervous it came out "Dodd."

"Please come in."

I walked in as if I was being led past the pearly gates, mesmerized as much by this ideal of womanhood as by the incredible space into which I was coaxed. It might have been Gloria Vanderbilt's home, or, indeed, one of the nicer salas in Heaven. If my conscious brain was working at all it was chewing on the question, who is this ravishing dowager and what does she have to do with J. Nozoufist?

"Please sit," she gestured toward the plushest piece of furniture I had ever seen. I could have lived in it.

A gentleman appeared as if a bell sash had been pulled.

"Would you like some refreshment?" this lovely woman asked, all flickering eyes and teeth.

"No. Uh, actually, yes, some ice tea, if available," I managed.

"Ice tea, Noah," she spoke to the superannuated butler, and I assumed he really was the Biblical patriarch.

"I'm sorry, Mr. Brackett. How rude of me. I am Cecilia Quisby. My name may be familiar to you, though I'm well aware that it is not me who you are here to see."

I didn't know her from Betty Grable but I smiled and nodded. She seemed to know a lot more about whatever was happening than I did and in such situations I always find it best to keep mum until things begin to take shape. It didn't take long.

"You are looking for Jim," Cecilia Quisby shimmered.

"Yes," I said. "I'm from Ardent Pub—"

"Yes, I know. Jim sent you his book. I told him we could look elsewhere, but, well, Jim has a sort of stubbornness to him, which…"

She drifted away momentarily and I took the opportunity to try and win some respect from this imposing woman.

"Frankly, Mrs. Quisby—"

"Cecilia."

"Cecilia. Frankly, I think, just maybe, Mr. Nozoufist has written something really remarkable here."

"No," Cecilia Quisby spoke quickly and then caught herself. "I mean, really? It's, its good?'

"Um, yes. I believe it is quite good."

"Well, I'll be damned, excuse my Alabama backyard French," she said and sort of fell back into the couch, wherein she could have fallen quite a long way.

"Jim is a real writer, then?"

"I believe so."

"Hm," she said and she lay there, in a repose rather unladylike for someone so elegant, though it gave me ample time to run my eyes over her aged but stately figure. She was a supernatural being.

"Mrs. Quisby—Cecilia—who is Jim Nozoufist? Is he here? I would really love the opportunity to speak with him about his book and about the possibilities I think—"

"Jim's not here at the moment, Todd," she spoke, familiarly, and she rose up to a more upright posture and placed a warm hand on my knee. It burned through my cheap suit pants. Up my leg went the heat of torment.

Letting the fluster pass, I took a difficult swallow of ice tea, which Noah had delivered I know not when, but which, magically, appeared near my right hand.

"Is Jim Nozoufist your husband, Ma'am?" I don't know where the Southernism came from, triggered no doubt by her mention of Alabama.

She let loose a cachinnate fanfare. "Oh, my, no," she said. "Jim, well, Jim, works for me."

"As?" I asked without thought.

"Oh, odd jobs. When a woman reaches my age she needs some seeing to. Jim does a little driving for me, a little grocery shopping, that sort of thing."

"I see. Well, I don't want to take up too much of your time. When can I speak to him? It's rather urgent," I added, self-importantly.

"Noah," Cecilia Quisby spoke in conversational tones and the man was suddenly there. "Call Jim and have him come straight over."

Noah nodded, I think, and left the room.

Cecilia smiled her bright white smile at me and we sat in silence for a few moments and I sipped at the ice tea without tasting it.

After a while she scooted a half-inch closer to me, leaned forward and replaced the hand on my knee, perhaps a measurable space higher on my thigh. This woman knew men. She knew me and she had me and she knew she had me. I didn't care. It was literature a-calling and, for the moment, even the sexual flirtation of such an attractive woman took a backseat.

"Todd," she said, as if about to let me in on a family secret. "Prepare yourself for Jim. He may not be what you were expecting."

"Ok," I said, though I wasn't aware of expecting anything.

A moment later there was the sound of activity coming from the kitchen area.

"I believe he's here now," Cecilia Quisby said, rising from the couch. Putting space between us was both a relief and an agony.

What emerged from the rear of the apartment was indeed not what I had expected no matter what I had expected. Neanderthal was an unavoidable reference term and had I Tourrette's syndrome no doubt I would have spoken the word aloud. Jim Nozoufist was a man about the same age as Mrs. Quisby, though through grime and facial hair it was difficult to ascertain much about the man. He was positively pithecoid. Surely this was just some poor homeless gull they brought up to impersonate the author. His dungy attire—ankle-length, soot-grey raincoat, unbuttoned formerly white shirt, oversize achromatic pants, squalid, unlaced hightops—reminded me of the costume Ian Anderson of Jethro Tull used to sport in his early rhythm and blues days, a sort of crazed, exhibitionist, street person affectation. Indeed he somewhat resembled Mr. Anderson in the uncouthness of his wild appearance. Aqualung with an Olivetti, I thought. No one could have been more out of place in Cecilia Quisby's elegant apartment.

"Jim, come here," Cecilia beckoned with a bejeweled hand. "This is Todd Brackett from Ardent Publishing. He's here about your book."

No change of expression occurred on the exanimate face of the feral fellow. Did he understand? Was he capable of more than animal instinct?

He shuffled forward and extended a meaty and distinctly unclean hand. I took it gently but he squeezed like an Irishman in a pub contest and when I drew my smarting body part back I found myself imagining all sorts of disease, scrud or double scrud. I wanted to bolt for the bathroom.

Professionalism reigned.

"Mr. Nozoufist? As Mrs. Quisby said, I'm from Ardent and I've had the pleasure of reading your manuscript, your, um, novel, *Anima*, and I'm quite taken with it. I believe you have a real gift. I have taken it upon myself to contact you personally, not standard procedure perhaps at Ardent, but I was moved to do so by the particularity of your work, by its special otherness, which it is my belief may just be something very special in the world of contemporary letters." I felt as if I was talking to an actor standing in for the real author. At no time during my speech did I believe this was the author of the book I still had clenched inside my jacket. I also felt orotund and absurd in my language and as if I was talking over the poor man's head.

There now emerged from somewhere inside the whiskers and grime on Mr. Nozoufist's facade a deep growl or grumble. Bubbles of saliva formed in his mustache. Fear flashed through me—perhaps he was an epileptic, perhaps he was about to bite my neck—but I glanced at Cecilia and she was smiling beatifically. This calmed me somewhat.

"I'd like Ardent to publish *Anima*," he said.

I nodded and was about to open negotiations—whatever those were going to be—when he sputtered further.

"Cecilia sent the check. We've paid," he said, and looked to his patron for reassurance. Cecilia moved to him and took his filthy arm in hers and placed a kiss on his hispid cheek. He smiled, a horrible smile, a monster's lascivious grin.

It suddenly occurred to me that Jim Nozoufist did a little more than some grocery shopping for this woman. There was a warmth between them one sees in movies, that romantic shorthand which says, *intimacy*. It made me feel unwell for some reason.

"Mr. Nozoufist, rest assured that all is satisfactory in your prepayment and the contract that denotes. Ardent would be proud to publish your novel. Ardent would be more than proud. Ardent should get down on its collective knees (here a brief flash of Sherri's lovely face threw a blinding flare over my vision) and beg to publish *Anima*. What I'm saying is—"

And, here I was at the moment of truth, the moment I had been dreading. What was my plan? Did I think I could parlay this man's talent, this wild man's exotic talent, into some kind of score for Todd Brackett? What were my motives? I had convinced myself that they were pure and that the main thing, the *important* thing was to get this book into print and into wide distribution, where it could, rightly or wrongly, upset the placid and smug and dull ship of state which was modern fiction.

"What is it, Todd?" Cecilia asked with genuine concern in her voice.

"I think *Anima* may be the greatest novel of its, of our, time."

I said it. I laid it out there like a taunt and I did not know, in this extraordinary company, where such a taunt would lead. I did not know who would pick it up.

After a pregnant moment, our aberrant author spoke.

"You do work for Ardent, don't you?" It was somewhere between a growl and a barroom challenge.

"Yes, yes," I assured. "But, this book, this marvelous book, is something quite uncommon. Quite frankly, it is too good for Ardent. I mean, we are fine for what we do, but, Mr. Nozoufist, Jim, if I may, *Anima* needs one of the big boys. It needs a Knopf, a Farrar Straus & Giroux. It needs a Gary Fisketjohn. It needs a Liz Darahnsof. It needs paperback rights, foreign rights, electronic rights, Hollywood representation, for Christ's sake!" I was sweating. "This is a major book. A searingly significant, important book." I finished with a deep breath as if I had sprinted here from Newark.

"I don't understand a word you're saying," Cecilia Quisby let out. "And I'm sure Jim doesn't either. With your Fiskyjons and your Jews and your Darryn Soft, Mr. Brackett, Todd, we are simple people. What are you suggesting?"

I didn't know. Could I tell them I didn't know? That even I was out of my depth?

"I don't know," I said.

"Ardent's good enough for me," the musty giant now spat out and strode out of the room so quickly it left me speechless. I looked at Cecilia Quisby—she smiled like the opening of the moon—and a few minutes later I was walking back toward Ardent, shell-shocked. The manuscript was still tucked under my jacket and my arm was cramped from the tension of holding it there. I had never even brought it out, examined it in front of its exotic creator, showed him that I knew my way around a work of fiction. I only then understood that that was what I had desired—to prove myself to the author of such an eccentric masterpiece. I had expected to be parlaying with someone along the lines of Mervyn Peake or Alexander Theroux.

Cecilia Quisby was right. I hadn't expected Jim Nozoufist. I hadn't expected a madman. And, now, where were we?

Sherri was playing coy when I returned to the office, playing at avoiding my eyes but giving me uncertain, saucy side-glances at every opportunity. I sat down at my desk and stared straight ahead. My head was full of expensive perfume and deodorized penthouse air and Cecilia Quisby's squeezable bosom and her hand which generated heat like a magnifying glass and the sweet rot of old flesh and fetid clothing and the incredible, exploding encyclopedia, which hovered above it all, that book called *Anima*. I finally remembered to unclench my arm and release the manuscript and I lay it in front of me atop the numerous unopened envelopes that would make up Ardent's Spring list.

I believe Sherri hissed or made some noise, which was not quite human speech, and I slowly turned toward her. She smiled a delicate, infirm smile.

My heart beat hard once or twice—there was pain there—should I worry? And then I opened my arms and Sherri Hoving slid across the room and onto my lap and her warm mouth covered mine and her tongue swelled into me and I lost, momentarily, all my worries as my blood careened around in my body looking for the place it was needed most. It found my loins.

Sherri felt the stiffening there and she loosened her kiss slightly and looked into my eyes. Her hand went South, where the trouble was, and opened my tensions to the air and it was that handjob at my desk—that release—in the middle of a most troublesome workday, which began to crystallize things for me. Which began to set a course for myself, for Sherri Hoving, and for our demented ward, the foul and priestly Jim Nozoufist.

Through Cecilia Quisby I set up a meeting with our author for the following day at a coffeeshop near Ardent and I asked Sherri to join us. My reasons for doing this were a bit confused, but it's safe to say, I wanted a witness. I wanted backup. And I counted on her to be true to her pseudo-lover and I counted on her unique capacity for organization, something this situation was in desperate need of.

I sketched the situation for Sherri and throughout my extravagant tale she looked at me wide-eyed, her moist mouth forming a series of variations on ohs and ovals. At the end of my recitation—and I told her almost everything, including my reticence about seeing this work of literature go through the mill which was vanity publishing—her doe eyes blinked once or twice and then she was all business. I told you she was the glue which held Ardent together and that professionalism took over and she immediately began making notes and gathering together a file, a file which would remain a secret between her and me, under the name "Anima, Nozoufist." The Anima, Nozoufist file. I believe she felt that this secret was further cement to our "understanding," though, for the time being, the personal was a back burner for me.

We arrived at the coffee shop about fifteen minutes early, such was our excitement and nervousness to set this thing into motion, whatever this thing was to be. With Sherri's encouragement our plan was simple, at least as far as step one went. Beyond step one was a haze of possibility, a scrim over the future which seemed murky and confusing and even perhaps a little dangerous, though I didn't at the time have anything to be afraid of. We sat over our dry bagels and weak joe and our conversation was scant and clipped, airy like a tattered flag. The fifteen minutes passed and then another fifteen and Sherri looked at me with an anxiety in her boyishly resplendent features which was overflowing with sympathy and concern. I believe she might have, for just a moment, believed I had made up Jim Nozoufist out of whole cloth, however exotic that cloth would have to be. I admit that I even had the passing notion that I had imagined the man, something from some primitive consciousness welling up like a bad dream, something unreal, a bit of undigested beef perhaps.

Just as exasperation began to take over I saw through the shop's wide glass window the madman author striding our way, crossing against traffic as if he were indestructible, walking almost totally erect. To say he burst into the coffeeshop is to resort to cliché, but Nozoufist practically thrust the door off its hinges, so exaggeratedly violent was his ingress. Sherri jumped in her seat as I stood to beckon the Yeti over. Jim wore the same outfit I had seen him in earlier. Sherri wore a look of what might be described as professional doubt, mixed with, I think, bemusement.

The waitress eyed us askance now but took our order for another cup of their dishwater coffee and a round of eggs and toast for our guest.

"Jim," I began, "This is Sherri Hoving from our office."

"Pleased," Jim grunted and put a hoary hand out, which missed Sherri's delicate attempt at a handshake and ended up gripping her forearm as if this were a meeting of two Vikings.

Step One was this: we were going to convince Jim Nozoufist to make us his independent agents. Sherri had sketched out a contract which gave us full power to place *Anima* where we thought best and make what demands we could, reaping only a measly 15% of whatever profits befell us. The important thing, the *only* thing, was to get *Anima* into bookstores, onto library shelves, into the right critics' hands, to get the damn thing *recognized*. The inchoate contract also gave full editorial decision-making to Todd Brackett, but with final say on any changes to the author.

Nozoufist seemed to chew on these terms at about the same frenetic and unwholesome way he dug into his toast and eggs. We could not look at him and spent the tense minutes looking at each other with, for want of a better word, affection. Our eyes may have been dewy.

"Ardent doesn't want it," he said, finally.

"No, no," I quickly corrected him. "Ardent would publish it in a heartbeat. Cash Cecilia's check and throw *Anima* out there. But, you have to understand Ardent would publish the ravings of any lunatic who could muster the money to pay their fees. They would publish that surly waitresses' love poems to her trucker boyfriend. Ardent is not about editorship. Ardent is about taking money from people who are desperate to have something, anything in print. *Anima* on the other hand is a life-changing work of the imagination. We can take it just about anywhere we want and get some real attention generated. We can make you famous, if that's not putting the inappropriate slant on it."

"Ardent is for the odes or autobiographies of retired doctors and lawyers, who have nothing better to do with the money they've made grinding the noses of the poor," Sherri put in. I squeezed her knee.

"Hmm," Jim Nozoufist said, maybe through his nose.

"We'll take full responsibility," I added. "If we fail to produce anything greater—but there is little chance of that—we can always fall back on Ardent."

"Ok, then," the mammalian author said, rising quickly from his seat. This time his handshakes hit their marks and he was gone, seemingly carried out by a gust of wind from the reek of New York, a wind up from the subways, smelling of urine and lost dreams and the foul decay of a once great city.

Sherri and I looked at each other. She couldn't suppress a tight giggle.

"Well, we got what we wanted," she said. "What next?"

"I'll make some calls," I said. "You make up a formal contract and we'll get that to Mr. Nozoufist and get this ball rolling." I smiled with a confidence that was the confidence of a child becoming an adult. I was making it.

Sherri and I walked back into the office holding hands like Hansel and Gretel, cooing at each other, snickering like schoolchildren. We were met by the grim countenance of our plenitudinous boss.

"Hello, Mr. Quillmeier," Sherri said, seriously suddenly, with more aplomb than I could have mustered.

"Early lunch?" he asked.

"Meeting with an author," I said, but from Sherri's darting eyes I knew I had blundered.

"We don't meet with authors," J. Quillmeier firmly informed me. "We publish their shitty books and cash their checks and move on."

"Is that on our logo?" I asked, sarcasm born of this newly acquired and foolhardy confidence.

Mr. Quillmeier glowered. He placed a chubby hand on a chubby hip and looked us over as if he didn't quite know what we were up to, into mother's cosmetics, perhaps, or sneaking out back with the airplane glue.

"Who is this author who demands such attention?" he asked.

It was a fair question. Unfortunately, it caught the two of us, answerless. We stared straight ahead. My armpits filled with moisture.

J. Quillmeier had us and let us run, cruelly, like hooked fish, which he only wanted the barb to dig deeper into. He stood before us like the Colossus of Rhodes for a few minutes while we fidgeted and cleared our throats.

"Was it perhaps James Nozoufist?" he asked.

We were stricken. We looked stricken.

"How—" was as far as I got.

"Cecilia Quisby is a very old and dear friend, my compatriots. She phoned me at home to find out how long until we could expect to see her man's book in the bookstores."

"Cecilia Quisby told me she tried to talk Nozoufist out of publishing with Ardent," I said, floundering, fighting for my life.

"A blind. She sent the book in through the regular channels, but, still was not above a phone call to an old admirer to grease the works. Seems she had a visit, a peculiar visit, from our chief editor who did nothing but confuse her about our intentions. Quite inappropriate. Hence, the call."

"Ahem," I believe I said.

J. Quillmeier waited.

"Mr. Quillmeier, this book, by this friend of your friend, is, well, it's quite a book."

"And?"

"And I think, maybe, it's just, sort of, not for Ardent."

J. Quillmeier waited another painful minute, looked at me, looked with not a little disappointment at Sherri, and then spoke, with decisive finality.

"You're fired," he said, poking a sausage-shaped finger at my sternum.

"And you," he said, hesitating as he turned toward the soul of his publishing house, and in that moment of hesitation, Sherri Hoving, God bless her, moved in my direction and slipped her frabjous arm through mine in a show of confederacy. "Well, you're fired, too," he was forced to add.

He then rolled into the inner recesses of his private den, a bear who must certainly go into hibernation, at least temporarily, with no Sherri Hoving around to keep his affairs in order.

"Well," I said, exhaling for the first time in ten minutes.

"We're out on the street," Sherri said, with brave calm.

"But we have *Anima*," I said. And I think I really believed it was a charm, a shield, a mojo against the perilous future.

Of course, in the following days, there was a back and forth wrangle between myself and J. Quillmeier about who indeed did own the rights to the wondrous Gordian knot which was *Anima*. It was the most conversation I had with the man in the nearly thirteen months since I had come to work for him. He was a surprisingly savvy combatant. I say surprisingly, because, one must ask, what is he doing running this shill game for suckers if he has the smarts to do better work.

It was my, our, contention that the author had signed a binding contract with us (he actually had not at this time, but the contract was professionally drawn up by my amorous conspirator and awaited only a meeting with the author for the proverbial eyes to be crossed, etc.) and that he had no such contract with Ardent Publishing. It was J. Quillmeier's retort, as one might expect, that the check, which he had quickly cashed, from Cecilia Quisby, constituted a contract and one which he had already made moves to justify by putting the manuscript through the motions of getting into shoddy print and between two glued-together cardboard covers and hence turned into a proud Ardent book. I doubted this contention, simply because we had both copies of the manuscript, and though it was possible he had obtained another from

Cecilia Quisby, J. Quillmeier had not the means nor the wherewithal to get the whole process rolling by his own rolling self. At least, this is what Sherri and I fervently hoped.

We believed, though, that we had to move quickly.

We set up another meeting with Jim in the coffee shop (as we now began to call him whenever we referred to him, the familiarity meaning—what?—a confidence that he was ours, that we were going to ride his raggle-taggle coattails into literary stardom). We anticipated trouble arranging said meeting, but Cecilia betrayed no loyalty to her old friend JQ, and readily set us up with our author but she also did not offer *his* address. It was an unspoken part of the dealings that everything would be funneled through the glamorous and ladylike hands of Cecilia Quisby.

Jim was late again. Sherri and I sat in worried silence, holding hands lightly, fingertips to fingertips, across the tabletop, casting strained, grim smiles at each other as each additional five minutes ticked away. Finally, Jim was blown in, by that same ill wind, leaves and detritus seemingly swirling around him, his hair a tangled mass, full of birds' nests and insect larvae and perhaps the missing body of James Hoffa. He threw himself into the booth on Sherri's side, fairly slamming against her but not upending her tight smile.

"Ok," he began, as if he had called this meeting. He was all at once in charge and it momentarily upset me.

"What you got for Old Jim?" he asked, a piratical jolliness inflecting his voice, unlike anything we had heretofore witnessed.

"A contract," Sherri said, briskly, whipping it out from her briefcase and laying it on the yolk stained Formica.

Jim looked down at it the way first man must have looked at first fire.

"It says, basically, what?" Jim said, quickly, as if to hide his embarrassment at not understanding the legal jargon before him. "You own me. You own *Animus*. You get all the money."

I didn't know if he was kidding or not. I didn't know if he was capable of kidding.

"Of course not," I said. "Just as we discussed. We will do everything in our power, *everything* to see that *Animus* gets the publishing contract it deserves, including all foreign rights, paperback rights, etc. at the best house possible and for the most money available. We vow to do this not only on this piece of paper in front of you but, here, to your face, with honest and heartfelt integrity. We will get your book the attention it deserves and for that we get 15% of all profits."

"15%," Jim said.

"That's fairly common, low even. Understand, Mr. Nozoufist, we have given up all other work to pursue this. We have no other job but getting this book out and reaping the rewards it deserves. We have, you might say, put all our eggs in one basket, laid our whole lives on the line," Sherri put in.

Nozoufist looked at me with what I thought was a twinkle in his eye—he resembled briefly a deranged Santa Claus—and then at Sherri the same way. Suddenly he leant over and kissed my compatriot full on the mouth, pulling back like a drunkard who has just taken a large draught of a rich ichor. A smile opened up the box of snakes which was his visage.

"Let's do it," he said.

I was taken aback. But then I smiled just as quickly and took his callused hand into mine and gave it a hearty shake. Fellow-feeling flowed.

Sherri, recovering from her bestial buss, pointed a red-nailed finger at the line on the contract where Jim was to put his John Hancock and brought out a pen from her lap with which he would sign. Jim gripped the pen like it was a Louisville slugger. Just for a second I thought he might make a crude X on the space provided, but he signed with a flourish, his name a dance of curlicues and embellishment, ending with a singular paraph.

"Good," he said. And he was gone.

Although tangential to the tale, now might be the time to discuss the nature of the relationship so recently born between the lithe Sherri Hoving and your humble narrator. After that unexpected office manipulation of my *membrum virile*, I supposed, naturally, that we had embarked on that journey which takes a couple of ordinary human beings and transforms them into the *coniunctio spirituum;* in short, that we were now a fully feathered couple, free to partake of each other's intimacies, privileged to feel the human warmth and moisture at the heart of the creature called man (and woman). I thought, bluntly put, that we would be fucking and soon.

It was not to be. Instead we regressed. That workaday pizzle-pull was not repeated and when our tongue sucking grew too intense Sherri again began that coy retreat which had initially signaled to me that we were not to be, couplewise. It was frustrating and may or may not bear on the frustrations to follow. I am not a Freudian disciple and do not pretend to possess the ability to explain human endeavor in terms of inner chemistry, misfiring neurons, bad potty training, want of breastfeeding as a child. So what follows followed. My flesh-loneliness is, most probably, only a not-so-interesting sidebar.

The truth was we couldn't place *Anima*. Much to my chagrin and shock, even when we were able to get the thing into what I would have supposed to be sympathetic hands, we got kind dismissals, compliments galore, but no takers. Roger Giroux himself penned a quick note, calling the book a "spiritual cousin to *Confederacy of Dunces*," but his house passed on it, seemingly against his wishes, but it's hard to tell. And, besides,

I thought, Jim Nozoufist could write rings around that poor dead Louisianan. If he were alive, I guess I mean.

I was flummoxed. I was confounded and astonished. We tried half a dozen major houses, both Sherri and I calling in whatever tenuous connections we boasted and received little or no encouragement. Could it be that I was wrong about *Anima*, about its place in the line of literature which went from Homer to Rabelais to Sterne to Joyce and then, unerringly, I believed, to our own beloved dement. No, I was not wrong. This was a hell of a book, a world-beater. It was the times that were to blame. I was not the first to decry the shallowness which had overtaken the culture, from idiotic TV, to bright, shiny, big-spectacle movies as empty as raided graves, to art which only imitated art which had self-consciously imitated art before it but at least for a laugh, right up to and including the now conglomerate-controlled publishing houses, where there were only *acquisitions* editors, where there was the search for the next *Bridges of Madison County* ongoing, but not the next Thomas Pynchon. I knew it. I knew it all. Maxwell Perkins was dead, as dead as Marley. I knew it but I still hoped. Surely, there was a place for genius still, a place for something as fresh and new and invigorating as Jim Nozoufist and his cracked, portmanteau tome.

Six months passed in this way. Increasingly frantic phone calls, faxes, letters, cold-call visits to houses we only knew the names of. We worked out of Sherri's apartment, where it was comfortable and clean and she cooked wonderful meals of couscous and exotic vegetables. She told me to stop worrying about money and I did, for minutes at a time, but things were not going well. Soon we would have to admit that we had to look for work—continue our ceaseless search for a home for *Anima*—but, at the same time, do something, however menial, to pay the bills.

It was about this time when I got a call from Cecilia Quisby. She was concise on the phone, but not unfriendly, and she wanted the four of us to get together to discuss the future of Jim's book. I was to pick her up at half-past seven and proceed to her private club, where a dinner would be waiting for us, over which we could make some plans on what to do next. It sounded good. It sounded wrong. But, what choice did we have?

Also, she added, could Ms. Hoving pick Jim up, and she rattled off a quick address.

I arrived at Two Towers at seven fifteen, dressed in my best suit, which was a poor imitation of good grooming, nervous as sunlight. This time the doorman parted the waters for me immediately and I proceeded up to Cecilia Quisby's wondrous place of residence, feeling like a kid on a first date.

Knowing my early arrival was rude I rapped lightly on Cecilia's door. It took some 90 seconds or so—an eternity—before the door was opened and there stood Dame Quisby herself. I had, of course, expected Lurch and was embarrassed to find Cecilia at the door dressed only in a housecoat, albeit a sheer, sparkling housecoat. The shins which showed beneath the elegant hem of her garment, though aged, shone like ambergris and her toenails were painted a pale shade of lavender, which made my heart do a sad drumroll.

"I'm so sorry I'm early," I sputtered.

"Nonsense," she said, waving me in.

I shuffled in, a child, a nullity in her reflective radiance.

"I'm afraid Noah is off for the evening, so if you could just make yourself comfortable while I dress," she said gesturing vaguely toward all that was hers.

"Certainly," I said.

She wafted away toward her bedroom and I spent some time examining the art on the walls. All the names were familiar. All the paintings were authentic.

"We're not having much luck with Jim's book," she called from the recesses of her apartment. It was a statement, almost, but not quite, a challenge.

"No," I admitted. I began my rant about the unappreciated prophet, the overemphasized profit, etc. She cut me off with a reverberating contralto.

"La di da, Todd," she sang. "You underestimate yourself. You have literature in your veins."

I let a few moments pass. I had no answer.

"Is that not true?" she asked, this time the challenge more clearly delineated.

"Well, I've tried all I know. I've called in all my markers. I've—"

"Todd. Todd, come here," she spoke, as if I were her stubborn spaniel.

I walked slowly toward the doorway to her bedroom. I didn't want to go there. I was sore afraid.

I stood in the doorway but my eyes were on my shoes.

"Look at me, Todd," she commanded.

I raised my face, knowing what would be there. Cecilia Quisby sat on the edge of her bed putting her stockings on. They were the kind that stayed up only by the magic of their darker top halves. I was looking at quite a bit of the fifty-year-old Cecilia Quisby and I was thoroughly impressed by what she was showing me. Her body, covered here and there with bits of lace and whalebone perhaps, was a wonder, for all its wrinkles and extra flesh. The places of extra flesh seemed derived from Elysian fields, fruit from the garden Adam was born in. I could not help but survey it.

Cecilia Quisby smiled like a ring-dove. Her remonstration was temporarily halted so she could address this new question, the question of what she was going to do about the lust she had engendered in me.

"You don't think I'm too old and used," she said, a hint of

insecurity in her voice, but a voice which quavered like a taper. She lightly spread her arms and revealed herself all the more. She was an aged Delilah, but the temptations were nonetheless irresistible.

"You're the most beautiful thing I've ever seen," I said. And I meant it.

"Come here, Todd," she said, and, of course I did.

I stood next to the bed and she wrapped her arms around me and put her cheek on my zipper and held me there like a queen making time-honored use of some hierodule. I ran my hands over what parts I could reach—shoulders, her slightly furry cheeks, her still glossy though graying hair, the tops of her bare breasts—but I felt as if I were straightjacketed.

What happened between Cecilia Quisby and me should not be made public knowledge. Things occurred in that plush and mirrored bedroom which I will forever want repeated, will forever be tortured for wanting them repeated. She was a remarkable woman.

After our athletic endeavors Cecilia Quisby begged off on the remainder of the evening, citing fatigue, headache, surprise, new things she would have to digest.

"Could we do this tomorrow night?" she asked from amid her pillows and silks.

I hoped for a moment she meant, well, at any rate, she meant the dinner/meeting.

"Of course," I said. I bent to kiss her on the cheek as I left and she turned slightly, I thought away from my lips, but perhaps it was just an awkward parting. I left feeling wrung out. I had at least, for the first time in a while, if only for an hour or so, forgotten *Animus* and the pledge that hung over me like the sword of Damocles. I forgot it until I arrived at Sherri's and found her in tears, her clothing torn, a bruise swelling up under her left eye like an ugly toad.

When she lifted her face to me it brought a more frantic flood of tears. She sobbed like a nun with stigmata, my name spewing from her blubbering like a curse.

"Wh-where were you?" she asked.

"Picking up Cecilia—what the hell happened?" I sat down by her and put my arms around her only to be pushed away.

"He tried to rape me, you shit," she managed to get out.

"Who?" I said, automatically, though I knew. Of course I knew.

"That beast, you selfish jackass. That goat-footed author of that horrid, horrid book. I never want to see him again. I never want to see *you* again."

"Sherri, you don't mean that," I started.

She was suddenly, fiercely calm. She looked at me with the face of an unrepentant killer about to be electrocuted.

"I do, though. I mean it. He attacked me. He thought it was part of the *deal*. God knows what goes on in that beastly mind of his. And you, while you were sporting with that rich—" here tears took over again.

"He *told* you that, that I was bedding Cecilia Quisby?" I sputtered in mock outrage, my face coloring with shame.

"Get out, Todd. That animal tried to put his thick dirty prick into me and I will never forget that and never forgive you for it. Get out."

I started another weak protest but I was beat. I was beat all to hell. I didn't know who I was, where I was from, who was on my side or who wasn't, or even if I was on my own side. I wandered out onto the rebarbative sidewalks and meandered around for a few hours. I was as loose as the trash blowing up Fifth Avenue. I was as pointless.

What had happened was this:

Jim Nozoufist and Cecilia Quisby, apparently in frustration over our impotence, our ignorance, our inability to get *Anima* published, had re-established contact with Ardent Publishing and J. Quillmeier and had signed with him (in apparent disregard for the contract Nozoufist had with us, but we were weak as kittens afterwards—we were cowed, subjugated—and they knew it) to bring the novel out as the sole offering from Ardent in the Fall of that year.

They also, coincidentally, had made a more personal, more vindictive pact to humiliate us, use us, show us that power in the circles they frequented had to do with who had whose dick. In the case of Cecilia Quisby's seduction this amounted to a fairly memorable and aristocratic, almost feline, display of how a woman controls a man, how she has him like a leopard on a leash. In the case of the less sophisticated Jim Nozoufist this amounted to a savage attack on Sherri that included tearing her blouse and blackening her eye. Sherrifa Hoving would never press charges, for her own personal reasons, which I can only guess at. Shortly, after this, I heard she moved out west and was working for one of those fancy book houses, one which makes a living publishing books of immaculate glossies of baby-boomer memorabilia, books for *Architectural Digest* coffee tables, gorgeous books, empty as skulls. I never heard from her again.

Ironically, sadly, *Anima*, was never published. Either Cecilia Quisby and J. Quillmeier made their own secret concordat and shelved the book for reasons of their own or they came up with a better plan.

Six months later there appeared on the literary horizon a new publishing house, Quillmeier Books. Its sole first offering was a potboiler entitled *Run for It*. You know the story. It went into multiple printings, launched the publishing house making James and Cecilia Quillmeier the toasts of bookdom, sold to the Book of the Month club, went to NAL for a cool million mass market rights, and the movie version, starring Bruce Willis and Natalie Portman was said to be filming in Chicago, where they were having script problems which were to delay the actual release of the film until the fall of the following year.

Run for It, the book, was seemingly everywhere at once: in every chain bookstore window, in every glossy magazine's book review section, no matter how perfunctory (*People* called it "John Grisham with extra adrenaline."), in the laps of every commuter. Its author, a James Skald, had his handsome kisser spread across America like a new brand of cereal. Or a new hostage crisis; he practically had his own theme music. He was on Oprah, he was on Charlie Rose, he was on NPR.

And James Skald, household name, with a face now as familiar as Dan Rather's, seemed to have come from nowhere. Was he affected by his time with Jim and *Anima*? How could he not be? The book must have entered his DNA, like a virus, or a shot of an ecclesiastical adrenaline. Skald had a burnished, prizefighter's mug, somewhat ruddy, perhaps freckled (it was hard to tell through the makeup and TV lights), and his clean-shaven jaw was as chiseled and well-cornered as a bank building. Still, if you squinted and held up *Time*'s cover to the right light you could see a bit of wildness there, underneath the well-groomed and artificial map. Somewhere under the sleek surface of that face which had been configured for television to consume and disseminate there was something almost sinister, almost feral. It's the beast inside man, I guess. We all have it.

But, some nights, here in Pittsburgh, where I moved and got a job at another bookstore, some late nights, when I'm lonely and I'm thinking about the snake-like shapeliness of Sherri Hoving or the delights of Cecilia Quisby's venerable body, I'll pull out *Anima* and read sections of it to myself. Or aloud if I've had a couple of drinks. Or sometimes even over the phone to family or friends back home, who wonder why I've called after all these years just to spout off some baffling jabber into the plastic receiver they clutch to their ears as if they expect real communication from it.

And I marvel, still, still I marvel, at the magisterial sentences, at the distilled but cockamamie wisdom, at the fantastical, magical, misbegotten, empyrean *otherness* which is this novel, *Anima,* destined to die with me, to know only the life which I bring to it.

Acknowledgements

"How to be a Man" in Esquire/Narrative 4 and in *As a Child: Stories* (MadHat Press, 2014)

"Supermarket" in Orchid and in *Notes toward the Story and Other Stories* (Aqueous Books, 2012)

"God and the Devil: The Exit Interview" in Grey Sparrow and in *As a Child: Stories* (MadHat Press, 2014)

"Monster" in Gargoyle and in *Notes toward the Story and Other Stories* (Aqueous Books, 2012)

"Everything $20" in Whisky Blot

"The Slim Harpo Blues" in Blue Crow Magazine and in *As a Child: Stories* (MadHat Press, 2014)

"He's Gone" in Ping Pong and in *As a Child* (MadHat Press, 2014)

"Any Day is a Good Day that Doesn't Start with Killing a Rat with a Hammer" in Storgy

"The Hen Man" in Wandering Army and in *Listen: 29 Short Conversations* (Pocketful of Scoundrel Press, 2009)

"Adman" in Heat City Review and in *Listen: 29 Short Conversations* (Pocketful of Scoundrel Press, 2009)

"The Stranger" in Grey Sparrow and in *I'll Give You Something to Cry About* (Queen's Ferry Press, 2011)

"Chip" in Grey Sparrow and in *As a Child: Stories* (MadHat Press, 2014)

"His Last Work" in Art Times and in *Listen: 29 Short Conversations* (Pocketful of Scoundrel Press, 2009)

"Blue Positive" in *As a Child: Stories* (MadHat Press, 2014)

"Barbra and Chuck Said We'd Like Each Other" in Internet Fiction and in *Listen: 29 Short Conversations* (Pocketful of Scoundrel Press, 2009)

"Alan's Approach" in Strawberry Press and in *As a Child: Stories* (MadHat

Press, 2014)

"Hypnotic Induction" in Raging Face and in *Listen: 29 Short Conversations* (Pocketful of Scoundrel Press, 2009)

"Shadow Work" in The Pinch and in *Notes toward the Story and Other Stories* (Aqueous Books, 2012)

"From the Desk of Jojo Self" in Monkeybicycle and in *I'll Give You Something to Cry About* (Queen's Ferry Press, 2011)

"A Walk in the Woods" in Thieves' Jargon and in *Listen: 29 Short Conversations* (Pocketful of Scoundrel Press, 2009)

"Mystical Participation" Cellar Door and in *Notes toward the Story and Other Stories* (Aqueous Books, 2012)

"Conjuration: A Fabliau" in Summerset Review and in *Diddy-Wah-Diddy: A Beale Street Suite* (Ampersand Press, 2013)

"The Day the Change Came for James" in Prime Number and in *I'll Give You Something to Cry About* (Queen's Ferry Press, 2011)

"The History of the Memphis 4-H Group" in Otoliths and in *I'll Give You Something to Cry About* (Queen's Ferry Press, 2011)

"Aftermath" in Quick Fiction and in Uncle John's Flush Fiction and in *Notes toward the Story and Other Stories* (Aqueous Books, 2012)

"The Plot to Kidnap Stonehenge" in From the Asylum and in *Re-Telling* (Ampersand Books, 2011) and in *Listen: 29 Short Conversations* (Pocketful of Scoundrel Press, 2009)

"Waiting for the Train" in Five Points

"Publisher" in Southern Gothic and as a chapbook in the Overtime Chapbook Series (Workers Write Journal Press, 2007) and in *I'll Give You Something to Cry About* (Queen's Ferry Press, 2011)

Books by Corey Mesler:

Poetry

For Toby, Everything for Toby (1997) Wing & The Wheel Press

Ten Poets (1999) editor, only Wing & The Wheel Press

Piecework (2000) Wing & The Wheel Press

Chin-Chin in Eden (2003) Still Waters Press

Dark on Purpose (2004) Little Poem Press

The Hole in Sleep (2006) Wood Works Press

The Agoraphobe's Pandiculations (2006) Little Poem Press

The Lita Conversation (2006) Southern Hum

The Chloe Poems (2007) Maverick Duck Press

Some Identity Problems (2007) Foothills Publishing

Pictures from Lang and Fellini (2007) Sheltering Pines Press

Grit (2008) Amsterdam Press

The Tense Past (2010) Flutter Press

Before the Great Troubling (2011) Unbound Content

Mitmensch (2011) Folded Word Press

The Heart is Open (2011) Right Hand Pointing

To Writing You (2012) Origami Poems Project

Our Locust Years (2013) Unbound Content

My Father is Still Dying (2013) Flutter Press

Body (2013) Chapbook Journal

The Catastrophe of my Personality (2014) Blue Hour Press

The Sky Needs More Work (2014) Upper Rubber Boot Books

The Medicament Predicament (2015) Redneck Press

Stone (2015) Origami Poems (chapbook)

Opaque Melodies that Would Bug Most People (2015) After the Pause Books

Mountain (2015) Fairfield Press

Home (2016) Fairfield Press

Among the Mensans (2017) Iris Press

River (2018) Fairfield Press

Madstones (2018) Blaze/VOX Books

Alphabeticon (2019) Staring Problems Press

Dog (2019) Fairfield Press

Memphis (2022) Fairfield Press

Prose

Talk: A Novel in Dialogue (2002) Livingston Press

We Are Billion-Year-Old Carbon (2005) Livingston Press

Short Story and Other Short Stories (2006) Parallel Press

Following Richard Brautigan (chapbook) (2006) Plan B Press

Publisher (2007) Writers Write Journal Press

Listen: 29 Short Conversations (2009) Brown Paper Press

The Ballad of the Two Tom Mores (2010) Bronx River Press

Following Richard Brautigan (full-length novel) (2010) Livingston Press

Notes toward the Story and Other Stories (2011) Aqueous Books

Gardner Remembers (2011) Pocketful of Scoundrel

I'll Give You Something to Cry About (2011) Queen's Ferry Press

Frank Comma and the Time-Slip (2012) Wapshott Press

The Travels of Cocoa Poem Lorry (2013) Leaf Garden Press

Diddy-Wah-Diddy: A Beale Street Suite (2013) Ampersand Press

As a Child: Stories (2014) MadHat Press

Memphis Movie (2015) Soft Skull Press

Robert Walker (2016) Livingston Press

Camel's Bastard Son (2020) Cabal Books

The Adventures of Camel Jeremy Eros (2020) Cervena Barva Press

The Diminishment of Charlie Cain (2021) Livingston Press

Cock-a-Hoop: The Adventures, mostly, of Neill Rhymer (2022) Whiskey Tit Books

author's photo: Mark Hendren

COREY MESLER has been published in numerous anthologies and journals including *Poetry, Gargoyle, Five Points, Good Poems American Places,* and *New Stories from the South.* He has published over 25 books of both poetry and prose. His novel, *Memphis Movie,* attracted kind words from Ann Beattie, Peter Coyote, and William Hjorstberg, among others. He's been nominated for the Pushcart many times, and three of his poems were chosen for Garrison Keillor's Writer's Almanac. He also wrote the screenplay for *We Go On,* which won The Memphis Film Prize in 2017. With his wife he runs Burke's Book Store in Memphis (est. 1875).